# The Better Portion

## by
## Diane Straub

To Aggie,
In God's Love,
Diane
I Cor 13: 4-8a

DORRANCE PUBLISHING CO., INC.
PITTSBURGH, PENNSYLVANIA 15222

ISBN # 0-8059-4511-3
Printed in the United States of America

*First Printing*

For information or to order additional books, please write:
Dorrance Publishing Co., Inc.
643 Smithfield Street
Pittsburgh, Pennsylvania 15222
U.S.A.

# Dedication

*In memory of my mother, Florence Rogers, whose love and support kept me from giving up, and who always loved this kind of story. This one's for you, Mom.*

# Contents

**Part Five:**      **Passion Week — The Last Seven Days**

**Part Six:**      **The Risen Savior**

# Prologue

*...the first man Adam was made a living soul...*
I Corinthians 15:45b.

### The Fall

He opened his eyes and looked around. He didn't know where he was or how he'd gotten there. No thoughts filled his mind. Indeed he knew no words because there were none to know. Everything his eyes beheld was beautiful. He couldn't have described the beauty even if he'd known the words. He sat moment after moment taking it all in. Everything was pleasant to the sight. A thought somehow was projected to his mind, the first he'd ever encountered. He saw himself, though he didn't know it was him, standing up. Until then he hadn't known he could stand or even move. Gently a Force he couldn't see helped him to his feet. The image of himself again appeared in his mind. He looked about, seeing nothing that resembled it, even though many things moved about and grew in the area. He was in a place full of sounds, but he didn't know what sound was. The sounds were pleasant and his heart wasn't empty–yet.

He turned around as he looked about, taking in all he could see and hear until he saw something sparkling nearby. The Force gently prodded him to move one of his legs. He noticed that the one he didn't move held him as the first moved forward. Awkwardly, after the first was again resting on the ground, he placed his weight upon it and moved the second. He began to fall, and another part of him at his side instinctively moved out and touched something. The force gently communicated peace into his mind, and he knew it wouldn't allow him to fall. He stopped moving to examine this newly discovered part of himself. Like the things he stood upon, there were two, one on each side. Each one curved out slightly again, and there were several more things extending from it. He found they moved if he willed it, and for several minutes he stood watching as he opened and closed this new discovery which was his hand. He again moved forward, gaining confidence with each step, and finally reached the sparkling substance that had attracted him. He looked down into it, seeing the image he'd seen in his mind. His hand moved to his chest and then up higher. The image did the same.

Another image formed in his mind. It was himself again bending over the sparkling substance he was looking into. The image reached out to the substance and touched it. The Force gently prodded him to do the same, his hand went through the surface, and he jerked it back up in surprise. He didn't know how, but he sensed a change in the Force. It was still comforting and still prodding him to do as the image in his mind had done, but because he knew no words, he didn't know how to describe the mirth the Force was conveying to him. In his mind, he saw his image bend over and, placing the two hands together, pick up some of the substance he'd just touched. He began to see that the Force wanted him to act out what he saw in his mind, so he began to do as he saw the pictures in his mind do. The Force, in this way, showed him many things, how to drink, how to eat, how to sit and stand. If he hesitated, it would gently prod him, but it never forced him. It was always a comforting presence.

After a while the Force showed him an image of himself standing again. This time the image stood next to the sparkling substance that he'd learned to drink, and the other moving creatures came to him. Each time one did, he saw the hole moving in his top part that he'd reached up and touched with his hand when he first saw his image in the sparkling substance. He didn't know it was his head, he only knew that he ended there. He beheld the beauty about him from that place, and when he opened the hole that was his mouth and put something in it, it was pleasant. But this image wasn't putting anything into the hole. He did not—could not—understand what the Force wanted.

Then an image of himself again appeared in his mind. This time a Voice, pleasant, soothing, and authoritative, spoke to him. It was the first sound he'd ever noticed, and he only noticed it because it was the first sound that was different from those that had been around him from the beginning.

"Adam," the Voice said gently.

He turned around, looking in every direction. But where did it come from? It seemed to come from everywhere. Again the image of himself came to his mind and, simultaneously, the Voice repeated, "Adam."

The image in his mind had moved his lips as if to form the word as the Voice spoke. The image pointed to itself. He did the same and moved his lips, but no sound was made. He didn't know how to make sound; he didn't know he could. He opened the hole again, but this time something from deep inside welled up and came out.

He stood, a bit surprised at the sound that he'd made. The image appeared again, and the Voice repeated, "Adam."

This time, knowing he could make a sound, too, he repeated what he saw, imitating the movements the image made.

"Ah-dam," he said with an effort. he laughed at this discovery, and his voice rang out with joy. "Ah-dam! Ahdam! Adam!" he cried, jumping, prancing, and laughing as a small child with a new toy might do. The Force joined him, and Adam now recognized the earlier change in the Force as something similar to how he was now feeling. The Force was laughing with him, enjoying the new discovery as much as he. The Force. What was this thing, this protection, this provider? What was it called? He had no words to form the question with, yet it was inside him.

"I am God-Creator," the Voice said. Simultaneously, in his mind, Adam knew that was the answer to his question. "I am Lord. I am Father." Adam felt in his body simultaneously with the word "Lord," a feeling of firm command, and with "Father," gentle comfort. He knew the Voice was all these things.

Innocent as a newborn child, his mind formed other questions he had no way of asking. The God-Creator answered him patiently each time, teaching him with images, words, and feelings. Then the image of himself came back with the other creatures coming up to him. This time Adam understood. The God-Creator wanted him to name each one. As this realization grew within him, the other creatures that moved began to approach him one by one, and Adam named them all. As he did this, he saw each kind had two, and he sought to find one like himself, but there were none. A void filled his heart as he realized there wasn't another like himself. Last of all, he put his hand to his chest.

"Man," he said and fell silent, not understanding that what he felt inside was loneliness. But the God-Creator knew, and compassion for the man caused Him to place Adam into a deep, deep sleep. All other creatures, including man himself, were made of dust and particles. But the God-Creator didn't want to give man another creature like that. Man had been made completely in His image and likeness. If He made another out of dust, it would be the same as man, but if He took out a part of man and made a creature, together they'd be completely in His image and likeness. So the God-Creator opened Adam and removed one of his ribs. This creature would be distinct; it would be female and would have strong creative and nurturing instincts. Her capacity for love would, in ways, be greater, and in areas of caring for the man and their young, she'd know instinctively what to do and how to do it. The man would be protector and leader, and the female would look to him and support him with her love. His weak points would be her strong points and her weaknesses, his strengths. They would be one—and yet two.

When she was complete, the God-Creator caused Adam to awaken. Adam stood and looked about. Nothing had changed.

"Adam," the God-Creator said and placed an image in Adam's mind of himself turning around. Adam did as the image instructed. There, behind him, stood the most beautiful creature he'd ever seen. Her skin seemed to shimmer, and her hair glinted in the sunlight that fell upon them both.

Adam caught his breath for a moment before speaking. "You are of my bone and of my flesh. Because you came out of me, we are one. You are woman. I shall call you Eve," he said.

The God-Creator saw that all His creation was good and instructed them all to multiply and replenish the Earth. He gave man charge of everything. Though Adam and Eve grew in intellect, they remained innocent. Completely free of cares, they roamed through the trees and fields. There were no restrictions either on them or around them, save one: a tree the God-Creator had shown Adam before Eve was formed.

"Eat not of it," the God-Creator said. "Of all else eat freely, but do not eat of this one tree." Adam did as he was told and named the plants and shrubs and trees and gave names to the rocks and other pretty stones he found. All this happened before Eve was made. By the time she came, all had been named, and he showed them to her. She marveled at their beauty. They laughed and played together among the foliage, and none of the other moving creatures did them harm.

One day the woman was alone near the tree that was forbidden. She saw a serpent in the tree, and it spoke to her. Never having seen it before, she didn't know it was not really of their garden, though Adam could have told her. He'd named all the creatures and, besides Eve herself, only he could talk the language that they spoke together and with the God-Creator. But she wasn't aware of this, and she didn't realize that the serpent was an evil one and not of their garden. She hadn't yet seen all the creatures that lived among them and didn't know this one had come to do her harm.

"Hello," it said, speaking in the language that she spoke.

She stood, staring up into the tree. She didn't answer at first.

"Come closer," it said.

She moved a step closer. There seemed to be something different about this creature. He wasn't like the others she'd seen.

"Come. Look. Is not the fruit on this tree good?" It stretched its long body out and touched a piece of fruit with its forked tongue.

"I don't know," the woman said. "The God-Creator said we mustn't eat of it."

"You must not eat of the fruit of the garden?" The voice was taunting, seductive.

"Oh, yes. I mean, we may eat of all of the fruit, save that of this one lone tree, lest we die."

"Die?" the serpent hissed. "Die!" it cried out again. "You surely shall not die. You will be as gods and know everything. This fruit would give you power and knowledge, not death." He lured her to eat of the fruit, careful to hide his deception behind the cloak of a friend. Finally she listened to him and forgot the warning she'd been given by Adam. She reached up and touched a fruit. She didn't even need to pick it; it fell into her hand. She looked at it. It was beautifully shaped, and the texture of the skin was pleasant. She smelled it. Its fragrance was appealing and seemed to call to her. She opened her mouth to eat, and, as she did, the serpent hissed and sucked in a quick breath. But she didn't notice. The flavor, at first, was pleasant, but as it reached her belly, the pleasantness vanished. The garden seemed to change in an instant, and when she looked at her body, her skin no longer seemed to shimmer. She became ashamed of her nakedness. Fear entered her. She'd never felt it before; there had been no reason to fear before. She didn't want to be alone in this, and she felt alone.

"Adam," she called. When he approached, she held out the fruit to him.

"You're different. What have you done?" he said.

"I ate of this fruit. It's good. Here. Try." She held it out to him again.

He looked upon her and knew she was no longer one with him. She'd eaten of the forbidden fruit, and the glow of life had left her. She no longer shimmered as he did. He remembered the loneliness he'd felt before she came. He couldn't bear to have that again, so he took the fruit she offered and ate it. His life, too, was gone. Shame came upon him...and guilt...and fear. The God-Creator was coming. Fear built up inside them, and Adam picked two gigantic leaves. He gave one to Eve and held one over himself.

"The God-Creator must not see that our shimmer is gone," he said.

"Where are you, Adam?" The Voice came gently to their ears as they crouched down in fear beside the tree. "Your life has come back to me. What have you done?"

Adam stood slowly. "God-Creator, I've eaten the forbidden fruit."

"Why? Why, Adam? All that's here was yours to eat of freely. Why did you eat of the one tree I said not to eat of? You had all these others to choose from."

Adam lowered his head and felt tears of remorse and sadness course down his cheeks. "The woman. She gave it to me. She ate, so I ate also."

The God-Creator looked at Eve, who then stood and pointed to the tree where the serpent was still coiled around a branch. "The serpent said it would make us as gods."

The God-Creator felt anger and sadness. They'd already been like Him. They needed no fruit to eat to become what they already were. He said to the serpent, "For this, you'll be cursed above all other creatures. You and the woman will be enemies, and her offspring and yours will be enemies. They shall stomp on your head and you shall bite at their feet."

To Eve He said, "With greater pain shall you give birth, yet you'll yearn for your husband, and he'll be in authority over you."

To Adam He said, "Because you ate of the fruit that was forbidden, no longer may you live in the garden I prepared for you before you were created lest you eat also of the Tree of Life and live forever as you are. The fruit of the ground shall no longer be easily gotten. The ground shall be cursed, and the fruit of it shall come only from much toil. You shall fight it, and it shall fight you." He led them out and placed guards around the garden, and man could no longer enter or look upon its beauty. Adam and Eve lived long in the world, working hard with the earth that was cursed. Eve gave birth to many young until finally both of their bodies ceased to function and the physical part of them followed their spirits and they died. But, though they left the Earth, the curse continued that had been caused by the fall of man until the God-Creator would send a Savior for all mankind.

Four
      Thousand
            Years
                 Later...

*...the last Adam was made a quickening spirit*
I Corinthians 15:45b.

# Part One

## Inauguration
## The First Year

*...behold, I will bring forth my servant the Branch*
Zechariah 3:8.

# *Chapter One*

## Forerunner

It was finished. Jesus laid down his tools and inspected his handiwork. The trunk was finished. For days he'd worked on it. He nodded in satisfaction. Yes, it was perfect. A knock on the door drew his attention. As he turned to answer it, his brother James entered the house.

"God's peace, James," Jesus said. Grinning, he greeted his brother with a kiss.

"Well, brother," James said. "Is it ready?" James had come with their Uncle Cleopas's cart to help Jesus take the trunk to its new owner. He stepped close and fingered the carvings on the lid. "This is truly a work of art. Aunt Salome will be more than pleased."

"Yes," Jesus said. "I think she'll like it. Thank you for offering to help and bringing the cart."

"It's the least I could do for my older brother. Do they know we're coming?"

"No. I want it to be a surprise."

"Well, let's get it on the cart."

James lifted one end of the large trunk, and Jesus picked up the other. Together they carried it outside, carefully laid it in the bed of their uncle's cart, and started their journey. Their aunt and uncle lived only a short distance away. The brothers traveled in companionable silence for a few minutes.

"Aunt Salome will wonder why you did this." James was curious himself. There was no special occasion, no obvious reason Jesus should be giving their aunt a gift.

Jesus glanced over at James. "I think it's more that you are wondering." Jesus laughed at James's sheepish grin and shrugged. "Her life is hard. She deserves to have something beautiful given to her once in a while; it will make her feel appreciated."

James took this in silently. It was just like Jesus to do this. Last year it was their mother's other sister, Maria, Uncle Cleopas's wife, who benefitted. The children of the family were always getting toys Jesus had made for them, all for no other reason than to show he cared.

They arrived at the house of Zebedee and Salome. Jesus knocked on the door, which was opened by a woman in her early forties. She smiled and embraced him.

"Peace, my son," she said.

"Peace, Aunt. I brought you something," Jesus said as he backed away so she could see past him to the cart where James stood with his hand upon the trunk. Her hands flew to her mouth, and she looked from Jesus to the cart and back to him, tears filling her eyes.

"Who is it, Salome?" Zebedee said. He came out to greet the young men as his wife walked as if in a daze over to the gift Jesus had made. The three men watched as she lovingly fingered the intricate carvings on the lid. James broke the silence. Turning to Jesus, he said, "Come. I'll help you carry it in."

By that time their cousins had all come out and were exclaiming about the beauty of the trunk. Salome turned to Jesus and clasped him to her, then placed a hand on each of his cheeks. "You are truly a gift to us all," she said.


The morning sun beat down upon the earth, spreading its bright rays over the hill commonly known as the Mount of Olives. At the eastern foot of that hill stood Bethany, a little village not far from Jerusalem. The quiet day was filled with normal activity and the usual hubbub of the village filled the air as a young woman made her way to the well which supplied the village with water. Her long white veil fluttered, and her gown would have billowed around her without the girdle holding it to her waist. Carrying a water jar on her head, she walked gracefully among the playing children and scurrying beasts contributing to the chaos. The pungent scents of perfume, sweat, animals, and the ripe fruits and vegetables sold by merchants added to the atmosphere, but these were also normal and the woman seemed unaffected by it all as she reached her destination.

"Good day, Martha," a woman already at the well greeted her. "Peace be with you."

"Good day, Miriam. Peace be with you also. What news have you today?" Martha lowered the water jar and began to fill it as she listened to the latest gossip and news.

Miriam, being the wife of a traveling merchant, gathered much information that otherwise wouldn't reach the ears of the women who met daily at the well. For many it was the high point of their day. Lately the news had been lively, for a new preacher in the desert had begun to make waves among the Jewish population. Miriam was talking of him now.

"They say locusts and wild honey are all he eats. He looks like a wild man, what with the camel's hair clothes and unshorn head and all. No one seems to know who he truly is. They call him John the Baptist because he's begun baptizing of late."

"What does he preach?" Martha asked as she finished filling her jar.

"Repentance mostly. Says the kingdom of God is at hand. I've heard that some of the priests think he might be the Messiah."

"The Messiah?" Martha raised her eyebrows. *Lazarus would be interested to hear of this.* She made a mental note to tell him. "Why do they think he's the Messiah?"

"I'm not really sure. I don't know the sacred Scriptures myself, but my husband does. He thinks they could be right. Lord knows we need deliverance," she said as they saw two mounted riders approaching on the road heading east for Jerusalem.

The riders drew their reins and dismounted as they reached the well. One, dressed in the garb of a slave, approached the well and drew water. The other rider stood by, holding the horses' reins. He was a tall, broad-shouldered Roman soldier, bearing the insignia of a centurion.

He smiled broadly at the women. "Peace be to you," he said.

"Peace be to you, my lord," Martha answered as she watched him take the cup of water offered by his servant. The women stood in silence, watching as the centurion and his slave watered their horses and remounted.

The centurion looked down with a kindly face. "May God be with you," he said, waving farewell.

"And peace be with you," Martha said as the men rode away.

"Well, I like that. Acting as though he's one of us," Miriam sniffed indignantly.

"Oh, he was just being courteous and friendly. I believe it was rather nice of him." Martha paused. "He treats his slave well. Did you notice?"

"You have the innocence of a babe," Miriam said. "The Romans aren't our friends. I hope the priests are right about this John the Baptist, then we'll see what happens when he declares himself." She turned to go. "God go with you."

"And the peace of God be with you," Martha nodded a farewell and, raising her water jar to her shoulder, started back to the house where she, her brother Lazarus, and their sister Mary lived.

The large crowd gathered around the wild-looking man as he exhorted them. "Repent," he bellowed, "you vipers. How dare you come here. Who sent you? Your pride tells you that you're sons of Abraham, but I tell you now, God can raise up sons out of these stones. If you are truly what you say, show your fruits or be quiet. Don't tell me you're good. I want to *see* it." He raised a tanned arm, pointing at the Pharisees, Sadducees, and scribes standing before him as he preached. Looking out further at the rest of the crowd, he continued. "If your brother lacks bread and you have surplus, give some to him. Don't just say you care about your brother in need. Act like it."

A man stepped up out of the crowd. "I'm a tax collector. What shall I do?"

John looked down at him from the rock he stood upon. "Do not steal. Take no more in your collections than what's required by law."

A group of soldiers, one a centurion, stood nearby. The centurion spoke up. "And us? What of us?"

"Don't threaten people to get things from them, don't accuse them falsely to your own ends, and live within the means your wages permit."

A Levite approached him. "Lord, are you the Messiah?"

John stood silently a moment, pitying the man and the crowd before him. They were searching, seeking, hungering for the one who would give them answers. "No," he said loud enough that all could hear.

"Then are you Elijah?" the man asked.

"No."

"Then who are you?" someone else called out in the throng.

"I'm the voice that cries out in the wilderness, *Make way for the Lord Whose king-*

*dom is at hand*, as spoken of by Isaiah."

Another priest approached him. "If you're not the Messiah or the prophet, why do you baptize?"

"I baptize only with water to show repentance. But one comes—in fact he's among you—of whom I'm not worthy to even loose the sandals of. He'll baptize you with Spirit and fire. He'll separate the fruitful among you from the unfruitful."

Though he said that he was not the one, they continued to question and prod him, seeking to get him to admit he was who they wanted him to be. But John held fast, claiming only to be a proclaiming voice. He continued to warn and exhort the people, and word spread about him throughout the lands of Judea, reaching to the northern lands of Galilee.

Martha entered the house and saw her sister Mary lying on a mat in the living area of their home. Her long dark hair was still braided, but her veil had been removed and her girdle unfastened. Martha's lips drew into a tight line as she lowered her water jar.

"Well, I see you've finally decided to come home." She managed to keep her voice calm and undemanding as she turned to address the girl on the mat. "Where have you been?"

Mary drew pictures on the floor with her finger as she held her head with her other hand. She didn't look up as she answered, "Oh, out." She waved the hand she'd been leaning on, as if to dismiss the subject.

"There's work to be done. I can't do it all alone."

"Well, I'm back, aren't I?" Mary snapped, looking up at her sister.

"Yes, and now that you're here, you can help me grind the flour for today's bread." Martha fought to keep her voice calm and pleasant. It was getting increasingly difficult to live with Mary. Martha sensed there was something wrong, but she didn't know what it was or how to help her sister. Mary's disappearance since noon the previous day was only one of several similar instances of late.

There had also been a change in her personality. Before that had begun, other things had been evident: She'd grown lazy and had taken to boasting about herself, exaggerating tremendously. She'd always do exactly the opposite of whatever was asked of her and could never be counted upon to keep her word. During the nights she stayed at home, she was restless or plagued with nightmares if she slept.

Martha didn't know what was causing all of this and was greatly concerned for Mary, but whenever she tried to talk to her sister about what it might be, Mary only stared at her in a patronizing manner and either walked away or changed the subject. Martha had begun to suspect what was wrong, but Mary was her sister. How could she accuse her of that? She forced her mind away from the thought before she finished it. She wouldn't accuse her sister of any sin like that; it was preposterous.

Mary had no reason to resort to such things. She was a beautiful girl with large black eyes, soft lips, and a heart-shaped face. Anyone would think her fair to look at.

Besides, Mary was always in attendance at synagogue; no one who attended synagogue would do that. She dismissed her suspicions once again and, picking up the bowl filled with barley, headed outside to the millstones.

"Are you coming?" she said, stopping at the door.

"Oh, I'm too tired; I don't feel well. I'll lie down for a short time longer. If I'm feeling better, I'll come out later. All right?" Mary used her most convincing tone of innocence and attempted to appear to be in pain as she rubbed her head and placed her hand on her stomach.

Martha started back into the room. "Have you got a fever?"

"No, I think it's only my time of the month," Mary said. "I'll be, all right, if I'm able to lie still for a short while."

"Well," Martha said, turning back to the door, "if you're sure...."

"Yes, I'm quite sure," Mary said, managing a feeble smile. "I'll be fine shortly." She laid back with a faraway look in her eyes.

Martha went back out the door after giving Mary a concerned look. "Okay. I'll be outside if you need me."


The blue-green water gently rocked the boats as the men prepared to cast their nets. In the distance the hills glowed with a pinkish hue as the sun set, casting its fiery light upon them. The two boats, placed several yards apart, bobbed in the water from the movements of the men as they threw the nets over the sides. They pulled the cords and drew the nets back, emptying them and then throwing them back out.

They worked in silence for the most part, until the boats were full, then they rowed back to shore and began sorting the edible from the inedible fish. After that was taken care of, there were nets to be mended and deliveries to be made. As they sorted, the silence gave way to friendly conversation. The four men were not only fishing partners, but good friends as well.

"I hear your cousin John is making a ruckus down in Bethabara," Simon said; he was a tall, muscular man in his twenties with light brown hair and grayish-blue eyes. He was addressing the two men from the other boat who were brothers. Their father, Zebedee, often joined them in their trade, but he was absent this day.

"So they say," James, one of the brothers, said. He threw his net behind his younger brother to get it out of the way and began sorting fish. "He's always been outspoken, but father says he's gone fanatical this time. He insists on living in the desert and keeps claiming the kingdom of God is here."

"Is he the Messiah?" the fourth man asked. He was Andrew, the brother of Simon. Though he was the elder of the two, he was shorter and less commanding, both in appearance and attitude. His face was eager as he placed the question.

Everyone, or almost everyone, expectantly awaited the promised Savior. Because of the oppression of the Romans, they anxiously sought out anyone who even vaguely seemed to fit their expectations.

"Of course not," John said. "He's just finally cracked is all." Their blue eyes twinkled as the two brothers grinned at each other and then looked over at the other men.

John, whom they called the Baptist, was a distant relative of James and John through their mother, Salome. They couldn't conceive of anyone in their family being chosen by God to do anything, not even Jesus, their mother's sister's eldest son, who was unusually wise and had a certain special quality about him. It was in the family history that he'd been born in Bethlehem during the census nearly thirty years earlier, which was from where the Scriptures said the Messiah would come. He was of the line of David.

Mary, their aunt, had been pregnant when the census was ordered. She'd gone with their Uncle Joseph to register, but a lot of people were of the line of David. Besides, Jesus was just a carpenter; he couldn't be considered a radical intent on reestablishing the throne of David. And John the Baptist was a Levite, not of the house of Judah at all.

"I think I'd like to hear this John," Andrew said. "I'd like to hear what he has to say."

"We need you here, Andrew," Simon said. "Not gallivanting all over Galilee or Judea looking for the Messiah." He threw a fish overboard and the others could tell he was getting irritated.

Simon didn't like to discuss religion, especially not the Messiah. The others didn't like to question him about it because he usually got unaccountably upset. It wasn't that Simon didn't attend synagogue or that he was impious. He felt what he believed was his own personal business and that he didn't have to discuss it with anyone else. As a result, he disliked others discussing it around him as well. Andrew's insatiable interest in the Messiah irritated him.

"Now, Simon," Andrew said good-naturedly as he leaned over and picked up a torn net to mend. "I don't gallivant all over Galilee and Judea, and I'll only be gone a day or two. You can do without me until then."

"I think I may join you, Andrew," John said. "Get Philip and father to help you, Simon. We'll see if we can pick up some orders while we're down that way."

Simon scowled and turned to James. "Well, what about you, James? Going to make it a threesome?"

James grinned. Simon, for all his bark, had little bite to add to it. "No, I'll pass this time and stay here with you. I've heard John speak already."

Andrew looked over at John. "When do you think we should go?" he asked.

"How about tomorrow?" John said.

"Fine with me. Tomorrow it is then."

# Chapter Two

## The Baptism

That evening in Bethany, after their meal was ended, Martha sat alone with her brother Lazarus in their living area. Mary had once again disappeared without a word, and Martha was growing concerned. She wondered if Lazarus had noticed any changes in Mary. She was trying to determine if it was only her imagination, not wanting to bring the subject up before she was sure what she suspected. Did she even have the right to accuse her own sister?

"You seem deep in thought, Martha. Does something trouble you?" Lazarus's voice was gentle. He was a quiet man.

"Yes, my lord, I'm troubled, deeply troubled, but I dare not speak of what, for I'm not certain of the truth behind my concern."

"Is it of Mary that you speak?" He turned his kind, wise eyes upon her.

She bowed her head in silence. She couldn't lie to him, but she was reluctant to voice her true thoughts.

"It is of Mary, I see," he said. Martha thought she detected a note of concern in his voice. "I've been worried about her also. I've heard unpleasant rumors. No one has mentioned her name to me, but when they think I cannot hear...."

"Lazarus, what shall we do? She's so young. Her heart is broken that she's not yet wed, but that will never happen if this is true." Martha looked imploringly at her brother.

He, as head of the family since their parents' death, was the one to make all the decisions. Martha had stayed, putting off her own marriage, until Mary was grown enough to leave. But the man Martha had been betrothed to had been killed suddenly before that time came, and Mary hadn't yet been sought after by any man of whom Lazarus approved. So the three of them remained in the house they'd been born in, for Lazarus was unmarried as well.

"You know that if it's true and she's caught, she'll be stoned."

Lazarus sighed, "Yes, I know." His younger sister was a trial. She was barely eighteen, beautiful, and vibrant. It was beyond him why no young man of good standing had approached him for her, but none had. Martha was plainer, less appealing, but she was a good worker and would make a good wife. He sighed.

Martha decided it would be better to change the subject. It was enough to know that Lazarus was aware of what was happening with Mary. Surely he'd say something to her. "Miriam told me there's a new preacher up in Bethabara."

Lazarus's eyebrows went up. "Is there now?" he said.

"Yes, she told me of him this morning. She says many of the rabbis believe he's the Messiah."

"That's interesting. Did she tell you what he was preaching?"

"That the kingdom of God is at hand. He's baptizing in the Jordan."

"He is? In Bethabara, you say? Maybe I'll go tomorrow and hear what he has to say. But it's time now for sleep." He rose and helped Martha lay out the mats upon which they slept. Soon after they were settled, Martha heard the familiar snoring telling her Lazarus was asleep, but she lay awake late into the night thinking. Mary still didn't return.


Mary lay awake listening to the even breathing of the man beside her. Was this love? She didn't know. She only knew that when he held her and caressed her she felt wanted and loved. But was it real love? What was love? She didn't know.

She looked over at him. The feelings he'd aroused within her were so pleasant, and yet the emptiness remained. Would it ever leave? Would she ever find love, acceptance, and inner peace? Her eyes filled with tears, which ran down her cheeks. She felt so alone, and what she was doing didn't take the loneliness away.

At first it had only made her feel guilty, but she couldn't control it. It was like something was compelling her to sleep with men. It felt good when she was doing it. After a while the guilt left and it no longer bothered her. At first she'd been careful not to be away from home too long, fearful that Lazarus and Martha might suspect something. Now she was no longer afraid of being caught. She knew she could tell them any silly little lie and they'd believe her because they wouldn't want to believe the truth. She began staying away for longer periods of time. She always made sure the men she picked weren't married. She did have some pride left.

She wondered if this man beside her felt anything toward her. This wasn't the first or even the second or third time with him. He'd sought her out and wanted her more times than any other man so far, ten times at least. She smiled. Maybe he did care. Why else would he keep asking her to come back?

She turned onto her side and, leaning on an elbow, kissed his cheek. His even breathing stopped and his eyes opened. He gently pushed her back on the bed as he leaned over her to kiss her and run his hands over her body.

The now familiar feelings began to course through her body. She couldn't let herself believe that all he wanted was to relieve his urges with her. She believed he cared because she couldn't face more rejection.


Martha quickened her pace to keep up with Lazarus. The bag in her hand weighed heavily on her arm, although its contents were light. She shifted it to her other hand as she struggled along the road at Lazarus's heels.

*I'll say one thing for Lazarus*, she thought, *he doesn't waste time when he has a purpose.*

He'd decided to seek out the Baptist almost immediately after Martha related what she'd heard at the well. She'd decided, out of curiosity, to join him, and they'd made as much haste as possible in preparing for the journey.

It had only been one day since she'd told him. It would have been sooner, but they'd attempted to find Mary first. However, Lazarus grew impatient to be gone, so Martha had agreed to give up the search, against her better judgment. Mary had no way of knowing where they had gone.

Martha came out of her musing in time to hear the tail end of a conversation Lazarus was having with a group of travelers they'd met and joined with for company,

"They say this Baptist fellow cares not a bit for what the leaders think of him," one of the men said.

Lazarus raised his eyebrows.

"And some haven't taken kindly to it," another added. The rest mumbled in agreement.

"Who?" Lazarus said,

"Ah, sir," one of the men lowered his voice and came closer to Lazarus as he spoke, "this John has taken to telling even Herod what he thinks of him."

Lazarus glanced over at Martha, then looked back at the man. "What does he say?"

"He's telling Herod that he can't marry his brother's wife even though she's divorced because it's incest."

"Oh?" Lazarus said.

The man lowered his voice so it was barely audible and looked about them cautiously. "Herodius is pressuring Herod into doing something about John permanently." His eyes were wide as he nodded his head.

Martha gasped, "But the Jewish leaders say he's the Messiah," she said. "Herod couldn't slay the Messiah."

The small man who had given them this news placed a finger to his lips and looked her squarely in the eye. "Messiah or no, Herod may try if she presses. I hear he's very taken with her beauty and her daughter's beauty as well." They had to strain to hear as he added, "And I've also heard she has no conscience." He shook his head. "None at all."

The crowd parted to let the man pass. He walked calmly, smiling a greeting to those whose eyes he caught, never seeming concerned with the reactions of others. The way he moved, his bearing and sureness, the depth of his eyes, and the warmth of his smile drew adults as well as children to him. He stooped to touch a child's head and smiled as she looked up at him with brown eyes, large and innocent. She returned his smile shyly, and then ran off to play with the other children who had come with their parents. The people were gathering to hear John the Baptist preach and witness his baptizing. He slowly made his way to the Jordan. Today was his day.

"You vipers," came the now familiar lashings of the Baptist as he lit into the Sadducees and Pharisees, the priests and rabbis. His exhortations rang through the air as he spoke out, unafraid of the consequences his words might bring.

John looked at Andrew to see what his reaction was to the fiery preaching. Andrew stood spellbound, listening intently to every word, so John also turned his attention to what was being said. He must've missed something because the crowd had gathered closer to the river. The baptizing had begun, but he couldn't see who it was in the water with the Baptist.

Suddenly the sky seemed to part, even though there were no clouds, and a sound like rolling thunder was heard. A point of light descended down upon the person in the water with the Baptist. The crowd parted to let the man through. John gasped. It was his cousin Jesus.

Lazarus stood only a few feet away from the preacher, listening closely to every word he said. This one was different somehow. He watched the faces in the crowd as the Baptist held them spellbound. Then a man approached.

He was slender yet well built, his broad shoulders hinting of physical power beneath his clothing. His brown hair was shoulder length, and he had a bearded face, but it was his eyes that attracted Lazarus's attention. They were as blue as the sky on a clear day, and a light seemed to radiate from them. They were wise eyes, yet they appeared to twinkle with suppressed merriment, as if their owner was about to laugh at any minute, and they glowed with warm compassion as well. Their depth was unfathomable and they appeared ageless, yet the man they belonged to was about Lazarus's age, or he seemed to be. The Baptist spoke with the stranger, and Lazarus was close enough to hear what was said between them.

"You are the one," the preacher said, surprise in his voice, The man didn't answer, and the Baptist continued. "I perceive I should be baptized by you, yet you've come to me. This shouldn't be."

The blue-eyed stranger spoke then. "We must do this. I have to fulfill all that is right."

The Baptist turned without a word, and the stranger followed him into the Jordan River.

Looking out over the crowd before him, John the Baptist felt a surge of compassion. Daily, when he spoke to them, the question came. Daily he answered it: *No, I am not the one you seek.* Yet they came and asked again. It was like they couldn't hear him. It was asked again today; again he'd answered no. Why didn't they believe him? Couldn't they see he wasn't the one? No one had preceded him. He was doing that for another. As he looked at the people, he saw Jesus approaching. It had been many years since they'd seen each other. John watched in awe as Jesus came up to the river and the skies seemed to part. A light, as a dove, came down upon Jesus. It was the sign John had been promised by God. Jesus was the one he was to precede.

Then a Voice from the sky, like the rolling of thunder, said, "This is my beloved Son, in whom I am well pleased."

# Chapter Three

## The Rejection

On her way back home Mary paused to watch some children playing leapfrog. The children were young, four or five. As she watched, their innocence struck her. Where had her innocence gone? When did it leave? She felt old, much older than her eighteen years. It wasn't pleasant.

She'd always thought becoming an adult would change how she felt about herself. She'd thought that suddenly she'd wake up one day and life would bless her with love and happiness. But now she was an adult—at least she did adult things—and that hadn't happened. Instead, she felt just as empty and unhappy as she had been when she was ten and her parents had died.

When they had died within two months of each other, something inside her had died, too. She never laughed after that, not true laughter, anyway. Her world had centered on her parents. She'd worshipped her mother and wanted desperately to be like her; she'd been her father's pet. When they were gone, she found herself without any emotional foundation. She'd placed it all on her parents, and they'd taken it with them. As a result, she began searching in other places for the acceptance she didn't feel at home any longer. That search had led her to do things that would horrify her brother and sister if they knew of them.

*Will I ever be happy again?* It was a question she often asked herself. She'd found momentary happiness when men made love to her, and she was able to make herself believe they wanted her because they cared for her—until they got tired of her and told her they no longer wanted to see her. That hadn't happened with this one, not yet anyway, and Mary prayed that it wouldn't because she loved him and wanted him to love her back. She knew her brother wouldn't approve of him, but if she became pregnant, surely Lazarus would agree to let them marry then.

She'd get pregnant. It would be scandalous and all Judea would talk, but she didn't care. *Let them talk.* She'd slept with too many men by now to have any delusions about her reputation. In fact, at first she'd wondered how all these different men knew about her. She'd found herself lying with a different one every time. But as time went on, she became more selective, realizing that they came to her because there were so few women with whom they could do the things she'd do with them. She could have her choice.

At least that was how she saw it, so it puzzled her when they'd end it as though she were nothing to them. Why, when she'd given them everything she could, would they do that to her? She sighed, deciding it was impossible to understand the male mind, and resumed her walk back home.

When she entered the house, she noticed Martha was gone. *Good,* Mary thought. *If I start doing something and am busy when she returns, maybe she won't question me.* Mary began to do some of her chores, expecting Martha to walk in at any moment, but she didn't come. Finally everything was done, but Martha still hadn't come, and it was even past the time Lazarus usually came home when he was out. If she'd known they were going to both be gone, she'd have stayed where she was and not come home. She'd just leave again; they could wonder where she was all they wanted. She wasn't going to waste her time wondering where they were; she had more important things to do.

As she made her way back up the hill, she thought of him, anticipating his reaction. He wasn't expecting her this evening. He usually told her when she left him when to come back, but he hadn't said anything this morning. That was odd. He'd never done that. She figured he must have forgotten. She dismissed the thought and hastened her steps, taking the back streets to his house. When she reached it, she raised her hand to knock, but before she could, the door flew open and there he was.

"What are you doing here?" he asked as if he were afraid someone would hear him.

She quickly recovered from her surprise at this unexpected welcome and smiled radiantly. "My brother and sister were gone, so I came back to—"

Grabbing her arm, he closed the door behind him and took her into the alley next to his house. "I didn't say to come back tonight."

"But, I—"

"I think you should leave," he said.

She threw her arms up around his neck and tried to kiss him, but he drew his head back and pulled her arms from about him.

Confused and hurt, Mary looked up at him with tears in her eyes. "But I love you. I thought you'd be pleased to see me."

"I'm not, and I didn't want to see you tonight."

"But—"

"Go!"

"When can I come back?" The tears flowed down her cheeks as she looked up at him. "When can I see you again?"

He pursed his lips and looked down at the ground. "I'm not going to see you again, Mary," he said slowly.

"What? Why?"

"I'm making arrangements to become betrothed to a girl whose family is very prominent. Her father is here now. That's why you must leave and not come back." He turned without waiting to see her reaction and left her standing alone beside the house.

She stood dumbfounded, her head whirling from shock. She couldn't comprehend, at first, what had just happened. When she finally grasped what had happened, her body began to shake. She crossed her arms over her chest and crumpled to the ground, weeping uncontrollably.

"Oh, God, no, not again. Why didn't he love me? Why doesn't anyone love me? Why?" She pounded her fist on the ground, repeating the word over and over. In her grief she did not feel a sharp stone cut her hand; her emotional pain was stronger. Again she'd been thrown away instead of getting the love she craved.

She thought about killing herself, but knew she wouldn't. She lacked the courage to even try. This realization made her weep all the more, and she lay in the dirt and mud that her tears had caused, crying until she could cry no more. Silence enveloped her as the moon and the stars shown overhead, casting shadows of the buildings about her.

The next day John took Andrew to John the Baptist and introduced them.

"John, this is my fishing partner, Andrew. He's heard of you and asked to meet you. He has questions about your work."

The Baptist turned his eyes onto Andrew, who had expected a look of fanaticism, but found those eyes contained only peace in their clear, green depths.

"Greetings, Andrew," he said with a nod. "What is it you want to know?"

"What's your purpose? Why do you baptize? Who–"

The Baptist raised a hand and said, "Wait, please. One question at a time. Be patient with me, my friend. I will answer them as best I can." An amused twinkle reached his eyes as he continued, "I am called to precede the long-awaited Messiah. It is he who will usher in the new Kingdom. I baptize those who have accepted my message of his coming. He was here yesterday." His face took on a dreamy, faraway look, and he inclined his head toward Jesus, who was passing by them as they spoke.

"Here comes the ultimate sacrifice, God's Lamb. He's the one I've spoken of so often. Even though we're related, I didn't know it was him until yesterday when he approached me. God had told me I'd see the Spirit come down upon him like a dove, and I saw it just as He said. It happened yesterday. I didn't even know it was him," he repeated, his voice filled with awe, "but I saw the sign. This is the Son of God."

Andrew and John questioned the Baptist some more, thanked him, and walked back to the inn, both contemplating what they had just heard.

"Well, what do you think, Andrew?" John said as they walked back to the inn that evening.

"I think I'd like to meet this Jesus," Andrew said. "The Baptist seems to think very highly of him."

"Well, that can be arranged. He's my cousin also."

Andrew stopped and looked incredulously at John a moment. "Is there anyone you aren't related to?"

"Yes, many people," John laughed. "Until John spoke today, I had no idea Jesus was anything special. His mother and mine are sisters. He's only a carpenter, as far as my family knows."

"The Baptist doesn't seem to think so."

"John doesn't know Jesus as I do." John paused and looked at Andrew a moment before he continued. "But if you like, I'll introduce you. We'll seek him out tomorrow."

The next morning, John and Andrew were standing with the Baptist, talking to him. They asked him where they might find Jesus. He looked past them as if he weren't aware of their presence. "There goes the one, the Lamb of God."

Jesus was walking by them. They looked at each other and John nodded to the Baptist. "Thank you, cousin," he said as he took Andrew's arm. "Come on, Andrew," he said in a low voice.

They followed Jesus through the marketplace in an attempt to catch up with him, but his steps were too brisk, so they called out, "Master." Jesus stopped and, turning, waited for them to reach him. He seemed not at all surprised to see John, and both men felt as though he'd expected to meet them. He asked them what they wanted.

"Jesus," John said a little breathlessly, "This is Andrew, one of my fishing partners. He wanted to meet and talk with you. Where are you staying so that we might come by later?"

Jesus smiled at them. "You needn't wait until later," he said. "Come. I'll show you where I'm staying. We can talk now."

He led them to a small cottage on the outskirts of the town. Andrew and John looked around as they entered. Although no one was present, there was evidence of a meal being prepared. Jesus brought them water to wash themselves with and laid out mats for them to recline on.

When they were settled, Jesus smiled and said, "Now, John, what is it you want to speak to me about?" This began a turning point in John and Andrew's lives, and they left that evening awed by the man with whom they had just spent time.

When Martha and Lazarus entered the house, it was very still. It was clear Mary had been there, so neither of them thought much of her absence when they arrived. Martha took the water jar and said to Lazarus, "I'm going to the well for some water for this evening." Lazarus nodded as she headed for the door.

After returning with the water, Martha prepared their evening meal. They ate in silence, getting up periodically to look out onto the street. Darkness had fallen and still there was no sign of Mary.

"Lazarus, I'm worried. We've been gone for more than two days, and she wasn't here, when we left. She's been here since, but I'm sure it wasn't for long after she realized we were gone."

"Don't worry. She's obviously been here," Lazarus said, but he was also concerned. "Would you like for me to go out and look for her?"

At Martha's worried expression and silent nod, he rose from his place and went over to her. Placing his hands on her shoulders, he kissed her forehead. "I'll find her," he said gently, then he turned and was gone.

Mary lay in the shadows, a sob periodically coming up in her throat. Finally she pushed herself to a sitting position. Leaning on her hands, she looked about her. She'd seen these surroundings so many times, yet now they seemed different. Her mind began to whirl again, and she lowered her head between her arms as they held her body up. Slowly she got up off the ground and started walking. She had no idea where she was going. She just walked, half-dazed, heading nowhere. She walked for what seemed hours, not knowing or caring where she was going. Eventually, lights and laughter drew her to a house. People were there. She didn't know them, but they were there and she needed them, needed someone–anyone–to take away the hurt.

As she approached the house, a man came out of the door, staggering toward her. As he came closer, he reached out and grabbed her. The odor of strong wine surrounded him. He held her a moment, leaning his head on her shoulder. Then he lifted it up and blinked his eyes twice, shaking his head.

"Well," he said, looking at her approvingly, "aren't you a pretty one? Where's Joshua been hiding you at?" He grinned and tightened his right arm around her as he drew her to the house. Mary's left arm automatically went about his waist as she let herself be taken into the house.

"Josh, where are you? Oh there you are. Where you been hiding this here little package?"

He staggered again as he spoke, and Mary felt certain that if she let go of him he'd fall. She looked at the man he'd called Josh and her heart leapt. He was a handsome man with dark brown hair and ice-blue eyes. His beard was full and he had broad, muscular shoulders. She felt the electricity between them and began to give him a welcoming smile just as another woman approached him from behind. She was beautiful with large, exotic eyes and sensual lips. Her black hair was unveiled and flowed down nearly to her knees. The woman's arms went about his body, and her hands traveled over him, massaging his muscular chest before she came around to his side, her right arm remaining tightly about his waist. He laughed and placed an arm over the woman's shoulder, giving her an affectionate squeeze as he did so. Obviously the woman felt he belonged to her. Mary's smile faded.

"Now, Jabez, you flatter me. I'd never be able to hide one of such beauty from you. She's a gift of the gods." Joshua laughed and so did the woman. Jabez looked at Mary and laughed also.

"So a gift from the gods." He started to slump to the floor, and Joshua moved quickly to catch and help him to a mat in the corner.

As he did, Mary's eyes traveled over the room. It was filled with people who were laughing and singing. Some were drunk, and some were necking and petting. No one paid any attention to anyone except the one they were with. The lovers didn't seem to mind the lack of privacy, and no one else seemed to think it strange that something so intimate was going on right in front of them.

After taking care of Jabez, Joshua came back. Standing in front of Mary, he crossed his arms.

"Now, my pretty miss, what can I do for you? What brought you to my house?" The woman came and stood beside him, caressing his backside with one hand as she held onto his large arm with the other.

Mary couldn't think of what to say. This was obviously not a place Lazarus and Martha would want her to be. She'd heard of places like this through the men with whom she'd slept, but was unaware that one existed right in Bethany.

"Maybe you could give me your name?" Joshua, obviously amused at her confusion, managed to suppress a grin.

"Mary," she said so softly it was barely audible.

"What? Speak louder."

"Mary," she repeated, raising her voice.

"Well, Mary, why are you here?"

"Maybe she's looking for a good time." The woman spoke for the first time and laughed.

Joshua looked down at Mary and raised his eyebrows. "Are you looking for a good time?"

Mary, unsure of what they meant, stood silent a moment. Then, as if something inside her snapped, she decided; she'd find out what this good time was. She didn't really know or care what would happen to her in the meantime. No one else did, so why should she? Maybe she'd find what she'd been looking for ever since her parents' death.

"Yes," she said. "I'm looking for a good time."

# *Chapter Four*

## The Meeting

Lazarus walked down the street toward their house. He'd been every place he could think of that Mary might be, but no one had seen her; at least that was what they told him. He wondered how to tell Martha. This would upset her greatly. Her concern for Mary grew daily, and it was only because he didn't want her to travel alone that he'd agreed to come back home so soon from Bethabara.

He entered the house, hoping against hope that Mary would be there, but only Martha sat by the lighted lamp, her head down and her eyes closed as if she were praying. At the sound of his footsteps, she looked up expectantly. The hope on her face vanished as she saw he was alone.

"She's not here?" he said, knowing the answer before the words came out.

Martha shook her head. "No. You didn't find her?"

"No, I didn't find. her. No one has seen her, or so they say, but I sensed they know something." He sat down and looked at Martha's worried face. Reaching over, he patted her hand. "I'll look some more tomorrow if she hasn't returned. Don't worry, I'll find her."

"Here, drink some more of this," Caleb said as he placed a cup to her lips.

For three days Mary had been finding out what a good time meant. She'd thought she'd done everything there was to do when making love, but she found she'd only scratched the surface before. It was delightful. She'd been with every man who wasn't taken by the end of the second day and decided Caleb was the one she liked best, not including Joshua.

Joshua was his own man, and she gathered that he chose his women, not the other way around. If Joshua wanted you, he had you. If he didn't, you waited until he did and satisfied yourself with another man in the meantime—all except Daphne. Mary wasn't sure if she was his mistress or not, but if Daphne wanted Joshua she usually got him—and Daphne always wanted Joshua. As a result, he spent most of his time with her.

"Who's Daphne?" she said as she kissed Caleb's cheek so it would seem she only had a passing interest.

"She's a Greek, from Antioch," he said, moving his head so she could kiss his neck. Instead, she stopped and sat up.

"A Greek? What's she doing here?"

He pushed her back down and began fondling and kissing her. "Who knows? She just showed up one day about a year ago." He stopped and looked down at her. "Why are you so interested?"

She shrugged her shoulders. "Oh, I don't know. She just seemed...different...and I wondered about her. Joshua seems very taken with her."

Caleb chuckled. "He should. She's his wife." He laughed even more at the shocked look on her face. "Why are you so surprised?"

"He made love to me!"

"So has just about every other man who's been here the last three days."

"But he's married."

"That's nothing, most of the men here are." She started to sit up again, but he pushed her back. "Now don't get excited. We're far enough out on the outskirts of town that no one ever bothers us. How about going to the roof?"

The roof was where the couples went when they decided to make love. It was usually only after dark so that no one would feel anyone was watching them, and only four couples at a time went up so that there was some semblance of privacy, each taking a corner. She would have agreed readily before, but finding she'd been sleeping with married men unnerved her.

"Are you married, Caleb?" she asked, afraid of the answer, but determined to find out.

"Me? No. I have too much fun. Why get married if I know pretty women like you?" He grinned and touched the tip of her nose with his finger. Then he kissed her as he whispered, "Now how about the roof?"

She looked at him, uncertain that he'd told her the truth.

"Well?" he prodded as he nibbled her neck.

"Okay," she said softly.


Andrew was excited. This Jesus was more than special. Even John admitted there was something about him, something John hadn't noticed before, for all his boasting of being Jesus' cousin. On their way back to Bethsaida, they discussed the previous evening which they'd spent with Jesus.

"I can't get over it, John. It's too good to be true. In our time the Messiah appears. Just too good." Andrew shook his head in wonder.

"It's not so much that to me. What I'm finding hard to get used to is that it's Jesus, my own cousin. I thought I knew him well. We've always been each other's favorite. He's only a few years older than me, but I've always looked up to him and respected his judgment like he was an elder. I never really wondered why. Now I know. The Messiah. Wait until James hears this."

They continued talking excitedly. Something inside them told them this was important, and both were determined to get their brothers to return with them to Bethabara.

For several days Lazarus searched. He even began knocking on the doors of people with whom he wasn't well acquainted. Somebody must have seen where Mary went. He walked dejectedly to the next street. He was far from the part of Bethany where well-known friends lived now. Surely Mary didn't know anyone here in this out-of-the-way district.

He knocked on a door and a woman answered. Had she seen Mary? Lazarus described her. The woman shook her head; she'd noticed no one of that description recently. Giving him her apologies, she wished him God's peace and shut her door. As Lazarus turned away, he noticed an old man sitting in front of a house across the road.

"Good day. God's peace be to you, father," Lazarus said as he approached the man.

"And peace be to you, my son," the old man said. He looked ancient and withered, all except his eyes. They were large and brown and twinkled as with the light of youth, the light of life. Alert and wise, Lazarus sensed that they saw and knew all. If anyone on this street had seen Mary, this man had. He asked if the old man had seen her.

"Yes, I've seen her here several times," he said. "You're too young to be her father. Is she your wife?"

"No. She's my sister. We've been very worried about her. Today marks the seventh day since we've seen her."

The old, kind face looked at him in pity. He told Lazarus of seeing Mary, of her visits to the house at the end of the street where a young man lived alone.

"Did she stay long on these visits?" Lazarus said.

"Yes. Sometimes I'd see her come in the evening and she didn't leave before I retired. In the morning, when I came back out, I'd see her pass by."

"Are you sure you didn't miss her leaving and returning the next day?"

"Young man, I may be old, but I miss nothing. My body may be withered with age, but these," he pointed to his eyes, "see as clearly as a youngster's. I didn't miss anything."

Lazarus turned to go. "God's peace be with you, Father."

"Wait. I'm not finished."

"Go on." Lazarus turned back to listen politely. Hadn't the old man said enough? He'd already confirmed the rumors Lazarus had been hearing.

"It's been about seven days, you say?" At Lazarus's nod, the man continued. "About five nights ago she came. She was running and happy when I first saw her, but she didn't stay long. When she passed again, I saw in her eyes what shouldn't be seen on anyone so young. Her clothes were disheveled and mud was on them and her face, but it was her eyes that I speak of, not her attire. Her eyes had the look of one possessed and her face of one who's lost forever. Find her, young man. Find her before it's too late. Something happened to her down there. I fear your sister may be in trouble within her soul. If she is, it will manifest itself in her actions if she's not helped," the old man looked him straight in the eye, "and helped soon."

Lazarus left the old man and went down to the house. He knocked on the door and the young man appeared.

"Peace be to you," Lazarus said.

"Peace be to you. How may I help you?" The young man seemed polite.

"I'm looking for my sister Mary," Lazarus said.

"Mary?" the young man questioned, as if he had no idea who Lazarus was talking about.

"Yes," Lazarus said. He proceeded to describe her.

"I'm sorry. I haven't seen her," the young man said. He started to close the door, but Lazarus stopped him.

"I know you've been seeing her and that she was here in the evening five days ago. Just what exactly is your relationship with my sister? Where is she?" Lazarus, though a gentle man by nature, was capable of backing himself up physically when he needed to.

"Look, I admit I was seeing her, but I told her I didn't want to continue seeing her on the very night you mentioned. I haven't seen her since, and I don't know where she is."

When the young man didn't continue, Lazarus said, "You didn't answer me completely. What are your intentions toward her?"

The young man smirked, "My relationship with your sister was as with a harlot, but she received no payment. If you want to find your sister, try Joshua's. Most women like her find their way there eventually."

Lazarus was so stunned by the young man's words that he didn't try to stop the door from closing this time. Mary? At Joshua's? Lazarus knew where Joshua's was. All the men in Bethany knew of Joshua's, although the decent men of the town didn't go there. Mary wouldn't go there, but where else had he to check? Joshua's was one of the few places left.


Lazarus's steps quickened. He hoped no one he knew would see him. He hoped he wouldn't find Mary, but he knew he had to check every possible lead.

The house was on the outskirts of town, not far away from the street he'd just left. It was in the direction of Jericho, as far away from Jerusalem and the Jewish leaders as possible. Places like Joshua's, although popular with men in search of women, weren't popular with decent people and especially not with those who obeyed the law. In the laws of Moses, a woman caught with any married man was taken out and stoned to death along with the man with whom she was found. Mary was in grave danger if she were there.

He knocked rapidly on the door when he reached the house, but apparently no one could hear his knock. He tried again to no avail, so he braced his shoulder and pushed the door with as much strength as he could muster, expecting to have to break it down. The door wasn't boarded, so it opened easily.

Lazarus stumbled forward into the house. He managed to regain his balance without falling over, and the effect it gave made it appear as though he'd entered the room in an angrier mood than what he actually felt. He appraised the room and his eyes fell on Mary just as she looked over at him with horror-filled eyes.

"Simon, I tell you, he's the one, the Messiah." Andrew leaned forward, anxious to make Simon see that it was really as he said.

Simon just shook his head and looked at James and John. "He's crazy," he said.

"No Simon, I was there, too," John said. "Believe me, I wouldn't believe it if I hadn't been there either. Jesus is my cousin and a more unlikely prospect—"

"But who knows the mind of God?" Andrew said. "The Romans would suspect someone more obvious. Surely this is the Christ. Just come with us, Simon. Come and see for yourself. You and James come. Bethabara isn't that far, and he said he'd wait for us."

Simon's eyebrows went up. "You told him we'd come?"

"Yes, it was the only way we could be sure he'd wait—"

"You had no right to do that," Simon said. "You know how I feel." He paused in exasperation. "Now I can't say no because you gave my word for me." Simon glared at Andrew.

"I knew you'd come," Andrew said. "You'll not regret it, Simon; you'll not regret it at all." Andrew looked triumphantly over at John.

"And I suppose you promised I'd come too, John?" James knew his brother well.

John grinned at Andrew and turned to James. "Sure. I told Jesus you only stayed here to keep Simon company. What excuse would we give if you didn't show up and Simon was with us?"

James turned to Simon, "We've been corralled, Simon. There's no getting around it for either of us. We're going to be preached at whether we like it or not."

Simon sighed. "You're right."


Mary lifted her head from where it was resting on Caleb's arm. "Oh," she said and raised a hand to her eyes as she let her head fall back.

Caleb chuckled as he silently put the wineskin to her mouth. He could tell she was not used to strong drink.

"Caleb, I feel funny."

"It's nothing to worry about. You're just a little drunk." He kissed her face, progressing toward her mouth as his hands roamed her body and she began to sigh in response then laugh when he tickled a sensitive area as he kissed her neck.

Suddenly the room went silent. Looking up, Mary saw everyone staring at the doorway. She turned her head to see what had caused the silence. There, in the doorway, stood Lazarus.


Lazarus was driven more by fear than anger at first, until he saw her. Then his anger, finally kindled, rose up. He stared at first. The man with whom she was lying had his hand on an area of her body where no man had a right to touch if he wasn't married to her. Her legs were bare, showing most of her thighs. Her veils were gone from her head, and her hair was loose and flowing. No decent woman would ever be seen as Mary appeared before him now; decent women always stayed modestly covered, never even showing their hair outside their own homes.

The anger rose within him. Unchecked, it flared out, and he roared and bellowed as if he were insane—insane with anger and pain in the knowledge that the rumors weren't just rumors: his sister, his precious little Mary, defiled and carousing with these men. He hollered at her, not knowing what he was saying in his anger.

She quickly responded, silently leaping to her feet and gathering her discarded clothes. She clutched the bundle to her chest as if to hide herself and ran past Lazarus and out the door, not even taking the time to dress.

As Lazarus turned to go, he shook his fist and vowed he'd kill anyone who ever went near Mary again. Mary stood outside the door waiting for him. Though now fully clothed, she was shivering, but it was more from fright than the chilly night air. When he came out, he grabbed her elbow and jerked her along, walking almost too fast for her to keep up. He didn't care if he hurt her; he was too angry to care. He'd raised her, cared for her, provided for every one of her needs. Martha had given up a husband and children of her own to help him. They'd devoted their lives to raising this insolent brat who showed her gratitude by sleeping around and shaming them. At that moment, he felt he could never forgive her, never get over the pain she was causing him. He shoved her brutally, pulling her behind him, nearly dragging her along the ground at times. He paid no attention to her pleading. She deserved the pain.

# Chapter Five

## The Desert

Andrew dropped back to walk beside John so they could talk. Simon and James weren't being very cheerful company. Both of them were still sore at being tricked into a trip to Bethabara.

"I don't see why we can't just wait until he comes back to Galilee," James said.

John gave him an angry glance. "A lot you know. And what if he went off someplace else instead?"

James shrugged. "I wouldn't care. I think this whole thing is ridiculous. Jesus is no more the Messiah than I am."

Andrew could see that John's temper was about to flare, so he intervened. "Just wait until you talk with him, James. He may have changed since you last spoke with him."

"I doubt that. Jesus has always been wise: that I can remember. That would be nothing new."

"But it's not wisdom that we're taking you there to see," John said. "There's been a change in him. I can't describe it, There's something different about him, something that wasn't there before." Seeing James's raised eyebrows, he said, "Well maybe it was, but it just wasn't as noticeable."

"Fine," Simon spoke up. "We're on our way to see that your cousin has undergone a change. We all do that. People are always changing."

"But not like this," John said. "Wait until you meet him. You'll see."


"Jesus," Andrew pointed to Simon, "this is my brother, Simon.

Jesus smiled and greeted him with a kiss on each cheek. "Peace, Simon." He looked deeply into Simon's eyes before he spoke again. The other four men stood, waiting silently.

There was a sense of authority emanating from him that they'd never before witnessed in any man.

James cringed at the memory of his thoughts on the road. He hoped Jesus wouldn't find out what he'd been saying. There was a difference. John had been right.

"So you are Simon, the son of John," Jesus said, his eyes surveying Simon. "I shall call you Peter, which means rock."

The others grinned as Simon looked down sheepishly. Though they laughed at this unexpected way Jesus had with Simon, they couldn't deny that Simon himself began changing on that day. Never again did they call him Simon, but always Peter. Peter was no longer skeptical of the promised Messiah.

Mary sobbed. "Lazarus, please, you're hurting me. I can't keep up. My sandals--"

"Do you think I care?" Lazarus stopped. Turning to her, he shook her arm to emphasize his words. "You care nothing for anyone but yourself, you ungrateful brat. You hurt Martha and me daily with your lazy, philandering ways. I tried not to believe the rumors, but they were true. You've disgraced us, lied to us, and betrayed us. You deserve some pain."

He resumed walking, pulling her along with him, pushing her ahead of him in narrow areas. He paid no attention to her cries of pain when her bare feet met sharp stones. What did he care that she'd left her sandals behind? Her pain now was nothing compared to what she'd inflicted on him and Martha. Mary fell to her knees and he pulled her, yelling as he did, ignoring the fear in her eyes. He'd never seen her react in fear toward him before, but he was too angry now for it to register. He ignored her pleas until they were nearly home, when Mary sat on the ground and would go no further.

"Get up." He glared at her.

"Only if you'll listen to me." Although she feared this stranger she was with, Mary was determined to have her say.

"All right. What is it?" There was no mistaking the indifference in his voice as he looked down at her.

"Lazarus, I promise I will not go back there, and I will not shame you and Martha further."

"You swear?"

"I swear."

He held his hand out to her. "Then come on," he said. "We won't tell Martha where I found you and cause her deeper pain. "

Mary took his hand and he pulled her up. He was still too angry to be gentle, but at least he was no longer yelling at her.

After John, Andrew, and their brothers departed, Jesus left Bethabara which was near the Jordan River where John had baptized him. He needed time alone to think and pray. Seeking complete privacy, he traveled south after reaching Bethany, two miles east of Jerusalem. Deciding the desert was where he'd be the least likely to be bothered, he went into the barren foothills of the Judean wilderness. He found a cave which seemed to be the abandoned home of a religious sect known to live in the wilderness. This sect, though not as fanatical as the revolutionary Zealots, still set themselves apart, believing they alone were the true people of God and all others were His enemies. The original inhabitant had left no comforts behind except a jar containing a small amount of stale water. Jesus raised his eyes to heaven.

"Thank You, Father, for providing the water I need to survive during this time I spend with You. You know why I've come and what I desire to know. Since I was a child You've guided me and shown me bits of what was and is to be. I now ask that You reveal my full ministry to me so I might know what I must do. I thank You, Father, that You will do this."

He lowered his head in his arms and visions began to come. He saw crowds of people all looking in one direction, and the vision then centered upon what they looked toward. There was a group of men, and in their center he saw himself, sitting upon a rock. He could see himself speaking, but couldn't hear what was being said. Some of the men about him seemed familiar, but he couldn't see them clearly enough to identify them. The vision changed, and he saw scene after scene of what he knew was his future. At last he saw his own death and he knew its full reason. The time taken to see all of it seemed only a few moments, but when he raised his head the sun was setting. It had been early morning when he'd entered the cave. He drank a mouthful of the water, then went outside.

He sat at the cave entrance watching a small group of conies scamper through the rocks. In the sky there were one or two vultures, and he could hear a desert partridge. He watched two scorpions together for a while before returning to the cave. He'd decided to make it his nightly shelter. There were bears, wolves, and jackals around. Although he didn't fear them, he didn't want to be in the open where a shepherd traveling with his flock might see him. The predators were a sign that a flock might be near.

He lay down and slept, waking before dawn. Again he took a mouthful of water, then watched the sun rise on the new day. "Father, You've given me visions; now tell me what they mean. I see myself teaching and healing many people. I know I'm to speak of Your Kingdom. I thank You that You'll reveal Yourself to those whom You've chosen."

If anyone had been near, they'd have thought him mad, for he talked aloud as if carrying on a conversation, first speaking, then being silent, with his body held as if he were listening intently to someone.

He continued on in this fashion and another day passed quickly and another and another. Each day God revealed more to him until he understood what his full purpose and ministry was. It was no surprise to him. Throughout his life he'd known he was special, for his mother had told him of the circumstances of his birth, but he hadn't fully known what it was he was to experience and suffer. Now he did, but it didn't frighten or sway him. He knew the suffering would be momentary. Now was the important part.

He found himself in a communion with God deeper than he'd ever experienced before; he never wanted it to end. As each day passed he learned more, and all the Scriptures he'd learned and studied all his life were made plainer to him. He'd always thought of God as Father instead of God; and now he knew why. God was his Father, and he was God's image on earth. His purpose was to reveal his Father to others and tell them of the Eternal Kingdom God had set up for mankind.

After Jesus had been in the desert for about two weeks, a being appeared before him. The being was beautiful to look at, but Jesus knew him for what he really was: Satan's spirit revealed to him.

Satan smiled an evil smile. "Greetings, Jesus."

Jesus didn't answer but looked calmly at the smiling face and cold, lifeless eyes.

"You've been here a long time with nothing to eat. You believe you're the Son of God, do you not?"

Again, Jesus was silent.

"Ah, you do. If you're God's son, you don't have to be hungry. Command this stone to turn to bread." He pointed to a round flat stone on the ground in front of the cave in which Jesus was sleeping. The stone was shaped much like a loaf of unleavened bread.

Jesus looked calmly from Satan to the stone, then back again. "The Scriptures say, `Man shall not live by bread alone, but by every word of God.'"

Satan's smile vanished, and his eyes narrowed to slits. He then transported Jesus to a mountain which provided a plain view of all the known kingdoms in the world. Waving his hand out over the view, Satan spoke again. "I'll give you these kingdoms and their power. It was turned over to me and is mine to give. If you'll worship me, it's yours."

Jesus knew this wasn't true. "I rebuke you, Satan", he said, his voice growing sterner. "The Scriptures say, `Thou shalt worship the Lord thy God and serve Him only.'"

Satan scowled. Then, transporting Jesus again, he took him to Jerusalem and set him on a high gable of the temple. "If you're truly the Son of God, throw yourself down from here, for the Scriptures say, `He shall set the angels about thee to protect thee and they shall keep thee from even falling and stubbing thy toe.'"

Jesus countered, "It is written, 'You shall not tempt the Lord your God.'"

Instantly Jesus found himself back in front of the cave in the wilderness, and a great peace came over him. He slept and awoke refreshed. Satan wasn't through, however, and he returned several times during the remaining month with the same temptations, varying only the order in which they were offered.

After Jesus had spent forty days in the desert cave, Satan returned one last time and presented everything he could conjure up to Jesus who, using the Scriptures, rejected him and all his tests. At the end of it, Jesus knew his ordeal was finished for the time being because God's angels appeared to him and comforted him by praising him for withstanding Satan's wiles.

Although he hadn't eaten anything during the time he spent in the wilderness, Jesus was strengthened and encouraged, and he set out to return to Galilee to begin gathering those he knew God would call to follow him.

# Chapter Six

## The Wedding

In Capernaum, where their fishing trade was flourishing, the four partners and Zebedee, the father of James and John, were busy mending their nets. It had been six weeks since they'd been to Bethabara. Although he'd been greatly affected by Jesus, Peter was beginning to doubt again that they'd really found the Messiah.

"If he really is the Messiah, why isn't he doing something about the Romans? Why isn't he proving himself? And where is he anyway? No one's seen or heard from him since before we left Bethabara." He threw out the questions they'd all been thinking, but the others didn't want to admit they were beginning to doubt.

"Now Peter," Andrew said, "he may have a good reason for not declaring himself openly yet. He can't do it all alone. He needs a following first."

"That's right," James said. "And with Herod up in arms about the Baptist, now is not the time for Jesus to be stirring everything up."

John the Baptist had begun preaching in Galilee a few weeks earlier. He'd bellowed the usual accusations at first about vipers and sons being raised up of stones. Then he began in a new vein. He'd alluded to it while they'd been in Bethabara, but they were surprised to hear him openly berate Herod for breaking up his brother's marriage and then marrying his brother's former wife the day of the divorce. There were rumors that Herodius, his new wife, was seeking a way to get John quieted permanently and that Herod was planning to arrest him.

"Well," Peter said, "it seems to me he'd at least show himself to someone."

"He will when the time comes," John said. "Jesus has a way of always knowing the right time to do things." He picked up his nets and headed for the boats. "Coming James? Father?"

James and Zebedee followed him, leaving Peter and Andrew alone. "Well, I suppose we should get out there, too." Peter rose, and Andrew picked up his net and followed him. They were all busy throwing out the nets and hauling them back in to be emptied when Peter looked up and saw Jesus standing on the shore watching them.

"Andrew, look," Peter said. He looked around to call out to James and John, but they were too far away to hear him, having gone to shore to mend a torn net.

Andrew looked to where Peter was pointing. "It's Jesus," he said. "Let's go in and see what he wants."

They rowed the boat in and drew it up on shore. Getting out, Andrew said, "Master, what is it you want?"

"Come and follow me and become fishers of men," Jesus said. He began to walk along the shore toward the boat James and John were in. Andrew and Peter left their boat, nets, and the catch they'd made and followed him as he walked to the other boat. Jesus nodded and greeted Zebedee as befitted a nephew to his elder, then he turned to James and John. "Come with me and I'll show you many things," he said.

The brothers looked at each other and then at their father. Without a word, they got up and, stepping out of the boat, followed Jesus as he went toward the main area of town. He entered a house, and they followed him into it. To one side were carpenter's tools, the tools of his trade. The other side of the room had normal living quarters. He laid out mats for them to sit upon and produced water for them to wash their hands and feet. The men settled themselves down and looked expectantly at Jesus. Questions burned in them. Where he had been the last six weeks was foremost in their minds, but they became aware as he talked with them that they wouldn't learn the answer from him.

He shared his evening meal with them and told them many things they didn't understand. He had a way about him that was refreshing. He spoke differently from anyone they'd ever heard before. What he said wasn't new, but how he said it was.

While Peter and Andrew were enthralled, James and John were more awed by his words. This was Jesus, whom they'd grown up with, played with, fought childish fights with, cried with, laughed with. They'd shared family sorrows and family joys, yet it was as if they'd never known him. He had the same laugh, the same frown, the same mannerisms, the same ability to put someone at ease that had always characterized Jesus. But something was different, and they couldn't pinpoint what it was.

At last it was time to retire. He invited them to stay, saying, "Tomorrow, there's a wedding in Cana. I'll go and you must come with me."


It was the fourth day of the wedding feast, and there seemed to be no end to the celebrations. Andrew, James, and John stood to one side of the garden outside the house. They were watching Jesus and Peter give piggyback rides to the small children to amuse them. A small tot came up to John and tugged at his robe. When John looked down, the little boy raised up his arms in a silent plea to be lifted up. John looked over at his brother and Andrew. He shrugged as he picked the boy up and placed him on his shoulders. The child laughed with glee and pretended to whip John with a stick as they romped around the yard. All the men were laughing, and a crowd of wedding guests was gathering to watch the antics.

Jesus' mother approached him. "The feast is still at its height and they're nearly out of wine," she said.

He took the child from his shoulders and placed him on the ground. Straightening back up, he looked at her and said, "What would you have me do? You know it's not time yet for me to begin my ministry."

Confident that Jesus would do what he could to help, his mother turned to the servants nearby. "Do as he tells you."

The servants looked expectantly at Jesus, wondering what he could possibly do to help the situation. Jesus walked across the garden to the wall. There were six water pots, each capable of holding twenty to thirty gallons of water, which was used for the Jewish cleansing ceremony. "Fill these," he said.

The servants obediently lifted the pots and carried them out of the garden and down the road to the community well. When they returned, they set them in front of Jesus, who took a cup and filled it from one of the pots. Handing it to the servant nearest him, he said, "Now take this to the Master of Ceremonies."

The servant took the cup of water into the house and gave it to the Master of Ceremonies, who had to taste all of the wine before it was served to the guests. The Master of Ceremonies' face changed from mild interest to surprise when he tasted it. He took another taste and then looked around until he spotted the bride-groom among the guests. Going over to him, the Master of Ceremonies said, "What is this? Usually the best wine is served first, but you've served the poor wine first and left the best until now."

The bridegroom, having no idea what the Master of Ceremonies was talking about, stood speechless. Andrew, who had followed the servant in and had witnessed all that had taken place, went back to the garden without waiting to hear what the bridegroom had to say.

He took Peter, James, and John aside. "Do you know what?" he said. "The Master of Ceremonies said that the water was wine," The others just looked at him incredulously.

"That can't be," James said. "It was water. We all saw the servants take the water pots out."

"But I tell you, he said it was wine," Andrew said.

"It couldn't be," Peter said.

"There's only one way to find out," John said. "Let's taste it."

They went over to the water pots and drew out some of the water. Each one gasped and looked inside his cup after tasting it.

"It *is* wine," Peter said.


"Would you believe it, Martha? The water the servants gave the Master of Ceremonies was wine when he tasted it!" Miriam was relating to Martha more of the gossip she'd heard from her husband. This time it was Jesus who was in the news. "The whole of Galilee is buzzing about it."

Martha only half listened to the rest of what Miriam said. A miracle had happened in Cana. Could the words spoken between the Baptist and the blue-eyed stranger have referred to something connected with this? She was sure this Jesus was the same one she'd seen at Bethabara. There had been rumors that he'd begun preaching, and she thought his baptism had been so unusual that it could be no one else.

Martha decided to speak to Lazarus about going up to Cana. Maybe this Jesus was still there. Maybe he could do more miracles. Maybe he could help Mary. She quickly finished filling her water jar, said farewell, and headed home. She wanted to catch Lazarus before he left for the day.

She hoped he could help Mary. Her sister had changed so much that she wasn't recognizable even to those who had known her all her life. She was more sullen and irritable than ever and did nothing but lie around when she was at home. Since the day Lazarus had found and brought her home, she no longer stayed away all night, but frequently left during the day for several hours. She was always evasive when questioned about where she'd been. Many times she snapped and said that it was none of Martha's business.

When Martha entered the house, Lazarus was gone and so was Mary. That was another thing that troubled Martha; Mary was sneaking around now. She knew Martha wouldn't tell Lazarus she'd gone out, so she waited until he left in the morning and then she left. Martha, not wanting to cause friction in the family, was caught in the middle.

She didn't know where Lazarus had found Mary because neither Lazarus nor Mary ever mentioned that day. Lazarus had been angrier than Martha had ever seen him when they'd arrived home. She still didn't dare bring the subject up, although it was now seven weeks since then. He was very stern with Mary now, and Martha sensed it wasn't wise to feed the fire of his wrath by telling him trivial things about what Mary did during the day.

Heaving a sigh, Martha took the bowl filled with grain out to the millstones. Today would be another day that she'd do the work alone.

# *Chapter Seven*

## The Cleansing

Mary ran down the side street to the main road. She was later than she should have been if she wanted to beat Lazarus home. She never had this problem when she was with Caleb, but today Joshua had wanted her. She'd cherish this day. It was the first time he'd wanted her since that dreadful day when Lazarus had come to the brothel and dragged her home.

She stopped a moment and closed her eyes as she clutched her hands to her breasts, breasts he'd touched only a few moments before. Just thinking of it sent tingles through her body. Caleb never affected her this way. Caleb had to do a lot just to get her even slightly aroused, but Joshua only had to speak to her and she melted. She would have preferred to forget all about Caleb, but since that day several months earlier, none of the other men would come near her. Lazarus had seen to that with that stupid threat he'd made.

Suddenly she remembered she was late and began running again. No time to daydream now; she had to beat him home or he'd question her and surely find out where she'd been. Maybe Martha would even break her silence and tell him it had been going on almost ever since he'd found her at Joshua's. Mary didn't want to find out what Lazarus would do if he ever found out she'd gone back after her promise not to.

When he'd dragged her home, she'd wept and promised never to go back there or do the shameful things she'd been doing. She had managed to keep her promise for almost a week, but the compulsion was stronger than her fear of Lazarus. She had to go back. When she'd showed up at Joshua's again, Caleb had been both surprised and pleased, but the other men had looked at her askance and none of them would have anything to do with her.

She'd explained to Caleb she could only stay a certain amount of time and then must leave so she would be home before her brother. Caleb had been very understanding and even reminded her when it was time to leave. But today Joshua had finally taken her to the roof, and they'd spent the whole afternoon there. She hadn't dared—or wanted—to tell Joshua she must leave and so had stayed until Caleb had stuck his head up over the stairwell, hissing at her that if she didn't leave, her brother might come looking for her again.

Right away Joshua had told her to go. She knew he was angry that she hadn't told him she had a time limit. She'd heard him swear when Caleb told him as she went down the stairs. She hoped he wouldn't stay mad.

She stopped running at the beginning of their street. It wouldn't do for her to come in breathless from running. Then Lazarus would surely know she was doing something he disapproved of. Maybe Martha was covering for her; she hoped so. After all, this was the first time, since that day, she'd not been home when he returned. Maybe he wouldn't question her.

When she reached the house, her heart sank as she heard Lazarus's voice inside. She squared her shoulders and opened the door, beaming a smile as she said as cheerfully as she could, "My, the day was so beautiful, I didn't realize how late it was." Neither of them seemed to notice how nervous she was and she began to relax. Silently she congratulated herself as she realized that she'd gotten away with it. This time, anyway.


Martha balanced the water jar on her head and walked as quickly as she could back to the house. Jesus was to be in Jerusalem in a few days, Miriam had told her. She had to convince Lazarus that they should attend also. Although it was only a couple of miles and Lazarus usually never missed Passover in Jerusalem, Martha feared that he might decide not to attend this year. It would be her luck.

Whenever she wanted something even half as badly as this, something always happened to keep her from having it. She was growing more concerned about Mary every day and wanted to approach Jesus about her. Martha was hearing more and more about Jesus and his healings, especially now that John the Baptist was imprisoned.

Herodius had finally gotten her way and the desert preacher was locked up, but many still believed him to be the Messiah. Lazarus was one of them, but Martha believed Jesus was the Messiah. John had never healed anyone or delivered them of a demon. Miriam was constantly relaying stories about how Jesus easily performed these acts more and more frequently. Martha was determined to go to the temple in Jerusalem on Passover to see Jesus and ask if he could help Mary.

In her haste and excitement, Martha nearly dropped the jar as she crossed the threshold. She caught her balance in time, however, and set it down in its usual place. Then she set about making dinner and tidying up the house. Mary always managed to make a mess before she left, and Martha always had to clean up after her before she could do what daily chores there were. All of this was building resentment inside her, but she dared not complain. Too many questions would arise that she wouldn't be able to answer.


As they entered the temple, Jesus' mother and sisters approached a table to purchase doves for their sacrifice. Jesus stopped, and his eyes slowly traveled from one area to another, anger growing in them.

James and John started toward a booth, but Peter held out an arm to stop them. He nodded, indicating Jesus, who was removing some ropes from a nearby stall. They watched silently as he tied the ropes together. John went over to his aunt and, pointing to Jesus, drew the women away from the merchants. The men surrounded the women as they watched the quiet, gentle man they were with change before their eyes into what seemed to be an angry fanatic.

"Cheaters," Jesus shouted. He flayed the improvised whip in all directions as he scattered the oxen and sheep out of the Court of the Gentiles. After every animal was chased out and their owners were frantically following them, Jesus dropped the whip and turned to the table nearest him. It was covered with money, for it was where people could get change if they needed it. He reached out with one arm and wiped the table clean, then proceeded to pick it up and throw it across the hall.

He turned to the merchants his mother and sisters had been dealing with only moments before. "What right have you to turn this, my Father's temple, into a common merchant's booth? Do you take pride in turning a place of worship into a thieves' den?"

"What authority do you have in turning us out?" one of the men behind the tables shot back. "Give us a sign that God's behind you."

Jesus stopped and looked at him a moment before answering quietly while gesturing toward himself. "Destroy this temple, and in three days it will rise again."

The Pharisees standing there, outraged at Jesus' actions, cried out, "This temple took forty-six years to build, and it still isn't finished. You would have us believe you could do it in three days?" They laughed at him.

Ignoring their laughter, Jesus turned and entered the temple, followed by those who were with him and others who were curious about him. Seating himself, he began to teach.

"Do not concern yourself with the cares of this world. Consider the wild animals and how the Father provides food for them. Neither be concerned with what you shall wear. The flowers dress the fields with their beauty. Don't you think our heavenly Father is even more concerned with what you shall eat and wear? He is the provider of all."

At the front of the crowd a young boy sat. The boy looked normal at first glance. Then he turned and Jesus saw that one arm was no more than a stump with a hand at the boy's shoulder. He beckoned the child to him and looked at the crowd. The boy's parents, Jesus' new disciples, the smug Jewish leaders, those just curious about this man who dared to speak out against the money changers and cheating merchants, were all watching.

Jesus took the boy onto his lap. "What is your name?"

"Zechariah," the boy said.

"Zechariah, the Father loves you very much." Jesus reached over and touched the stump on the boy's shoulder.

The crowd gasped. The hand was growing into an arm. The boy's brown eyes grew big as he watched his arm become whole. Many in the crowd dashed out and reappeared later with a friend or loved one in need of healing. Jesus did not disappoint them. He continued to teach and heal throughout the day, and the Jewish leaders choked on their laughter as jealousy began to grow in their hearts.


Martha stood next to Lazarus in front of a merchant's booth. They were waiting to purchase their sacrifice for the Passover feast. Suddenly, the animals scattered and ran. Martha turned and saw the stranger they called Jesus wielding a whip, his face contorted in anger.

She moved over to a corner and watched the drama unfold and listened as the Pharisees and others questioned him. Lazarus had disappeared, but she was sure he'd also be noting what transpired.

After Jesus entered into the Sacred Enclosure, Martha searched for Lazarus. Knowing he wouldn't just leave her, she guessed he'd followed Jesus inside, so she also entered and went to the Court of the Women. She found out later from Lazarus what Jesus did after they were inside. She knew she had to talk to Jesus about Mary.

Caleb walked through the gate to the city. Not being a very religious man, he cared little for most of the Jewish celebrations, but Passover was an exciting time to be in Jerusalem and he went there solely for excitement. He followed a crowd that had journeyed through Bethany and noted that several were traveling with a man who seemed intriguing. Caleb couldn't place his finger on it, but the man was different, special somehow. Once he turned and his clear blue eyes were looking directly at Caleb; they seemed to know everything about him, even his most minor thoughts. Every act he'd ever done seemed to be laid bare, yet the eyes were warm with compassion. They haunted him constantly afterward.

He followed the group to the temple. In all the times he'd been in Jerusalem during the Passover, Caleb had never gone to the temple. He didn't come for the religious aspect, but this time was different. He was drawn by those eyes, that man.

He followed the crowd into the Sacred Enclosure and witnessed the miracle with the boy's arm. After several more healings, Jesus taught some more. He told a story familiar to them all. It was the story of the prodigal son; only Jesus didn't tell it the way the rabbis told it. Always, while growing up, Caleb had heard how the prodigal son was not forgiven because he was undeserving, but this was not how Jesus told it. Instead, the son was not only welcome back, but he was also forgiven by the father. The story made Caleb want to hear more. The judgmental attitude of the Jewish leaders was what had kept him away from the temple for so many years. But this Jesus did not teach judgment; he taught forgiveness and love.

The week passed quickly, and before Caleb knew it, it was over. For the first time, he'd spent the whole time at the temple. He couldn't stay away. This man called Jesus was special. Caleb knew he had to see more of him.

# *Chapter Eight*

## The Outcast

Mary half skipped through the streets, humming as she went. Today had been a beautiful day, one of the best in a long time. Daphne had been gone, and Joshua had poured all his attention on her; he hadn't even looked at another woman and had taken her almost directly to the roof. He always made her feel so good. This had to be love. She'd forgotten her determination to keep away from married men. When she was with Joshua as she had been today, she forgot Daphne even existed. He was so wonderful. She closed her eyes as her memory traced his features–so large, so handsome. An unconscious sigh escaped her lips as the memories flooded her mind.

She was jerked back to the present when a man screamed at her to watch where she was going. Her eyes popped open, and she saw that she'd nearly upset a cart full of produce the man was selling. Quickly, she swerved to avoid it and resumed her daydreams. Thoughts of Joshua again flooded her mind as she passed familiar houses and streets. She walked slowly, savoring every moment as she remembered it. She had time; she was early today.

Jesus opened his door at the sound of a knock. There in the shadows stood a man he vaguely recognized as being in the temple during the Passover feast.

"Yes?" he said. "How may I help you?"

"Teacher, may I enter?" the man said.

"Assuredly." Jesus stood back so the man could pass him. He recognized the man in the better light and saw it was the Pharisee named Nicodemus. Jesus gave him water to clean himself from his journey. "Please sit. Here's a basin to wash with."

"Thank you." Nicodemus gratefully took the basin and cleaned himself. Jesus sat across from him, patiently waiting for him to speak.

"Master," Nicodemus said. "I know you've been sent by God to teach us, for no one could otherwise do the miracles we've witnessed by your hands."

Jesus smiled. "Truly, Nicodemus, you haven't yet witnessed the greatest miracle. It's to be born again. For without that, you cannot enter God's kingdom."

"Born again? How can a man ever be born again? He can never go back into his mother."

"It's just as important that your spirit is given birth, as well as your body. When you're born of a woman, your body is born. When God's Spirit gives you light, your spirit is born. That's being born again." The puzzled look on Nicodemus's face prompted Jesus

"You're a teacher and you don't know this? How can you teach spiritual things if you don't understand something you can see, hear, or feel? I've given you an example that you're familiar with, and you don't understand or believe me. How could I explain a heavenly experience to you? No one can enter heaven except the Son God sent, and as the serpent was raised up by Moses, so must that Son be raised. Whoever believes he's God's Son shall be born again and live forever. God hasn't sent His Son to condemn, but to save the world because He loves the world so much. The Son was sent so that the world might not perish. Anyone who believes this will live. Those who don't will die because of their unbelief and their desire for evil. Those who love evil can't witness light because the light reveals the evil he loves. Those who don't love evil aren't afraid of the light; in fact, they're drawn to it, and what they do as a result is from God."

Nicodemus sat in silence a while as he pondered what Jesus said. Then, without a word, he got up and left.


Martha looked up quickly from her work. She thought she had heard a noise in the house. It was too early for Lazarus to return home. Was it Mary? Before she could investigate, Lazarus appeared in the doorway to the garden.

"Where's Mary?" His eyes surveyed Martha doing a job meant for two people.

Martha remained silent. What should she tell him? Mary had left, as usual, immediately after he had. She had no idea where she'd gone. "I sent her to get some water."

Lazarus's eyes gazed at her a moment. Then he said, quietly, "You're a poor liar, Martha. The water pot is still where it should be. I passed the well on my way back and Mary wasn't there, nor was she anywhere in sight. Where is she? Why isn't she helping you?"

Martha lowered her head and looked at the ground. "I don't know where she is. She left after you did and didn't say where she intended to go."

"Did she at least say when she would return?"

"No," Martha barely whispered. Lazarus frightened her even more with his present calmness than he had when he was uncharacteristically angry.

"Has she done this often?" When Martha gave no answer, he repeated, "Has she gone off like this often?"

Martha raised her head and looked at her brother. Tears welled up in her eyes as she realized she could no longer protect Mary and keep peace in the family. "Yes, Lazarus," she said. "She's gone often." There was no need to say `every day'; `often' sounded bad enough.

Anger flared in Lazarus's eyes. He turned and entered the house. She knew he wouldn't let this pass.


Lazarus sat staring at the entrance to the house in front of him, his arms folded over his chest and a scowl on his face. He'd been hearing rumors again about Mary. That was the reason he'd gone home early three days ago. He wanted to find out if they were true. He sat brooding, waiting for her to come out. Finally, he decided to enter the brothel and take her out by force again. He disliked doing anything while angry, but he'd no longer tolerate Mary's actions.

Mary raised her head at the commotion she heard from the stairwell.

"What is it?" Caleb questioned. He stopped and turned in the direction her eyes were focused. There stood Lazarus.

"Get dressed," Lazarus said. His face was flushed with anger. "And you," he turned to Caleb, "I ought to kill you, but I won't; I'll let God take revenge. She's not worth my efforts anymore."

Mary quickly rose and picked up her gown.

"Mary," Caleb said in a low, sad voice. She turned and looked at him with fear in her eyes. "I'm sorry."

She just nodded and gave him a weak smile. With shaking hands, she fastened her girdle and covered her head with her veils.

Lazarus stood watching, anger emanating from him like a tangible thing. Caleb watched silently. When Mary finished, she glanced down at him before turning toward Lazarus. She saw in his green eyes a glimpse of something more than just sympathy, but she didn't have time to think about it before she felt Lazarus's hand grab her arm. She looked up into the snapping black eyes of her brother. His usually handsome face was contorted with rage. He shook her once, then shoved her ahead of him toward the stairs.

"Move," he said.

Biting her lower lip, she hurried off the roof. She knew Lazarus was even angrier this time than he had been the first time he'd discovered her at Joshua's. That time he'd hollered, but this time his controlled voice and actions were even more frightening.

Lazarus followed closely behind her. As they reached the door, he turned and addressed the room of people. "I told you before I would kill anyone who touched her again. I would do that now if I thought she was worth it, but she isn't." Turning, he shoved her through the portal.

Joining Mary outside the brothel, Lazarus grabbed her arm and propelled her forward. He felt about to explode inside, his anger bubbling out in heated words.

"Jezebel, Harlot. You are a worthless, worthless ingrate." He could not contain his wrath and Mary cried out as he squeezed her arm while dragging her through the streets. Lazarus's voice was loud and she saw neighbors peeking out doors and windows as they passed by.

A voice outside startled Martha. She turned to see Mary being pushed through the door by Lazarus.

"Mary! Lazarus!" she said. The looks on their faces frightened her. Mary was weeping and begging, but Martha couldn't understand her because of the frequent sobs and Lazarus's roaring voice. His face was livid, and Martha had never seen him so angry, not even the last time he'd brought Mary home.

"Get your things and get out," he bellowed. "I never want to see you again. Get out of Bethany and our lives. You're not worth even looking at."

Martha was appalled by her brother's words. Where had he found Mary? Silent tears rolled down her cheeks as she watched her sister gather her things and get ready to leave. What had she done?

# Part Two

## Popularity

## The Second Year

*The Spirit of the Lord God is upon me; because the Lord hath anointed me to preach good tidings...*

Isaiah 61:1.

# Chapter Nine

## The Servant

Andrew and Peter jumped from their boat and pulled it ashore just as John and James began to row back. They'd been out all night on a fruitless vigil. Peter was becoming discouraged. They had customers to satisfy; if fish didn't come into their nets soon, there would be no customers. There were other businesses out there, and they were catching fish.

Andrew followed him as he sighed in resignation and carried his net over to wash it in the clear water in the Sea of Galilee where they'd been fishing. In the distance a crowd was forming and they heard a familiar voice speaking out.

"Sounds like Jesus is teaching today," Andrew said.

"Yes." Peter was in no mood for conversation.

The others took note and kept quiet as they cleaned the nets. The crowd was drawing closer, and now they could hear not only Jesus' voice, but also could distinguish his words as well. He was speaking on faith. The fishermen had their backs to the shore and didn't notice that the people were crowding Jesus up to the water's edge. Out of the corner of his eye, Peter saw Jesus step into the boat he and Andrew used. He straightened up and Jesus beckoned to him.

"Take me out a few feet so I may sit and teach without being pushed further into the water, Peter." Jesus' voice was low. He had a way about him; he could make his voice loud enough to be heard by twenty thousand or could lower it so only one could hear. It was compelling.

So were his eyes; Jesus spoke with his eyes. They were a crystal clear blue when he was calm, but turned darker if he was angered or excited in some other way. They snapped or twinkled according to his emotions as well. Peter had been with him only a few times, but he was finding this man to be intriguing in many ways.

He climbed into the boat and went out a few feet from shore and sat, waiting patiently, until Jesus was through. The sermon was interesting, with many illustrations of what faith was, but the last thing Peter was expecting was that he was about to be used by Jesus for a demonstration. When Jesus stopped talking, he turned to Peter and Andrew, who'd also entered the boat.

"Let down your nets," he said quietly.

Peter was dumbfounded at first. "Lord," he said, "we've been fishing all night and have caught nothing." He paused. The sermon had been on faith. Did he or did he not believe what Jesus taught? He decided to try out what he'd heard. "But because you say to, I'll put out my net again."

Peter threw the net over the side and sat silently pondering what Jesus had been teaching on, not paying attention to the nets he'd just put out.

"Peter," Andrew said, waking his brother out of his musings. "The net is breaking."

Peter moved automatically to draw the net up as he called out, "James! John! Come, we need help."

James and John jumped into their boat and rowed out to Peter and Andrew. The four of them heaved the net up and divided the catch between the two boats, both of which began to sink. Peter, awed and frightened by the realization of what had happened, threw himself at Jesus' knees.

"Lord, I'm not worthy to have you near me, for I'm a sinful man."

"Peter," Jesus said quietly, "forget this kind of net and come with me to catch the hearts of men instead."

The men looked at each other and back at the fish at their feet in the boat. They silently rowed back to the shore where the crowd was dispersing. Without a word, they dragged the boats ashore. Leaving their nets with the freshly caught fish in them, they turned their backs on the boats and followed Jesus back to the house at which he was staying.


Caleb followed the four fishermen and the preacher. He'd witnessed the catch of fish and listened carefully to the words between Peter and Jesus. He wanted to know more of this preacher. He spoke true words, wise words, words with authority. He knew what he spoke of and wasn't afraid of controversial subjects.

Most of all, he portrayed God in a different way than Caleb had ever heard. God had always been a feared being, an untouchable being who would just as soon smite you dead as look at you or care about you. But Jesus called Him Father and spoke of Him as loving men as His children and caring for the needs of men. That was a new concept to Caleb.

He followed Jesus back to Capernaum and went to hear him every day. He wanted to see if Jesus lived what he said. Caleb had seen too much hypocrisy in the Pharisees and Sadducees to believe any of the Jewish leaders could be honest, but so far Jesus was, and Caleb was drawn to him. He saw the five men enter a house, so he found a spot close by and sat down to watch and wait for Jesus to show himself in public again.


Mary stopped at the inn in Sychar. She pulled her veil up over her face to conceal it as much as possible. She was sure her eyes and nose were still red from crying. It had been two days since Lazarus had told her to leave and she still couldn't believe it. Every time she thought of it, the tears began anew.

Both Mary and Martha had pleaded and begged, but Lazarus had remained firm. Mary was to go immediately with whatever she could carry of her belongings; the rest would have to stay. She wouldn't be welcome one more night in his house. He was adamant, and when Martha again began to protest, he told her in graphic detail where and how he'd found Mary. Martha was appalled and shocked, and she had stopped her defense of Mary.

*A fallen woman. That's what they think I am.* She'd never thought of herself that way, and even now she didn't. She only wanted to love and be loved. The men she knew all equated that with sex, so she complied. What else was she to do?

She had no place to go and no one to turn to for help. She'd gone back to Joshua's, but they refused to let her even enter the building. When she had inquired about Caleb, they had told her he wasn't there. She couldn't find him anywhere, so she'd decided she'd go where no one knew her and do what she had to do to live. She no longer cared what happened to her. Why should she? No one else did.

She spent a fitful night at an inn. Arising early, she was on her way before daylight had fully shown itself. Her feet were sore and her legs ached, but she was determined to get as far from Bethany as she could. She didn't know where she was going; she only knew she had to go north; maybe to Capernaum near the Sea of Galilee. Something in the back of her mind was directing her there. She'd forgotten that Caleb had been talking of going there because of some preacher he'd seen during Passover. Without consciously realizing it, she was following him.

Caleb sat listening intently to Jesus. For months he'd followed him, unable to stay away from this man who seemed to know everything. Caleb felt changed by just being near him and listening to him teach. This Jesus knew what he was talking about, yet he was gentle and full of compassion for the weak and sick. Caleb had never heard a cruel word or unwarranted rebuke come from his mouth. When Jesus spoke of God and heaven, it made Caleb want to know God better and have the relationship with Him this man had. Jesus always put God into human terms and used stories to illustrate his teachings. It made Him more real, and for the first time in Caleb's life, he felt like he wanted to be close to God.

Caleb half dozed in front of the house he thought was the home of Peter and Andrew. Suddenly his eyes jerked open. A movement at the doorway had caught his eye. Someone came through the door at that moment, and Caleb recognized Andrew, followed by James and John, then came Jesus with Peter. Caleb stood and prepared to follow them, wherever that would be.

As they moved down the road, it became apparent that they were heading for the synagogue. He debated with himself about going in and decided against it. He hadn't slept well the night before because of his vigil and was afraid he'd fall asleep during the teachings and embarrass himself. He settled himself down as comfortably as he could. Spotting a young boy a short ways away, he beckoned to him, and the boy approached him shyly.

"Yes, sir," he said.

Caleb smiled warmly to gain the boy's confidence. "How would you like to earn some money?"

The boy's face lit up and his eyes grew wide as he looked at the coins Caleb held out. He didn't answer, but only looked from Caleb's hand to his face in a questioning glance.

Caleb bent down so his eyes were at the child's level. "Do you see those five men over there?" He pointed in the direction of Jesus and his companions. The boy nodded. "I'll give you one of these two mites now. When you see them come back out of the synagogue, I want you to wake me. When you do, I'll give you the other mite." The boy looked up into Caleb's face and then at the coins in his hand. He eagerly nodded his head and took the mite Caleb offered him. Caleb sighed contentedly and leaned back to get some much-needed sleep.

Caleb shook his arm to ward off the animal bothering his sleep, but it did no good. He opened his eyes and found himself looking into the face of a young boy. Disoriented momentarily, he shook his head and blinked a few times. Then his memory returned and he looked at the boy, whose big brown eyes hadn't left his face.

"Master, they've come out," the child said.

"Thank you, boy. Here's your mite. Where are they now?" He handed the promised coin to the child and let his gaze follow in the direction the boy indicated. Jesus was surrounded by many people. Caleb got up, brushing some of the dirt and sand from his clothes.

"Is there anything else you'd have me do, Master?" The boy looked hopefully at the purse at Caleb's side.

"No, son, you've done enough. Thank you again. Now go and play, and God's peace be with you."

"And with you, sir."

The boy ran off to join his friends, and Caleb walked over to the crowd Jesus had drawn. He edged his way through until he was standing next to Peter. The Jewish leaders of the area had just begun talking to Jesus.

"Lord, we've come on behalf of Cornelius, the Roman centurion," one of the leaders said.

Jesus' face was expressionless. "What is it he wants?"

"His servant is ill," the leader replied.

"He asks that you heal him," another said.

"Lord, he's a good man, not like most other soldiers. He does a lot for us. He built our synagogue," the first man said.

"Paid for it all himself," the second added. "He does all he can for us. He deserves your help, if anyone does."

Jesus stood silently, looking at their faces. "All right, I'll come and heal his servant."

He began walking in the direction of the centurion's house.

Caleb stayed as close as he could, but it wasn't easy. Peter and the other three had formed a circle around Jesus to keep the crowd from trampling him. The Jewish leaders led the way up the road. Periodically they turned to make sure Jesus was still following them. When they were nearly at the centurion's house, a servant came out from it and stopped them. He walked past the Jewish leaders and stood in front of Jesus.

"My Lord," he said, bowing.

"Yes?" Jesus waited.

"My master sent me out to give you a message, Lord."

"Go on."

"He says to tell you he's not worthy for you to enter his house. He doesn't even feel worthy to come before you himself. That's why he asked the Jewish leaders to come to you on behalf of his servant. He sent me out to tell you it's not necessary for you to come in. He understands the authority you hold because he's also a man of authority and when he gives an order, it's followed regardless of whether it's to a soldier under him or one of his slaves. He believes you have that kind of authority over disease and demons."

Jesus was stunned. He stood in silence a moment before turning to the crowd and saying, "I haven't witnessed faith like this in any Israelite. I tell you all, truly, that many like this man will come to my Father's table who are not first choice, and many of those who are first choice will go where there's not a feast, but suffering instead." He turned back to the servant and quietly said to him, "It is done. Return to your master."

"Thank you, Lord." The servant bowed and returned to the house.

As the crowd turned to follow Jesus, Caleb heard a cry of joy come from the centurion's home. He turned to see the servant who'd just talked to Jesus calling out a window and waving his arms. Most of what he cried out wasn't clear, but from the joyous look on his face, Caleb gathered that Jesus had spoken truly and the ailing servant had fully recovered.

# Chapter Ten

## The Merchant

When Mary reached Nain, she stayed at the inn overnight, but when she was about to pay her bill she found she could not. She hadn't realized she'd used all the money she had for food and lodging. The innkeeper looked up and smiled at her, not knowing that she was unable to pay him. Mary quickly looked around the room. What could she do? Maybe if she explained to the innkeeper, he'd let her owe it. Then it dawned on her that she wouldn't be able to pay it later any more than she could now. She had no way of getting more money.

She was about to explain her problem to the innkeeper and take the consequences when a man in the corner caught her eye. He was old, older than her brother at least, but he dressed as if he were very well off. Instead of approaching the innkeeper, Mary changed her direction and headed for the old gentleman. If she gave him favors and he were willing to pay for them, what could that hurt? She'd be doing nothing she hadn't done many times in the past already. The way he looked to her, she'd be helping him as much as he'd be helping her. Even old men had needs, and this one looked ancient to Mary. His hair was even beginning to get streaks of grey in it.

He looked up as she walked toward him, and she smiled. He smiled back uncertainly as she stopped directly in front of him.

"Peace, my lord," she said. "Are you journeying far?"

"Hardly, I live in Nain," the man said. "I come in here every once in a while to pass the time."

"I see." Mary lowered her eyes demurely. "Doesn't your wife object?" She thought it would be wise to discover his marital status, figuring unmarried men would be more likely to pay. After all, why should a man pay for something he could get for nothing any time he wanted?

He laughed heartily. "Oh, I'm not married."

She responded with another inviting smile. "No?"

"No. But here, sit." He spread out his pillows so she could settle next to him. "What about you? A pretty woman like you must have been wed long ago."

Shaking her head, she answered, "I'm not married either. My husband was killed by a Roman soldier." She decided a white lie was in order and adopted Martha's fiancé Daniel, as her own. It would also explain any experience she had in bed.

"I'm sorry to hear that. Was he doing something to anger the soldier?"

"No. Not unless walking on the same road the soldier's chariot was speeding down was enough to anger the man." She managed to sound indignant and still be able to smile a wan smile.

"Ah," he said, "the impertinent militia. They've conquered us, so they believe we can be treated as animals. They regard our lives as worth less than an animal's."

"Yes, it seems that way." She sighed and looked down to hide the excitement on her face. It was working. She was gaining his sympathy. "And, as if that weren't enough, I'm on my way to Capernaum because I feel I had too many reminders of him where we lived, but someone has stolen all my money." She thought of what Lazarus had done to her, hoping it would cause her to cry. She needed tears to make her story more believable. It worked to a certain extent, although she found it difficult to cry.

"Now don't cry." He reached up and, using a cloth, wiped her cheeks with a shaking hand. "When did this happen?"

"Last night."

"Here?"

She nodded. She didn't trust her voice just yet. Her excitement might show. She needed to compose herself and make it sound tearful.

"Tell me." The sympathy in his quiet voice calmed her enough so she was able to act the role she was taking on.

"I stopped here to rest, and I had a purse full of money. Daniel, my husband, had left me a great sum of money, and I had it in a purse attached to my belt. This morning, when I awoke, the purse was still there, but the money was gone." She knew it was a believable story. Robbers didn't discriminate, and since the inn had no separate rooms and everyone slept together on the mats laid out, any one of a dozen or so people could be suspected of the theft, but none blamed because of the lack of proof. "Now I have nothing to pay the innkeeper with." She took the cloth he'd previously wiped her tears with and blew her nose for effect. "I just don't know what to do." She dabbed the corners of her eyes and handed the cloth back to him.

"No, you keep it." He shook his head and his left arm crept around her shoulders. "What's your name?"

"Mary." She looked at him innocently.

"Mary, I'm Marcus. I'll help you. I'll pay your bill for you here. It's not right that a woman should travel alone. You'll come home with me, and I'll have two of my servants pack up a donkey with provisions. They'll accompany you to Capernaum."

Caleb gathered his courage and stopped Peter as they entered Capernaum again. Peter seemed to look directly through him.

"What is it you want?" His voice rolled like thunder, and Caleb was struck at how much it matched his physical appearance.

"I'd like to accompany you wherever you go." Caleb's voice, though not soft, seemed so by comparison to Peter's rumble.

"Everyone would. Look at this crowd. They'd trample him if we let them."

"No, you don't understand; I want to learn. I want to be a part of it, not just follow like a dog."

Peter was about to answer when a soft voice behind them stopped him. "Peter, who is this you're talking with?" Turning, Peter saw Jesus standing with the other three companions and Nathaniel and Philip, who'd also joined their close circle.

"A stray, Lord. Says he wants to be a part of our group."

Jesus looked at Caleb, and Caleb felt Jesus saw every deed or thought he'd ever performed or had. Without realizing what he was doing, he knelt at Jesus' feet and, taking his hand, bowed over it, touching it to his forehead. "Lord, please allow me to serve you. I've seen all you've done. Never have I witnessed so many wondrous deeds. All my life I've searched for something or someone to believe in. Please don't turn me away."

Jesus looked in pity on the man before him. "What's your name?" he said softly.

"Caleb, Lord."

"Caleb, what may I do for you?"

"Lord, I..." Caleb stopped. What did he want? Love, joy, peace? Something to live for? Life? Could this man give it? If so, how should he ask for it? He looked into Jesus' face. "I want what you have."

"You want what I have, Caleb? I have no home or place to call my own. I go from place to place."

Caleb shook his head. "That's not what I mean. I want what you have, what you are." Caleb felt something ease up inside him. Jesus wouldn't fail him. He healed others of their physical infirmities, and he'd heal him of his emotional infirmities as well.

Jesus smiled, and Caleb sighed with relief and smiled back, "You'll have what you desire, Caleb, but it will only come with sacrifice and obedience on your part. If you come and be my disciple, you'll learn how and why I am the way I am. That's how you'll have what you want."

Caleb kissed the hand he held. "Thank you, Lord," he said. "Thank you. "


Marcus held Mary's elbow and steered her through the streets. He'd paid the innkeeper for her and was now directing them to his house. He stopped in front of a gate that was set into a large wall.

"Here's my home," he said.

She looked up. The house behind the wall was huge. She'd thought he was well off, but not rich. Now she knew. Did she dare go through with her plan? Would he have her stoned? Was he a religious leader or just a man of position?

"My," she said, "what a large house."

"Yes, I inherited it," he said. "My father was a tax collector."

She looked at him with what she hoped was a shocked look, but inside she leapt for joy. She was sure he wasn't a religious leader, not if he followed in his father's footsteps as most sons did.

"Don't be shocked," he said. "I'm not a tax collector. I just inherited the wealth of one. I'm a merchant, or at least I pay men to sell goods for me." He chuckled.

She raised her eyebrows. This was too good to be true. "Aren't you ever lonely, Marcus? I mean, this house is so large for one person."

He shrugged. "I have my servants."

She took his hand. Leaning as closely as she dared without seeming too obvious, she said softly, "But servants aren't good companions and don't fulfill all the wants and needs a woman can."

# *Chapter Eleven*

## The Washing

Mary stayed with Marcus in his home because of his riches and Capernaum left her mind. Although he was old, over twice her age, he was kind and very understanding. She felt puzzled that the emptiness that she longed to be rid of still lurked within her, haunting her every waking hour. She couldn't explain it to him, try as she might; words escaped her. He loved her, but it wasn't enough. Something inside her was unsatisfied.

Marcus tried everything to make her happy. He even suggested marriage, but Mary couldn't bring herself to make that kind of commitment to him. She didn't know if she loved him. She didn't know if she could ever love anyone, not even herself. She didn't know what love was.

Idly she walked to the main road that led out of town. In the distance she heard the loud wailing of professional mourners. Feeling curious, she followed the sound until she came upon a large procession passing through the street to the outskirts of town where the tombs were located.

Mary found herself not far from the litter. As she watched, another crowd approached from the northbound road. A man separated himself from the crowd and, stopping beside the litter, touched it, the men carrying the dead man stopped. A woman, weeping profusely, stood behind the body and looked questioningly at the newcomer.

His piercing blue eyes looked upon her in sympathy, and Mary heard him say softly to her, "Do not weep." Then he turned to face the corpse the men carried. He took the hand of the dead man and, without raising his voice at all, commanded, "Rise up, young man."

Mary's own eyes widened as she saw the eyes of the dead man open and blink several times. The stranger gently pulled on the hand he held, and the young man sat up. His mother, the woman the stranger had spoken to, went around to where the man stood by her son. She embraced the boy and, taking hold of the hand which held her son's, looked up into the stranger's eyes. She couldn't find the words to speak her gratitude. Others all around her had no such trouble and began exclaiming God had visited them and sent a great prophet in their midst.

Mary stood in awe as she watched the procession change from tears to profound joy. That man, the stranger, he had it. She knew he did. He had what she wanted more than anything. She could see it in his face, his carriage, his eyes. He had the fulfillment she craved. Somehow she had to have it, too.

Jesus was teaching on one of the hills not far from the Sea of Galilee. He'd left Capernaum for a while and had gone to teach in the other towns of the Galilee district. The news of his raising the boy from the dead had spread and a large crowd had developed, bringing with them all their lame and sick for Jesus to heal. His teaching was always full of examples with which the people were familiar. His comparisons to heaven and what God was like were more real, so that all who listened could relate to what he said. They drew the people like bees to honey.

The crowd was large, as usual. Caleb did the best he could to help the other disciples keep order and to keep Jesus from being trampled. Jesus himself seemed to take no notice of the number of people following him. It could be ten or ten thousand; he always acted the same.

Caleb watched him daily, all day. He never seemed to tire, yet Caleb knew that the pace Jesus kept had to take a lot from him. What was his secret? He'd seen Jesus angry before at the Passover and sometimes in the synagogue in Capernaum, such as when he saw merchants cheating the people, but never at any of the commoners who surrounded him daily. He was always patient and calm, his blue eyes taking in everything about him.

He had an uncanny way of knowing things without being told, and it unnerved all the disciples, not just Caleb. Their number was increasing daily. Some, like Caleb, were always present, but others, because of families and other responsibilities, were there only occasionally. And some, like Peter, Andrew, James, and John, were lucky enough to be with Jesus even when he ate and slept.

Then there were the children. Jesus loved them. He loved to be around them and to have them around him. Caleb had seen Jesus playing and laughing with them as if he were one of them. He'd also heard Jesus talk with them as seriously as he did the adults. The children loved him. Everywhere they went, children flocked to him and took turns getting on his lap. It never bothered Jesus, but it tried the disciples severely, because the crowd would press so closely they were afraid Jesus would get injured. Most of them lacked the patience Jesus displayed with the children and their parents.

After Jesus finished teaching, two men were standing near him; Andrew recognized them. Leaning toward Jesus, he said, "Lord, two of John's disciples are here." He nodded in the direction of the men, and Jesus turned as the men approached him.

"Lord", one said as he stopped in front of the rock Jesus was perched upon. "We come seeking answers."

Jesus raised his eyebrows. "What is it you want?"

"We're disciples of John the Baptist, Lord," the second man said. "He sent us to ask you if you're the one we're awaiting or shall we wait for another?"

Jesus sat silently a moment before answering. John had baptized him in the Jordan and had known then who he baptized. Apparently his imprisonment had caused him to become anxious that he might have been wrong. He smiled a sad smile, knowing the fate of his cousin wouldn't be good. He looked directly into the man's eyes.

"Tell John what you've seen here today," Jesus said slowly. "Tell him that the blind see, the lame walk, lepers are cleansed, and the deaf hear the Word of the Lord. The dead are raised and the Good News is told to all concerning God's kingdom. Tell him to rejoice and not doubt, for whoever doesn't doubt me shall be blessed by God."

The men bowed. "Thank you, Lord," the first one said, They turned and were lost in the crowd. When they left, Jesus sighed deeply. Turning to the people, he began to speak to them of John.

"What were you looking for when you went into the desert to hear John the Baptist speak?" he said. "Someone who was weak? No. But who then? Someone richly dressed? No. One who's richly dressed isn't found in deserts, but with kings. Who did you go to see? A prophet? Yes, but much more than that. For John was chosen by God, and it's he who the scriptures speak of when they say, *I will send someone before you who will speak of you and prepare for your coming.* For surely, it's true that of all who are born of the flesh, none are greater than John. But of those born of the Spirit of God, even the least of them is greater than John."

Mary followed the crowd out of Nain, drawn out by the realization that she needed something more and the certainty that the teacher called Jesus possessed what she longed for. Marcus called her ideas ridiculous and laughed at her, but she couldn't forget what she'd seen the previous day or felt in her heart. It was as if she thirsted and Jesus was the only one who had access to the liquid which could quench her thirst. She'd asked Marcus to join her, but he declined, stating he didn't feel well and would remain in bed that day.

As she walked along the road, she felt as though the procession carried her along with it. She didn't know for sure where she was going, but she knew it was where he was at. Everyone around her spoke of him and what he did, but Mary was more interested in him—in what he had—and she didn't listen to the talk of diseases of others being cured. She wanted freedom from the personal prison she felt she was in.

She watched him and listened to him speak. The peace radiated from him to her, only to bounce off when it reached her, as though it couldn't bear to touch her body. A few times he turned her way, and she felt as though his eyes saw her innermost thoughts and knew every speck of her being. Those eyes froze her, tore through her, yet they warmed and soothed her.

After his teaching, she moved toward him to try to speak to him and find out what it was he had. She got close enough to hear him speaking to two men about a third. Then they left and he turned back to the crowd and spoke to them again.

When he finished, arguments flared up between the common folk and the Jewish leaders. Jesus stood to leave, and Mary noted Simon, a prominent Pharisee in Nain, approach him. She heard him invite Jesus to his house and Jesus accept, then she turned to go. Her chance to speak with him was gone.

As she entered the house, she called out to Marcus, but he didn't answer. She entered their bed chamber and found him lying with his back to her on their sleeping mat. She shrugged and moved quietly about the room so as not to disturb him. He'd awaken shortly, and she could tell him about Jesus then.

But time passed and still Marcus didn't stir; in fact, he didn't move at all or make any sound, which was unusual. Marcus usually snored loudly while sleeping, no matter what position he was in. She went over and lightly shook him. No response.

"Marcus," she called softly as she shook him again, a little harder. Still, he didn't move or react at all.

A dawning fear came over her, and she bent low to listen to his breathing. She heard nothing. Panic began to grab at her, and she shook him with all her might as she called his name repeatedly, louder and louder. Soon servants were knocking at the chamber doors, but she couldn't answer; all she could say was his name between heaving sobs. She heard the servants enter as she slumped over him, crying loudly. She'd finally found someone who didn't reject her, only to lose him to death.


Mary lay motionless, allowing the servants to prepare Marcus's body for burial. They'd carried him out to another area of the house so she didn't have to sleep with a corpse.

Without a word, she rose from her mat. Crossing the room, she stopped at a chest Marcus had given her. He'd given her many things—clothes, jewelry, perfumes. The material things were, for the most part, stored in this chest.

She opened it. To one side, she had a collection of bottles holding ointments and perfumes. She selected a beautiful alabaster jar which held one of the rarest perfumes. She placed it upon the floor, then turned and took from the far corner on the other side of the chest a plain, long necked bottle which had been carefully wrapped to protect it. She selected a gown and a long veil for her hair. Donning the clothes, she coiled her hair in a bun at the nape of her neck and covered herself with the veil.

Picking up the jar and the bottle, she silently left Marcus's house and made her way to the one man she knew could give her comfort. She made her way to Simon's house.


Jesus reclined on the couch Simon indicated for him at the head of the table. Peter, James, and John had joined him at Simon's invitation, but were somewhat further down the table as lesser guests. Several other religious leaders were also already lying in their respective places.

As the meal began, Jesus raised an eyebrow and looked in the direction where his three disciples reclined. Peter shrugged and raised his brows as he met Jesus' gaze. Common hospitality dictated that water be offered so a guest could wash before dining. However, no basins were evident or even jars containing water. Jesus returned his attention to the conversation closest to him and said nothing about the lack of manners to his host.

A commotion stirred outside, and a woman entered the room with two flushed and anxious-looking servants following close behind, trying to stop her. Before they could catch her, she ran to the foot of the couch Jesus was lying on. In her right hand, she carried a small alabaster jar which held a pint of perfumed oil. In her left hand was a long-necked bottle which all present recognized as a tear bottle.

Murmuring among themselves, they each looked over at their nearest neighbors. Why would this woman bring her tear bottle and such expensive perfume to this man? The perfume could be a gift, but the tear bottle? Surely, he had his own already. The bottle was a possession everyone—even the poorest—owned. It was taken to any event at which tears would be shed, and the tears were captured from the faces of those who shed them. At the time of the owner's death, it was buried along with the dead person. It represented their whole life, and many felt it should be closely guarded because of that.

The woman set her burdens on the floor at her feet and removed her veil. Unbinding her hair, she let it fall to her hips as tears streamed down her cheeks. Jesus didn't move, but watched her silently, compassion filling his heart. This woman had been through much pain; of that, he was sure.

She knelt and picked up the tear bottle. Many of the guests gasped and looked on incredulously as she began to pour the gathered tears onto his feet. As she did, the tears her eyes shed fell swiftly, merging with the ones the bottle held. She reached behind her head. Drawing her hair over her shoulder, she began to wipe the dirt off Jesus' feet, kissing them frequently as she did so. She continued until every drop of her tears had been used. Then she picked up the alabaster jar and poured the oil over the freshly washed feet in front of her.

Peter, James, and John remained silent as they continued their meal, looking at each other with raised brows in reaction to the comments they were hearing.

"Outrageous," said one Pharisee.

"This is blasphemous," said another.

"Doesn't he know what she is?" asked a third. Jesus turned to Simon. "Simon, I'm wondering something. Maybe you can help me."

Simon brought himself up in a smug manner. "What is it, Master?"

Jesus, knowing Simon's haughtiness matched his thoughts, used an illustration to bring his point home and teach a lesson in humility to the Pharisee. He told of a creditor who had two men owing him. One owed a considerable amount more than the other, and the creditor released them both from their debt because neither was able to pay. When he finished the tale, he said, "Simon, which of them would be the most grateful?"

"Why, the one who owed the most, of course," Simon said, puzzled that Jesus would need an answer to so simple a problem.

Jesus nodded. "Correct." Then, turning, he indicated the woman at his feet and continued. "This woman has done for me what you, as a host, should've done. When I came in, you neglected to offer water with which to wash. She washed my feet with her tears. You failed to give me the courtesy and hospitality of an anointing for my head. She has perfumed my feet. Her sins may be many, but they're forgiven, for her heart holds compassion, but those who lack compassion have little forgiveness granted them." Turning to Mary, he said, "You've been forgiven."

She lowered her head as murmurs ran around the table, indignantly questioning Jesus' right to forgive sins. Ignoring the comments, Jesus told her, "Because of your faith, you're forgiven. Go with the confidence that your burdens have been relieved."

The woman looked up at Jesus, tears again welling up in her eyes. As the men watched her, she silently turned and left them.

Mary ran from Simon's to the house Marcus had said was hers to do with as she liked when he was gone. She went through the gate leading to the courtyard which surrounded the building. Without pausing for breath or to speak to anyone, she made her way to the bed chamber she'd shared with the only man who'd ever shown her true kindness and love—before that night, anyway.

Her mind was racing. She threw herself onto the sleeping mat and cushions and tried to calm her beating heart and still her mind enough to sort out her feelings.

He'd forgiven her. He'd been so kind. He had defended her to the very men who had the right to accuse her. She wished she could know him better. Her heart ached to be free of the inner turmoil she felt. She'd sought him out hoping he could tell her how to be free and only went away with a stronger yearning to be free.

And yet, he'd smiled upon her and defended her. She'd never been close enough to truly see his face before. His eyes, she'd never forget his eyes; they were pools of fresh, clear water. His voice was a soothing, cool wave—but not cold, not cold at all. His voice was warm.

She shook her head. Her thoughts contradicted themselves. His voice had warmed her when he spoke to her yet was soothing as a cool breeze. That was it. She lay back and contemplated the faces of the Pharisees, especially Simon's, as Jesus rebuked him and defended her. She didn't regret pouring out the contents of her tear bottle onto such a man as that. What did he say to her? Her burdens were relieved. What did he mean? Did she really go to him with faith?

She reflected on her reasons for going. She'd seen him raise a man up from the dead and had watched him perform endless miracles the following day. It hadn't been clear in her mind why, but she sought him out believing he'd have the answer for her inner turmoil also.

In a way, she'd been right. She felt lighter than she ever had before, but she still longed for love, longed for the emptiness to cease. Maybe if she saw him again, the next time she'd get that release. She laid her head back, closed her eyes, and tried to relax as she let her mind drift. She soon fell into the most peaceful slumber she'd experienced in many years.

# Chapter Twelve

## The Disciples

Lazarus turned to wait for Martha as she came panting behind him. He smiled as she stopped at his side. "Are you too tired to go on?" he asked.

"No, I can go further. I want to see the Master again today, too, if I can." Martha wiped the grime from her hands and face and straightened her veil.

Since Lazarus had thrown Mary out of their house, he'd been spending more and more time following John the Baptist. Then John was imprisoned, and Lazarus, along with many of John's other followers, began to follow Jesus at John's urging. Martha, finding increasingly less reason to stay in Bethany, had begun to join Lazarus in his travels.

They'd returned to Bethany for a short spell to conduct some business matters and check on the house. They were becoming familiar with many of his other disciples and even had become close to some, but Martha still wasn't able to bring herself to approach the Master about Mary. And she couldn't discuss her frustrations with Lazarus, who was still angry at the mere mention of Mary's name.

Lazarus waited impatiently for Martha. They weren't far from their destination, and he was anxious to see his friends and possibly have a word with Peter, James, and John about some things he'd heard while in Bethany. Martha finally joined him, and they began their journey.

"I saw Miriam at the well," she said.

"What news did she have?" Lazarus was sure Miriam would tell all she knew of anything that had taken place.

"She told of a young woman in Nain. She'd been living with a prominent merchant there who was found dead. The woman sought out Jesus and washed his feet. Her description sounded very much like Mary." Martha looked apprehensively at Lazarus.

Lazarus looked at her thoughtfully. "I've heard similar accounts," he said. "Some of my friends were there."

"Do you suppose she has begun following him?" Martha sounded hopeful.

"I don't know; no one has said. That is why I am anxious to get back. Peter, James, and John were there."

They looked hopefully at each other. Even though she was exiled from them, they both still loved her.

Lazarus and Martha found Jesus the day after the Sabbath. Looking around, Lazarus spotted a disciple he had come to know. Pulling Martha along, he headed for him.

"Well, brother, God's peace be with you." Lazarus grabbed the man, embracing him and planting the customary kiss on each cheek.

Caleb smiled and returned the greeting. "Lazarus, how goes it? How does Bethany fare?"

"Good, good. What of you? And the Lord? Have things gone well while we were gone?"

Nodding, Caleb said, "Very well, except–"

Lazarus frowned. "Except what? Tell me."

Pointing to a small clearing, Caleb said, "Come. I'll explain."

Martha followed the men over to the area indicated and sat down at Lazarus's side as their friend began.

"We were passing through a wheat field," he said, "and many of us were hungry. We picked some of it to eat along the way. But some Pharisees were watching and are coming down on the Master for it, claiming we labored on the Sabbath."

"What did Jesus say?" Lazarus said. He and Martha both leaned forward. "Did he get angry?"

"He reminded them of David and his men eating the shew bread in the Temple and that the priests work every Sabbath yet aren't condemned. He wasn't angry; I'd say it was more like exasperation."

Martha smiled and looked over at Lazarus, who was grinning widely as he said, "I wish I'd been there."

"Oh, but that wasn't all."

"No? What else happened?"

"Afterwards, we entered the synagogue and a man was there whose hand was withered. The Pharisees must be jealous of Jesus or something, Lazarus."

Lazarus couldn't hide the sarcasm in his voice as he said, "Now I can't imagine why. He's only drawn half or more of the common people to him, is all. And many were those the Pharisees, Sadducees, and other leaders were never able to reach."

Caleb grinned. "Well," he said, "they tried to bait him by asking if it was lawful to heal on the Sabbath."

"What did Jesus say?"

"He told them if a sheep fell into a hole, they'd not leave it until the morrow, and then he asked them if a man wasn't better than an animal. After that he said it was all right to do good on the Sabbath and healed the man's hand." He laughed. "You should've seen their faces. They looked angry enough to spit fire."

All three of them laughed at that. Then Lazarus said, "We must watch closely. My Pharisee friends have told me some of their colleagues are plotting revenge. They're accusing Jesus of working with the devil and doing his work and not God's."

"But that's ridiculous," Martha exclaimed.

"Ridiculous or not, it's what they say." Lazarus shook his head. "Who knows where their jealousy will lead?"

Caleb stood on the outskirts of the crowd waiting for the teaching to begin. As he waited, a man and woman hailed him down. It was Lazarus and Martha.

Caleb had recognized Lazarus right away when they first met through Philip, but Lazarus hadn't recognized him. Caleb never told him he knew Mary or reminded him he'd been with her the two times Mary had been found at Joshua's. For one thing, Caleb remembered the blaze in Lazarus's eyes when he'd found her. He'd probably been so angry he hadn't looked at anyone except Mary, and Caleb had grown a beard since then which helped to hide his features. Also, after knowing them as he did now, he didn't want to add to the pain they felt about their sister. They weren't like Mary had described them. After coming to know Jesus, Caleb understood them better than Mary did because he was more like them now than he was like Mary.

He thought of Mary often and wondered where she was. She was so beautiful. When he thought of her it wasn't with lust, as he'd thought of women in the past. Instead he remembered the way she smiled, her innocence, the way her eyes twinkled when she laughed. Her beautiful hair and face were imbedded in his memory. He wished she could share in the joy he'd found when he discovered Jesus, but Mary was gone. Not even Lazarus and Martha knew where she was. Or so he thought.

Caleb stayed with Lazarus and Martha during the teaching. Today it was about the Father and His love. Caleb had never thought of God as a loving Father until he heard Jesus speak during the Passover week when Caleb had first seen him. Now he was used to hearing about God and His love, yet it still amazed him.

Jesus said God loves us all. That was contrary to all the teaching Caleb had ever heard. He had always been taught that God only loved the Jews and that they had to earn that love by obeying all the laws. According to those teachings God was a harsh taskmaster, but Jesus portrayed Him as merciful and loving. You didn't need to change to receive His love. Caleb's heart burst with joy and a great peace came over him whenever he heard that. The feelings of condemnation and guilt he'd experienced whenever he attended synagogue were never present when Jesus taught.

After most of the people had gone, the three of them remained seated, discussing what Jesus had said. None took notice of a man approaching until his shadow crossed over them. Startled, they looked up into Peter's face.

"Would you like to come and eat with us?" he said.

"Us?" Lazarus couldn't hide his surprise. Martha was too stunned to even speak.

Peter grinned. "Yes. You. All three of you. Jesus wanted me to ask you." He continued talking as they approached the group surrounding Jesus. "We're staying at my house tonight, so I was elected to invite you." He looked at Caleb and, raising an eyebrow, gestured at Lazarus and Martha. "I believe we haven't been introduced, although we've noticed you often in the crowds."

"Oh, I'm sorry, Peter," Caleb said. "This is Lazarus and his sister Martha. They're from Bethany."

Nodding at them as they stopped near Jesus, who came over to greet them, Peter introduced them. "Lord, this is Lazarus and his sister, Martha, from Bethany. I'm sure you remember Caleb,"

"Yes, I do." Jesus' clear blue eyes caught and held each of theirs in turn and then looked back to Peter. "We must be going." He turned and, accompanied by Peter, led the way with Caleb, Lazarus, and Martha following.


Mary lay in bed unable to sleep. It seemed she'd been through this before. Only then she hadn't been her own mistress, but had been living with her brother and sister. She missed them, but they'd disowned her. So in her sorrow for Marcus, Mary sought out companionship where she could. She'd been called a harlot and everyone in Nain believed her to be a woman of sin because of her life with Marcus, but they didn't understand that she couldn't control herself. It was like she had no will of her own, but someone or something ruled her mind and body.

She could no longer bear to sleep alone, and the men of the town who would, sought her out to give her warmth–in return for their pleasures and their money. Even though Marcus had left her all that was his, she couldn't bring herself to use it to entertain other men. Although she no longer had material needs, the love still wasn't there and she searched for it with every man who came to her.

One was with her now. She looked over at him as he slept, one of his arms draped over her body as she lay within the circle of the other. One of his legs was still pressed between her thighs, pinning her onto the bed until he awakened or moved. This one was handsome, she thought, but not satisfying. He hadn't aroused the slightest bit of feeling within her and she wished he'd leave, but he'd paid her for the night and she couldn't turn him out.

At times like this her mind wandered, and she found herself dreaming of Joshua again. He'd always stirred her, and she yearned to have those sensations again and have her urges satisfied by a man who knew how. Instead she got men like this one. She sighed in disgust and tried to break free, but to no avail. She was trapped beneath him.

His arm moved over her and she felt his head rise to look into her face. She fought the nausea as he began to make love to her again. She felt trapped in a world of her own making, a prison of which she thought she'd never be free.


Martha hugged herself; she could hardly believe this was happening. Here she was in Peter's home listening to Jesus, watching him laugh and joke one minute and become serious the next. She wished it wouldn't end. She'd imagined him to be something other than what she was seeing. She'd imagined he was untouchable, but he wasn't. He was real; he was human.

He laughed and sang, told jokes and stories, held the babies and played with the older children. She shook her head. How could he be this way and still be able to perform the miracles he did? He was a mystery and yet not a mystery. To be around him was a delight, not only because of his personality, but also because he had an aura about him. He was different from any man she'd ever known. He was special.

She came out of her musings to laugh at something they were laughing at, not wanting the others in the cottage to know she hadn't heard the jest. Jesus lifted Peter's eldest son from his lap. Placing the boy on the floor, he gave him a playful tap toward his mother as she beckoned him to bed.

The men started speaking in a more serious vein, as the rest of the women settled down to listen after putting the children to bed. Martha's gaze traveled, and she wondered about these men who were closest to Jesus and why he'd selected them. James and John seemed obvious; they were his cousins, but the rest? She looked them over.

There was Peter. He was a strong leader, handsome, muscular, and outspoken. Andrew was Peter's brother. He was a silent version of Peter. He was shy with women, but outspoken if the topic was something he believed in strongly. Then there were James and John. Both resembled Jesus in looks, but not temperament. Jesus laughingly called them the Sons of Thunder because of their quick tempers.

Philip was a handsome youth not much older than Mary. Deep dimples and a mischievous twinkle in his eyes gave him a boyish appearance when he smiled. He seemed to hang on every word Jesus said and was wont to bring everyone he knew to hear the Master if he could persuade them. That was how Nathaniel, Philip's older brother, had come. Nathaniel had been skeptical at first until Jesus had described to him where Philip had found him when he told him of Jesus. Thomas was the most skeptical, however. He was the worrywart who never seemed to take hold of anything unless it was right in front of him. Matthew was a tax collector. They also called him Levi, and he was a man of some means; he owned a fairly nice house anyway. Simon the Canaanite was a Zealot and very outspoken. He clearly expected Jesus to take up arms against the Romans, but he held his peace about it around Jesus. Then there were the two silent ones, or so Martha pegged them. James, the son of Alphaeus, and Thadeaus who was also called Judas, but since there were two named Judas, everyone knew him as Thadeaus. And lastly there was Judas Iscariot, the keeper of the funds. Martha didn't know much of any of them, but they all seemed nice and devoted to Jesus.

She looked over at her brother and Caleb. They were both enraptured with whatever Jesus was saying and so she turned her attention back to him.

Lazarus stood listening to Jesus preach. Out of the corner of his eye, he saw a man he knew well in the area: a Pharisee. He greeted him, and together they listened to the rest of what Jesus had to say. Jesus was speaking on signs, and criticizing the people for their unbelief because they wanted him to perform more and more miracles to prove who he was. Then his teaching seemingly turned to another subject.

"No one lights a candle and then hides it," he said. "Instead he places it out where all can see the light. There's a light in every man. It's seen in the eyes, and those whose consciences are clear and good show the brightness of that light. Those whose consciences aren't good show a dullness, and their light is darkened because of the evil within them. Therefore, when the inside of a man is good, the whole body is good and reacts so. But if the inside is bad, their bodies are also that way. Let it be a warning, then, that your inner self

self is clean so your life is full of light. For if you're full of light within your conscience, then your whole body will be tuned in to the good inside you and you'll be as a candle giving off its glow, unencumbered by the darkness."

The Pharisee friend Lazarus was with asked him to go home with him for the evening meal. Lazarus accepted and was surprised to see the man turn to Jesus, who was walking close by.

"Master," the Pharisee said, "Come dine with me this evening in my home."

Jesus accepted the invitation, and they soon had gathered in the man's house. Several other Pharisees and teachers of the Jewish laws were also present, and Lazarus found himself reclining at the table with a dozen or so religious leaders. He felt slightly out of place and remained silent during the meal. But he stayed alert, watching and listening to everything that took place.

He noted the faces and reactions of the men dining with Jesus as he lambasted them for being more concerned with their outward appearances than with how they treated people and their lack of compassion for others.

"Master," one of the Pharisees said, "Why don't your disciples always follow the cleansing rituals we must follow?"

"That is just what it is, a ritual. You are more concerned with rules having to do with the outer body than with how clean you are inwardly. Appearances are everything to you; you care nothing for the true man."

Looks and murmurs of indignation traveled around the room as Jesus continued, "If you truly cared about others you would show compassion and understanding rather than judgment and would allow others to hear and act on what they hear instead of rebuking them for following their hearts, thus hindering the growth of their spirits because of your jealousy."

Lazarus noted many of the scholars and Pharisees were indignant and a great foreboding came to him that these men wouldn't long remain passive against the accusations Jesus made, no matter how true they were.

# Chapter Thirteen

## The Plan

Mary dressed herself in traveling clothes. Four months had passed since Marcus's death. She'd tired of her life in Nain and had acquired a small cottage in Magdala near the Sea of Galilee where she could live quietly and with privacy.

*Having money has its advantages,* Mary thought as she prepared herself to go to Bethany. She intended to somehow seek out Joshua and bring him back into her life more than he had been before. She was no longer the innocent child she'd been when they met. This time she'd get him for her own and it wouldn't be by chance. She added a few last touches and, satisfied that she was at her best, dismissed her servant and left the cottage to begin her journey.

It was the end of the day. Jesus had been teaching near the western shores of the Sea of Galilee. The crowd, instead of dispersing, seemed to be getting larger. Jesus turned to Peter. "Let's go across the lake," he said.

Several disciples, besides the twelve who always accompanied him, were standing nearby. Wanting to be with Jesus, they gathered into several boats beached close to Peter's larger one.

After boarding the small ship, Jesus laid a few pillows out in the stern of the boat and immediately fell asleep. He was drained physically because a lot of healings had taken place that day, and he needed rest to regain his strength. There was another reason he wanted to enter the boat; the east side of the lake was more desert-like, therefore containing less which meant less people to follow him and more opportunity for privacy and prayer. Jesus loved the people, but he also felt he needed time alone to talk with his Father and seek guidance and strength from Him. In crossing the lake, he sought both physical and spiritual rest.

At first the sea was calm, but suddenly, without any warning, a water spout appeared and great waves began to crash over the sides until the boat became dangerously full of water. The men tried to bail out as much as they could, but it was to no avail. For each bucket they emptied, twice as much came back in. The wind whipped around, and the boat became unmanageable. None of this disturbed Jesus, and he slept with a contented, peaceful look on his face.

"Lord!" Peter shook him as he called above the noise of the storm. As Jesus stirred, Peter said, "The boat is sinking. Don't you care that we might drown?"

Jesus slowly opened his eyes and looked up at Peter. "What is it, Peter?" he asked, raising himself to a sitting position.

"The boat is sinking, Lord," Peter said. "The wind and sea will be our undoing. We'll surely drown if it continues."

Exasperated, Jesus stood up and looked out over the water. "Peace," he said, and the wind calmed immediately. The waves still raged, however, and he gave a further command. "Be still." He moved back to where he'd been sleeping and said, "Where's your faith? Didn't I say we *would* reach the east side?" Without waiting for an answer, he fell back to sleep.

"Peter," Philip asked, "how can he do this? The wind and sea calmed at his word." The other men echoed him in murmurs.

Peter shook his head. "I don't know," he said, awed. "I don't know."

The cell had no window. The only light was a small hole in the wall near the ceiling for air and what light wasn't hindered by the shadows outside the walls. John's head rested upon his knees as he sat on the floor with his arms sagging above him. His wrists and ankles were chained to the walls, but the chains on his arms were long enough to allow him to sit if he desired even though it meant his arms would be stretched almost to their fullest above his head. He sat periodically to rest his legs and stood to rest his arms.

Herod had placed him there to quiet him, but it hadn't worked. He still accused Herod whenever he came down to see him. He came often, and John wondered about that. Maybe he was reaching Herod. He was allowed visitors at times from the outside, and he'd sent two of his disciples to Jesus. He'd been so sure when Jesus had come to him at the Jordan, but since his imprisonment, he'd begun to doubt. He couldn't control it, and only the reassurance from the men he'd sent to see Jesus had eased his fear that he hadn't accomplished God's purpose before Herod had chained him to the prison walls he now leaned against.

He heard the door open and looked up as a torch was placed in a holder in the wall. Herod stepped into the cell. The only time light was brought in was when Herod visited. Even when other visitors came, he had to ask who it was or rely on his memory of their voices. Now Herod stood before him.

"Greetings, John." His voice was apprehensive. Herod was always nervous when he came, yet something drew him to John's cell.

"Peace be with you, Herod." Although physically weakened by his predicament, John's voice was as strong and vibrant as ever. "To what do I owe this honor?"

Herod paced back and forth. "I've come to hear you speak of this kingdom you proclaim." John remained silent. "Tell me about it." Herod stopped directly in front of the man sitting on the floor. "Tell me how Rome shall be overthrown, John." He laughed, but the laugh was weak.

"Who said it would be overthrown?"

"Well, isn't that what the Zealots preach?"

"I'm not a Zealot."

"Then what are you?" The anger rose in his voice.

"I'm a beacon, an announcer, if you will."

"Announcer of what?"

"Of the coming of God's kingdom, the coming of the liberation of God's people."

"That's what I wanted you to speak of." Herod was excited, and his voice raised to almost a shrill pitch. "What is this kingdom, and how are you to be liberated?"

"It's not a kingdom of this world."

"Not of this world? What other world is there? What riddles are you speaking?"

"No riddles. You know the scriptures, or you should. You're a Jew. The scriptures are full of the prophesies of a Messiah."

"Messiah? You can't mean you're the Messiah."

"I didn't say that, Herod. I'm the forerunner of the Messiah, It's He who shall bring in the new kingdom, not I."

"How? And who is He?"

"I don't know how. As to who He is, you must find that out for yourself," John said. He wouldn't tell Herod of Jesus if Herod hadn't yet heard of him. John didn't want to jeopardize him with a premature declaration.

Herod continued. "Who is he? Or don't you know?"

"I know, but it isn't time for Him to declare Himself. I must stay silent until He does."

Herod continued to question him, at first only curious and then angered that John wouldn't reveal who the Messiah was. Finally in exasperation he stalked out, leaving John again to bide his time alone and in darkness.


The boat landed on the eastern shore of the Sea of Galilee. As Jesus stepped ashore, a naked man approached him. The man was dirty, and his hair and beard were mud-caked and tangled. Dark bruises were all over his body, which bore many deep scratches. Some of them were festering. The man snarled, and Jesus rebuked him, saying, "Quiet. Release him."

"We know who you are, Jesus, Son of the most high God." The voice coming from the man was gruesome and leering, and the tone was full of ridicule. The man was possessed by demons.

Jesus knew that it wasn't the man's will to be that way. He spoke to the demons. "Who are you?"

"Legion, for there are many of us," the leering voice of the demon spokesman said. He reached out to touch Jesus, holding his hand as if to claw at him. Then, apparently realizing what Jesus intended to do, his attitude quickly changed from being arrogant to pleading. The demons knew that they'd have to obey Jesus when commanded to do so. They begged Jesus to not turn them out into the abyss or make them leave the region, asking that they be sent into the swine feeding nearby instead.

Jesus nodded. "Leave this man now, Legion. Go into the swine if you must, but go."

The man's body convulsed for a brief moment and then relaxed, and he lay unconscious on the ground. The swine, however, turned into a raving drove, and the herdsmen couldn't control them. In their madness, the animals ran over the edge of a nearby cliff into the water below, drowning themselves and releasing their bodies from the demons.

The herdsmen looked over in the direction of Jesus and his disciples and saw the madman sitting up, his dazed eyes and face for once calm, his actions normal instead of lunatic. They looked into Jesus' face and saw his blue eyes gazing back at them calmly. Frightened, they ran away in the direction of Gadera, the nearest town.

Soon the people of Gadera came out to see if what the herdsmen claimed was true. They saw the madman, sane and dressed in some clothing the disciples had given him, sitting at Jesus' feet. The sight was too much for them. They couldn't adjust their minds to the miracle before them. Frightened of what else might come, they begged Jesus to leave their region.

Sighing, Jesus rose to go. The man he'd freed spoke to him. "Please, Lord," he said, in a voice entirely different from the one before, "let me go with you."

Jesus looked at him with compassion. "No. You'll do better to go back to your family and witness to them of the love of God toward you."

"I'll do that and more. I'll tell everyone I meet in all of Galilee what has happened to me because of you." He watched as the boats holding Jesus and his disciples once again returned to the water.


The city noises welcomed Mary, calling to her from every side. Merchants showed their wares. Children scuttled around her, chasing each other. Dogs barked and babies cried. The air was mixed with the scents of perfume, sweat, and human as well as animal waste. She turned from side to side to take in every sight and sound around her. She'd forgotten how busy Jerusalem was. It was a refreshing change from the quiet countryside to which she'd grown accustomed.

She'd gone to Joshua's, and they'd told her he wasn't there, he'd moved to Jerusalem. Although he still ran the house in Bethany, he no longer lived there. When she inquired about Caleb, she'd been told he hadn't been back since the night she'd last been there. Someone told her they heard he'd left Bethany for good.

She traveled the streets looking for the one on which Joshua lived. She soon found it and turned down it to search for his house. The houses on the street were run down, and sounds of drunken arguments could be heard, slough-eyed women in bright colors stood on corners, and here and there a drunk was passed out. As she passed down the street, a drunk reached out to try to grab her. She heard shrieking laughter coming from one of the windows. She managed to keep the man from touching her by side-stepping, and as she continued on he fell in the mud and was unable to get up.

Finding the house for which she was looking, she stood a moment contemplating what to say if he weren't alone. She'd been thinking about that throughout her journey and still hadn't quite decided what she should do about Daphne. She posed quite a problem, and Mary could think of no solution.

She knocked on the door and stood gazing back the way she'd come.

The disciples were gathered at Matthew's house for a feast. Many friends of Matthew's who were considered sinners by the Jewish leaders were present, as well as a few scribes and some Pharisees. Jesus reclined at the table between a tax collector and a publican of ill repute.

The scribes and Pharisees murmured to the disciples about the questionable dinner partners Jesus had chosen, and it was drawn to his attention.

He looked down the table at the closest Pharisee. "Do you have something you wish to say to me?" he said.

The Pharisee looked at him. "Yes, I do. You're known for being so good, yet you think nothing of sitting with these sinners. You enjoy it."

Jesus looked at him with pity, and he answered him slowly. "Only a person who's sick seeks out a doctor. Those who are with me are those who need forgiveness."

Peter was listening to the conversation. He said, "Lord, how often should I forgive someone who wrongs me? Seven times?" Peter thought he was being generous because Jewish law only required three times.

Jesus turned to him, and the others around them leaned forward to hear. "Oh, Peter," Jesus shook his head, "not only seven times, but seventy times seven at least." He went on to tell a tale. "There was a king who had a man owing him a great deal of money. The king threatened to sell the man, his family and all they owned to repay the debt, but the man pleaded for mercy and was granted it. Yet when this same man left the king's presence, he met up with another who was owing him a small amount. The man owing him begged for mercy, but he declined and sent the man to prison. When the king heard of it, he was very angry. He had the man to whom he'd given mercy whipped and imprisoned until the debt he'd owed was repaid. So will God do to those who refuse to be forgiving to those they should forgive."

Peter looked down, embarrassed that he'd asked the question. Everyone else turned the conversation to other matters, feeling uncomfortable with the topic and what Jesus had said.

The door opened, and Mary turned her attention back to it. There stood Joshua, as handsome as ever. Her heart leapt within her, but she forced her voice to remain calm as she spoke to him.

"Peace, Joshua. May I come in?"

"Mary, it's been a long time. Please, do come in." He stood aside as she walked past him and entered the cottage. "Won't your brother be angry?"

"Lazarus?" She gave a short laugh and shrugged. "Lazarus knows nothing and cares even less about my life now." She turned to look at him and held out her hands for him to take. "What of you? It's been so many months. Are you still married to Daphne? How is she?" She glanced around the room. "Where is she?"

Taking her hands, he laughed and said, "She's at the marketplace preparing for her journey."

"Journey?" Mary raised her eyebrows.

"Yes. She's going back to Greece for a visit. She's to leave in two months."

Mary's eyes widened and her mouth formed a silent "oh" as she let this news sink in. Quickly recovering her voice, she said, "Are you going with her?"

"No. Her visit won't be long, and I have a business to run." He looked at her and smiled. "Even though I don't live there any longer, I still watch it carefully. I don't trust anyone else. They aren't of the highest repute in society."

She grinned. "No, I suppose not." She looked up at him. He still could cause a stirring within her. She was determined more than ever to win him from Daphne.

Joshua smiled and reached over to release her veil. "Daphne left only a few minutes before you came. Why don't you get comfortable, Mary?" he said as he drew her to him.

# Part Three

## Opposition

## The Third Year

*...and the rulers take counsel together, against the Lord,
and against his anointed...*
Psalms 2:2.

# *Chapter Fourteen*

## The Birthday

Caleb and Lazarus had become fast friends. They'd worked closely with the Master, and that common bond drew them together. The Master. That was how they thought of him, and that was what they called him. They weren't as close to Jesus as the twelve, but they were closer than most others, and both felt honored at the distinction Jesus gave them.

The twelve were gone for a short time. They'd been sent out in pairs to prepare the way for Jesus in the cities he was traveling toward. At the present time things were relatively calm because the people hadn't yet discovered Jesus had returned from the east side of the lake. He was staying in one of the disciple's homes along with Caleb, Lazarus, and Martha until the twelve returned. Then they'd again be traveling from town to town.

Caleb looked over at Lazarus. They were alone for a while. Jesus had gone out by himself, and Martha had gone to the market. It was time, he felt, that Lazarus knew of his relationship with Mary. Caleb desperately hoped that Lazarus had listened to the sermons Jesus often gave about forgiveness. He didn't want to lose this treasured friend because of his past, but he knew he had to face him. It was better to do it now. He cleared his throat.

"Lazarus," he said, "there's something I must tell you."

His friend looked over at him questioningly. "What is it, Caleb?"

Caleb paused. He shook his head and covered his eyes with one hand, "I don't know how to tell you this. I love you. The last thing I want in this world is to lose your friendship."

Lazarus reached out and placed a hand on Caleb's arm. "Caleb," he said gently, "don't fear for our friendship. What is it that's bothering you? Whatever it is, it can't be bad enough to destroy our feelings for each other."

Caleb looked up at him. "I know Mary."

Lazarus's face, for a fleeting second, displayed the pain that it usually showed at the mention of her name. "I know," he said.

"You know?"

Nodding, Lazarus said, "It's no fault of yours that my sister came to that place. I recognized you at once, when we first met."

Breathing a sigh of relief, Caleb ran a hand through his hair. "All this time, I thought--"

"I know." Lazarus stood and began to pace in front of Caleb. "I've always shown anger and hurt when she's mentioned, and you thought I'd blame you. I don't. I don't even blame Mary. In the months we've known Jesus, Martha and I have both become convinced she's possessed and can't control her own actions. Therefore, how could we? How could you? Why would you want to stop her from giving you what you'd gone to Joshua's to get? It just so happened that you were with her both times I found her there."

"Lazarus, I–"

Lazarus raised a hand to stop him. "Don't worry about it. We've left her in God's hands. He's taking care of her." He sat and looked into Caleb's face. "I'm concerned for you, Caleb, and ashamed of myself. You haven't lost my friendship because of Mary. You never will. I've waited for you to come to me about her because I don't care for her way of life and I avoid discussing her when I can. I've wronged you because of my selfishness. If I'd acknowledged my recognition of you, you would have been spared months of inner torment. Please forgive me."

"Oh, Lazarus," Caleb shook his head and hugged the other man, "there's nothing to forgive. I'm honored with your friendship." He hesitated for a brief second, then boldly continued. "Mary didn't realize what a wonderful man you are or what a wonderful woman Martha is. She was too absorbed in her own unhappiness to see you both as you truly are. I hope for your sake, as well as hers, that your prayers and faith concerning her are satisfied."

Lazarus nodded confidently. "They will be."


It was midsummer, and the grass was spotted with various wildflowers. Among others, poppies, anemones, and chrysanthemums provided an array of color over the sloping green hills which rose slowly from the Sea of Galilee.

Martha quickly walked up the hillside. After telling Lazarus and Caleb she'd be visiting the market, she'd followed Jesus when he left the cottage at which they were staying. Mary had been on her mind so often lately. She wanted to talk to the Master about her, but until now she'd seen no opportunity to be alone with him. He wasn't far ahead of her and she was surprised at how easily he seemed to get away from the crowds which usually plagued him.

She followed him to a secluded area a couple of miles away from the town and stood behind a tree to watch him for a few moments. She'd always wondered what he did when he went off by himself and intended to watch him a few minutes before she let her presence be known.

He knelt near a rock which he leaned over for a few minutes. Then he raised his arms, and she heard his voice ring out in a song of praise that was commonly sung in the synagogue, then he was quiet again. Or rather she couldn't hear what he said. Before she realized it, he stood, turned around, and looked directly at her. He smiled and, holding out his right hand, beckoned to her.

"Come, Martha, something troubles your heart. Don't be afraid to speak to me concerning it. It's the reason you followed me, isn't it?"

"Yes, Lord." She went over to him and took his hand.

He led her to some nearby rocks and trees that seemed to form an alcove with a thick carpet of plush green grass. The rocks had a natural ledge wide enough for two people with enough space between them to keep a comfortable distance while seated. Jesus motioned to it. "Sit," he said as he perched himself on the ledge.

Jesus watched Martha as she sat silently for a few minutes. "Martha," he said, "don't be afraid to tell me the reason you came here."

"Lord, I've wanted to come to you about this ever since I first heard you speak." Tears began to flood her eyes, and her lips trembled. She turned her head and wiped the flow from her cheeks with her hand.

Jesus reached out and took the hand still in her lap. "Martha, you're valuable and precious to me. Don't be afraid. What is it?"

"It's my sister, Mary. Lazarus and I have...." She covered her face with her free hand and sobbed as Jesus held her other hand and patted her back. He said nothing, but waited for her to calm down and continue.

"I'm sorry, Lord; forgive me. I didn't realize that it still bothered me this much. Even Lazarus doesn't know how I worry about Mary. I dare not speak to him about her since he banished her from our home."

"When did this happen?"

"Shortly before we began traveling with you."

"I see. Why did he banish her?"

Martha's face became red, and she stammered in embarrassment. "She shamed us. He found her in a brothel." She began to cry again and hung her head in sorrow. "He dragged her home and told her to take her things and leave."

"And she left."

Martha nodded. "We've heard rumors of her. She's the one who washed your feet in Nain. She's fallen so low."

Jesus comforted her with his arm over her shoulder and didn't say anything for a while, letting her tears cleanse the hurt she was feeling. "You must not worry about her. Place her in the hands of the Father. He's her Father as well as yours and mine. He'll draw her to Him if you have faith and don't doubt that He's able to do it."

"I'd hoped you could help her."

"I could if she came to me willingly and was desirous of help. I can only heal when those needing it don't stay away from me by their unbelief."

Martha sat a moment, pondering this. "Is that why you couldn't do very much in Nazareth?"

"Yes. It's like when the wind blows at a doorway. If the door's open, the wind can pass through and freshen the inside of the house, making it clean. But if the door's closed, blocking the wind, the stale air remains. Unbelief is like a door blocking the wind."

"I see," she said. "Master, is it possible that Mary's door is open, or at least opening? She did come to you in Nain. I know she hasn't come back, and I've heard since then that she hasn't changed, but–"

"Yes, Martha, it's very possible. God's drawing her. Be patient. She'll come; I'm sure of it. Now you must go back. I want to stay here a little longer. I'll follow you shortly."

She smiled up at him and squeezed his hand before she turned and followed the path back down the hill, leaving him alone to pray.

Herod's steps were light and brisk. He always felt this way after seeing John. He didn't know why; he only knew that he enjoyed listening to him. He respected John and revered him as a holy and just man, but Herodius had been offended when John had called their relationship incest. Because of this, she'd nagged Herod until he'd given in and taken John prisoner. She continued to nag, trying to get Herod to execute him, but Herod saw no reason for it and told her so. Besides, if he did comply with her wishes, the people might react in a way he didn't desire, especially with Rome watching him. He had no love for Rome, but his title meant everything to him. If there were too many riots, he could be in trouble.

Lately Herodius hadn't mentioned it, and Herod was grateful, especially today. It was his birthday, and a feast was being thrown in his honor. He quickened his step.

Entering their living quarters in the palace, he saw his stepdaughter sitting near a window looking out over the city. At the sound of his steps, she turned and smiled. Herod braced himself. Salome was treacherous. At fifteen, she had the cunning of a cat and acted as deceitfully as a woman twice her age.

"Salome." He inclined his head and greeted her warily.

"Greetings, Herod. Good wishes to you this day." She fawned innocence in her manner, and only her eyes showed a fleeting glimpse of the malice of her offer. "Would you like for me to dance for you at the feast?" She paused. "As a birthday gift to you?"

He contemplated her offer. Salome was as beautiful as her mother and as deadly when crossed. He had no idea what her motives were. It wasn't unusual to be entertained in such a way at feasts, but the entertainment was usually for a price. He looked closely into her face. The malice, when he first came in, had been veiled before he could see it. He saw nothing in her face now but the fake innocence she intended. Believing that her offer had been true, he inclined his head in acceptance.

"I shall be honored."


Salome raised her arms. Swaying her hips seductively, she danced around the men reclining at the table with Herod. She purposely let the flimsy veils she wore gently stroke the men's bodies as she passed them, feeding their arousal with touch as well as sight. She centered her attentions mostly upon Herod, but drew away again and again toward the other men to tantalize his senses and desires.

She knew that more than one man there desired her body and Herod not the least, even though he was her stepfather. It was her intent to entice a declaration from Herod. Salome didn't know what her mother planned as yet, but she was willing to play along. It was fun to tease and then deny a man what the teasing seemed to promise. Salome enjoyed it. Her mother had taught her well. Men, she'd said, were to be used and manipulated to get what a woman desired, and sex was the tool a woman could use to control them. Salome had found this to be true, and she was doing her best to get Herod to proclaim a promise.

She ended her dance by dropping directly in front of him and bowing low to reveal her breasts beneath the low cut neckline of her gown. She raised her head and, looking directly into his eyes, smiled.

"Ah, Salome," Herod said. "You surpass the most skilled dancers I've seen anywhere. What is it you desire? Up to half my kingdom I'll grant to you."

Salome's smile broadened. "May I have time to think upon your generous offer my lord? It's such an overwhelming one, I'm not sure what to ask for."

"You may, but don't take long. Will you dance for us some more this evening?"

"Of course, but first let me rest and ponder what gift I desire. When I return, I'll tell you and dance again for your pleasure. May I be excused for a time?"

"You may." Herod leaned back, looking pleased.

Salome rose and left the hall, going directly to her mother's chambers. Opening the door, she entered and saw her mother being waited upon by several of her women servants as she reclined on a couch.

"Well, did you dance, my daughter?" Herodius said as she ate the grape that had been placed in her mouth.

"Yes, Mother."

"And Herod's reaction?"

Salome grinned. "He's offered me up to half his kingdom."

"You didn't make a request?"

"No. You told me not to. I came to ask you what I should tell him."

Herodius smiled wickedly. "What do you want? You want to please me, don't you?"

"Yes, Mother."

"And You wouldn't question any request I make?"

"No. I know you'd have good reason for any request you had."

"Then come here, child." Turning to the servants, she said, "Leave us."

The women left, leaving mother and daughter alone. Salome came and sat on the floor at her mother's side. Herodius absent-mindedly stroked Salome's head.

"What have I taught you about men?" she said, looking past Salome into space.

"That they're vile and are only good for us to get ahead with."

"You've learned well. You have Herod in your hands. Together, because of his promise, we can get our revenge on one who has criticized not only me, but also many others, unjustly.

"Who, Mother?"

"John the Baptist."

"You mean the prisoner Herod is so protective of?"

"Yes. He must die. He's filled Herod's head with lies and told him I have no right to be his wife." She leaned closer to her daughter. "I want you to request his head on a wooden platter. Don't fail me, Salome. It's the only way Herod will agree to do as I want him to. He won't go back on his word in front of his guests. He's too proud." She waved a hand toward the door. "Now go and tell Herod your request. When it's done, bring the head to me."

Salome obediently rose and went out to make known her desire to Herod as her mother threw back her head in wicked laughter.

# *Chapter Fifteen*

## The Beheading

Mary leaned over and kissed Joshua, then stood up and started to dress. Joshua watched her until she turned to him and said, "It wouldn't be good for Daphne to return and find you naked. Especially if I'm still here."

Joshua sighed. "You're right." He stood up and began dressing. When they both had finished, he gathered her in his arms. "You've changed. What happened?"

She smiled. "I've just decided I want something and I won't let anything or anyone keep me from getting it."

"What is it you want?"

"You."

He raised his eyebrows. "I believe Daphne will object. How do you know that I'm willing?"

"You're willing. You wouldn't have taken me to bed just now if you weren't. I don't care that Daphne may object. I have as much and more to offer you as she does."

He settled himself on the floor. "What have you to offer?"

She came over, sat down next to him, and ran a hand over his thigh. "I'm very well off now."

"Oh? In what way?"

"I own property and a business left to me by a friend when he died."

"What sort of business?"

"Traveling merchants work for me. I also own a house in Nain and a cottage in Magdala."

"You are well off." He nodded his approval, and Mary saw the interest increase in his eyes.

She drew her other hand up to play with his hair and leaned herself against his body. "I've learned to take what I want, and I want you. I know you're married, but wives don't have to be permanent. I intend to do all I can to persuade you that the one you have now will not be your wife for much longer. Now I must go. It wouldn't do for her to find me with you."

Before he knew what was happening, she was gone.


Herod looked down at the chalice in his hand. The men were laughing all around him. A movement near him caught his attention and he raised his eyes to see Salome standing before him. Without a word, she smiled and, lifting her arms, began an even more enticing dance than before. At the end, she again stood at his feet, still smiling seductively.

The room suddenly became quiet. All eyes and ears were upon them and their words; Everyone present was curious as to what Salome would ask.

Herod himself smiled when he saw her. "Salome," he said, "have you decided what request to make?"

"Yes, my lord, I have."

Herod raised his brows. "Well?"

Looking up to see if their audience was listening, Salome raised her voice triumphantly. "I would like the head of John the Baptist upon a wooden platter."

A murmuring arose from those around them. Herod froze. He glanced around at his guests and closed his eyes momentarily and swallowed. He had to grant it or lose the respect of everyone present; too late he saw his folly. Herodius had put her up to this; he was now certain of that, even down to the offer to dance. He realized now that Salome would never have offered of her own volition. She was too selfish for that.

He opened his eyes and looked toward the guard standing in the doorway. He beckoned him over to his side. The soldier approached and stood at attention in front of Herod. Salome looked smugly from Herod's face to that of the guard, curious to see the reactions of both.

"Go down to the cells," Herod said. He cleared his throat and continued, much louder than necessary. "Bring back the head of John the Baptist on a wooden platter. That's my stepdaughter's request."

Without a word, the soldier bowed. Barely glancing in Salome's direction, he went to carry out the deed.

"I hope you and your mother are satisfied," Herod hissed so only Salome could hear. "You've ordered an innocent man to his death."

Salome laughed and walked away. Her conscience, like her mother's, had left long ago.


Salome entered her mother's chambers, carrying the wooden platter with John's bloody head. Placing it on a table beside the divan where Herodius reclined, she bowed.

"Here's the head of John the Baptist as you desired, my mother."

"Ah, my beautiful, obedient daughter." Herodius took Salome's hands and drew her close. "You've done well."

"I know." Salome looked over at the table and shuddered involuntarily.

The servants tried not to show their revulsion and grief. Many had heard John speak and thought him a great man of God. Salome looked back at her mother and smiled. His sightless eyes and silenced lips could no longer accuse.

Herodius hugged her and returned the smile. "Go and rest now, my darling. You've pleased me tremendously."

Salome bent forward, kissed her mother, and left.

Herodius, after watching her go, commanded her servants, "Leave me." Not needing another invitation, the women were quickly gone and she was alone.

"Well, John," Herodius said. "Now what do you say? Nothing? Cat got your tongue? Ha. You'll never breathe another word against me. Oh, how I wish I'd dared to witness the act." Her eyes narrowed, and a gleefully evil look crept into them. She rubbed her hands together as she arose and began pacing in front of the platter, "I can picture it now. Did you beg? I hope you did. How wonderful it would have been to be there and see, but, alas, I could not."

Pouting, she picked up the platter and held it so the head was at her eye level. "I could not," she repeated sadly as she replaced it on the table. Then seeing a needle left by one of her maids, she grabbed it. Laughing wickedly, she opened the mouth of the dead man and drew out his tongue, stabbing it several times before leaving it there.

"Rot," she croaked, laughing hysterically. "Rot."

The third Passover since Jesus began his ministry was approaching. The twelve who had been sent out had returned. Their voices rose and fell as they told Jesus of their doings and the response of the towns into which he'd sent them. Martha remained silent, serving each one as she listened closely to their reports. Caleb and Lazarus also were intent upon the other disciples stories when a knock brought them back to the present. Caleb rose to answer, and the room grew ominously silent. It was late in the evening. When Caleb came back, he was followed by two men whom Martha recognized as the two disciples John the Baptist had sent to ask Jesus if he was the one they awaited. They were greeted by those already in the room, then they came and knelt at Jesus' feet.

"Lord," one of them said, "We've come bearing news."

"Go on," Jesus said, his face solemn.

"John the Baptist is dead." The man lowered his head to hide the tears that fell down his face. "Herod beheaded him."

There were several gasps. Shocked, the disciples silently looked at one another and then turned to Jesus. His face showed a deep sorrow, but he also remained silent.

Martha was the first to speak. "Whatever for? Just because he told the truth?"

"Tell us what you can," Peter said.

The two men looked at Jesus, who nodded.

Martha placed dishes of food in front of the two newcomers who told the story as best they could, repeating what had been said by the soldier who had been forced to perform the deed.

"We buried his headless body," the one telling the tale ended.

Jesus sighed. "You did well to come and tell us. Tomorrow we'll seek out a more private place. Stay here and join us. We'll go into the desert. We're all in need of rest and prayer."

"Lord," Peter said, "is it advisable for us to leave now? Wouldn't your presence comfort those who need reassurance because of John's death?"

"No, Peter. Few need my presence now. The crowds I draw could only do harm to us. There may be trouble because of this. If I stay, my presence can be blamed for the commotion, and the time hasn't yet come for me. It would be better if we went." Rising, he added, "Also you twelve are weary. I know only too well what strength this took from you, and only prayer and rest will rejuvenate you. You can't have either with crowds pressing in. Now we must sleep, for tomorrow we'll leave before the sun rises."


The place was a familiar one. Jesus often went there to pray when the crowds had drained him. The disciples hadn't fully understood why he'd needed the time alone until then. He led them in prayer and encouraged them to speak to God on their own and in their own way. At their request, he'd taught them how to do this and how to praise as well. As they did as he instructed them, inner strength returned to their bodies, their minds cleared, and their spirits began to soar to heights of which they hadn't dreamed. Before they realized it, the morning was half over.

James looked back toward the village. A crowd was forming and was heading toward them. He went over to Jesus and silently pointed it out to him. The others noted the gesture and turned to look also.

"Do you want us to send them away again, Lord?" Peter said.

"No, they're in need. They search for leadership, wandering as sheep with no shepherd to guide them." He sighed. "We've done well to come here this morning. By evening we'll have given out all we've gained here, but they'll be fed." He stood. "Let them come."

Instead of waiting for the crowd to come the complete distance, Jesus went down the slope a ways to a group of rocks to await them. The sun shone brightly in the sky, and the breeze from the sea played among the tall blades of grass.

Peter and the other disciples went down to stop them from crowding too closely to Jesus so that all might hear what he said. He spoke of God's kingdom to them. Then, after teaching and healing the sick for several hours, Philip and Caleb approached Jesus.

"Lord," Philip said, "evening is coming upon us. Send the people back to the villages so they can find food."

"Why send them away?" Jesus said.

Caleb watched silently as Philip and Jesus conversed.

"You feed them," Jesus said.

"How, Lord? It would take more than half a year's wages just to buy enough for a bite for each. There are five thousand men here and at least that many women and twice as many children."

What Philip said didn't seem to bother Jesus. He looked at the crowd and said, "How much food is here?" A couple of the men groaned as Jesus said, "Go and see."

The disciples dispersed into the crowd. After questioning for a good amount of time, they returned. All but one was empty handed. Andrew had a small boy with him who was carrying a basket.

The boy set the basket in front of Jesus as Andrew said, "Lord, this lad has five loaves of barley bread and two small pickled fish with him. But what is that with all of these people?" He threw his arm out to indicate the crowd before them.

"It's enough," Jesus said. The disciples just looked at each other as he continued, "Now, have the people sit in groups of fifties."

When the people were seated, they watched incredulously as Jesus broke each loaf into three parts. He then raised his eyes to heaven and thanked God for the provision. He handed each of the twelve, John's two men and Lazarus, a piece of bread. Martha and Caleb were each handed a fish.

"Distribute this food to the people. When they're fully satisfied, gather the scraps, that none of it may go to waste." Jesus' voice was calm and authoritative. Without looking at their reactions, he turned back to the rocks he'd been perched upon while teaching and waited for them to do as he'd said.

The men looked at each other and at Jesus. None dared to say what he was thinking, but it was written on their faces. Martha took the fish Jesus had handed her and began breaking off pieces and distributing them. The fish never seemed to grow any smaller, but at first she didn't notice, until she started hearing exclamations from Caleb, who was distributing his fish in the group next to hers. Then she began hearing the disciples with the bread making similar comments and looked down at her fish. It was still as large as when Jesus had given it to her.

The people in the crowd were also making comments. The pieces of food they'd been given didn't diminish as they broke off pieces to eat. When all the people had been given bread, the disciples came over to help Martha and Caleb hand out the fish, neither of which had diminished in size even though several hundred people had already been given some. Martha walked back in a daze to where Jesus sat. It was a miracle, and she'd participated in it. She was stunned. That small amount of food had fed at least twenty thousand people, counting the women and children—and the disciples were finding scraps.

# *Chapter Sixteen*

## The Bread

Darkness quickly came to the skies. Sitting in the stern of the boat, Martha watched the wind play upon the water, causing the waves to chop and swirl. She hugged herself as she thought of the events of the afternoon: to feed that many people with so little food.

She knew, of course, the story of Elijah and the widow–how the meal and oil had never failed as long as the famine lasted and Elijah stayed with the widow and her son–but that was three people and a different situation. This, Martha felt confident, was unprecedented. There was no way her mind could fathom it without using the word "miracle," and Jesus had taken it all in stride.

She could see him now in her mind as he sat calmly among the rocks while the twelve each brought him a basket containing many times more than what they'd started with. He'd looked at the baskets and then at the men and had quietly ordered them to enter the boat and cross the lake while he dismissed the crowds and went alone to pray.

Before Martha had entered the boat, she'd heard some of the people in the throng declaring they should make Jesus their king. She watched as he expertly maneuvered away from them and disappeared into the distance while the boat containing herself and the disciples slowly moved across the lake.

It was now past three o'clock, the fourth watch according to Roman reckoning. The movement of the boat and the inner excitement Martha felt had kept her awake. The wind was strong and the men were having a hard time directing their way in the water. They kept their comments low so she couldn't hear, but they couldn't hide the fear in their voices. The wind was making it nearly impossible, and Jesus hadn't joined them as he'd promised.

She heard one of the men cry out and looked out across the water where she saw everyone else looking. There upon the choppy seas was a figure, white against the black sky and even blacker water. Martha gasped; it was Jesus.


Peter looked up and saw a figure approaching them. It moved quickly; the wind and waves seemed to have no effect upon its progress.

As it approached, he heard it call out in a familiar voice, "Don't be afraid. It's just me." Jesus was walking on the water.

The others didn't believe it. They all, including Peter, had missed the point that Jesus had tried to show them by feeding the multitudes that day. They'd missed that anything was possible with faith. Something came over Peter, a sureness that Jesus could overcome anything.

Peter cried out, "Lord, if that's you, let me come to you."

"Come, Peter," Jesus said. He stretched an arm out in the direction of the boat.

That was all Peter needed. He felt as though he were in a dream. He pulled his tunic off and threw it down. Swinging a leg over the side of the boat, he stood upon the water as if it were solid ground. The others in the boat gasped incredulously. He walked for a short distance and then noticed the wind blowing Jesus' clothes about, heard it howling, and saw it playing with the water, causing waves and small water spouts to form. His eyes, which had been on Jesus, looked more and more often at the water. He felt the cool wetness begin to surround his feet as his mind lost the sureness it had held when he left the boat. Fear gripped him.

"Lord, help me," he cried.

"Oh, Peter, why do you doubt? Where is your faith?" Jesus said as he held out a hand to help him. They walked back to the boat and got into it. As Jesus' foot hit the bottom of the boat, they found themselves ashore at Bethasaida.

It was twilight over Jerusalem. The Temple grounds were quiet. They all sat silently staring at each other. There were only ten of them meeting together because they were the only men Caiaphas could locate on such short notice. He looked at the others.

"It's imperative that we do something about this Jesus who goes around calling himself a king and making himself equal to God." Caiaphas stood and began pacing the floor.

"But what can we do? The people all think very highly of him," Josiah said as he watched the high priest move nervously about the room.

"We must find a way," Annas said. As former high priest and father in-law to Caiaphas, he had a lot of clout when it came to Jewish laws. Caiaphas had many times turned to him for guidance, and he felt sure his word would carry weight now. "He's leading the people too much. He performs miracles and exerts himself on the Sabbath, a day of total rest. Only Satan would approve of that."

Several of the others nodded in agreement. Nicodemus didn't; he was appalled at what he was hearing. Ever since his secret visit to see Jesus, Nicodemus had diligently searched the scriptures to see what they said of the promised Savior. Many spoke of a gentle man who was to be born in Bethlehem. Nicodemus had done some checking up on Jesus and found he was not only of the tribe of Judah, but also had been born during the forced census some thirty-odd years earlier.

At that time, all the members of each tribe had been told they must register in the city of their fathers. Jesus had been born in Bethlehem, the city of David, while his parents were there registering. The scriptures said the Savior would come from that city and also that he'd be called the Nazarene. Jesus had been raised in Nazareth. Nicodemus secretly believed Jesus to be the long-awaited Messiah. He applauded his teachings and was awed by his miraculous works. Never had he heard Jesus declare himself a king nor was Jesus being blasphemous by calling God his father, in Nicodemus' eyes. He carefully watched all of Jesus' doings and was convinced every day this man was sent by God.

"Wouldn't it be wiser for some of us to go and hear what Jesus has to say before we judge him?" Nicodemus said.

Caiaphas looked thoughtful, then a slow grin lit his face. "Yes, that's what we shall do." He beamed at Nicodemus. "Thank you, Nicodemus. We'll send someone to question and entrap him with his own words."

"Look," someone cried as they reached the shore. "Look, it's Jesus, the prophet from Nazareth. Hurry, gather the sick."

Like magic, people began appearing from everywhere, carrying cots which held the ill, leading donkeys which bore the lame, leading those who couldn't see, helping those who couldn't hear. They sought to touch him, believing even a touch to be sufficient enough to bring the healing power into their bodies. None who came left disappointed; all were healed. Many needing healing in their spirits received that as well. Even if they hadn't been aware they'd been searching for fulfillment, the presence of Jesus fed them and quenched a thirst in their hearts. Many who came found a void was filled within them. They urged him to stay with them.

"Master, please come and stay in my home for a time. We have plenty of room."

"No, stay with us, Master. Our children are grown, and we'd like to have you with us."

"Yes, Lord, stay and be with us for a while."

Many others begged him, but Jesus said, "I cannot. There are others in other places who must also be reached." Their faces fell, and Jesus' heart went out to them, but he knew he had to go on toward Jerusalem for the Feast of Tabernacles. Those who could, followed him from town to town. Those who could not, returned to their homes with a song in their hearts and a memory in their minds.

Joshua looked up from where he was lying as he heard Daphne come in. "Ah, my pet. Did you get everything done?"

She smiled, "Yes, I'm nearly ready to leave now."

He reached up and pulled her down next to him and began rubbing her body. "I'll miss you, my sweet."

"Joshua, you'll never miss me. I know you well. You won't fail to find someone to warm your bed while I'm gone."

"You're being very flippant, as if you don't care."

"Oh, I care. I'd stop it if I could, but I know I can't. I won't be here to stop it. I must accept that you'll roam while I'm gone. I can only hope you'll think of me a little and not stray too far."

"I won't stray from you, Daphne, and if I should dally, it won't be anything serious."

She looked into his eyes. Many women had tried to take him from her, but he always came back. She smiled. She knew how to keep him from straying too far.

Jesus entered the synagogue in Capernaum. As he did, several people approached him, inquiring when he'd arrived in the city. Jesus looked at them quietly a moment before replying.

"You followed me and ask me this because of the food you received, not the healing and miracles you witnessed. You aren't looking for spiritual fulfillment, but physical satisfaction. You should be seeking the spiritual food, not the physical because the physical is only temporary, but the spiritual gives unending life. I can give you that life. God has given me His approval to do it."

The people about him looked perplexed. One man spoke up, asking, "What does God want us to do, Teacher?"

"Believe in me."

"Fine," the man said. "What will that accomplish? Our fathers believed in Moses and were fed daily from heaven. Can you do as much for us?"

"Moses didn't give that bread," Jesus said. "God did. And they died; I am the bread that lives. Anyone coming to and believing in me shall never hunger or thirst, but you don't believe. I'll never turn away from those who come and believe. I've come to do the Father's will, and those who believe in me shall be raised up on the last day."

Several men who Jesus recognized as being from Nazareth put their heads together as they whispered to each other.

Jesus declared more loudly, "Yes, I am the life-giving bread. Don't murmur about it. Unless the Father puts a desire into your hearts to come to me and believe in me, you won't come to believe, but those who do will be raised up at the final judgment. The prophets said, 'And they shall all be taught by God.' Anyone to whom God has spoken will come to me. No one has seen God except for me. And I tell you sincerely, whoever believes in me will live forever because I'm the bread that gives that life. The manna your fathers ate didn't give that life. I am the true bread from heaven. Any who believe and partake of my bread shall live eternally, and this bread that I give for the life of the world is my flesh."

Jesus shook his head as he looked around at them. Even though he'd told them this before, he knew they still didn't hear and believe him. "I'm telling you that unless you eat and drink of me, you'll perish, for my flesh and blood are the true life, and when you partake of them, you abide in me and I abide in you. You'll live because of me, for I live because of the Father. I'm the bread from heaven, not the manna your fathers ate. Those who partake of me will live forever."

The crowd buzzed at his words, and Jesus turned to his disciples, who were also talking among themselves.

"Are you upset, too?" he asked. "What would you say if you saw me rise up to heaven? It's the Spirit of God that gives life. The words I've spoken are spirit and life, but some of you are stumbling over them. That's why I said only those the Father speaks to and draws can believe."

Dismayed, he watched as several of the men who had been with him a long time backed off and withdrew. Turning to his twelve closest disciples, he said, "Well, are you going to go, too?"

Peter looked into the faces of each of the other men then turned back. Facing

Jesus, he said, "Lord, where? You give us life and a reason to exist. You're the Messiah. You're God's Son. We're nothing without you."

Jesus nodded, satisfied with Peter's answer. "I chose you, all twelve, yet one of you is a devil." As he said this, his eyes roamed over them and rested on Judas Iscariot.

# Chapter Seventeen

## The Transfiguration

Daphne paused after entering the brothel. Looking about, she scrutinized each man there, assessing which ones would be best for her purposes. That any one of them would deny her was unthinkable. None of them were in a position to quibble about what she wanted, since they all would be found guilty of the very thing of which she wanted them to help her accuse Joshua. At first she hadn't thought such drastic measures needed to be taken, but what she'd heard in the marketplace while preparing for her trip dictated otherwise: Mary had returned.

After discussing tactics, the scribes and Pharisees again sought Jesus out and approached him with what they believed to be a grave sin. According to the traditions which had been followed for generations, all Jews were to wash not only themselves, but also all pots, utensils, and tables before eating. Any neglect of this traditional law was a serious offense in the eyes of the religious leaders. They'd noticed that the disciples following Jesus were lax in this observance and pointed it out to him.

Jesus' eyes snapped when he answered them. "Isaiah was certainly right when he spoke of you. He said 'You show reverence with words, but your hearts don't follow your confessions. You put your man-made rules before those commanded by God.' That's exactly what you're doing here. Washing hands and pottery is more important to you than the laws of God set down by Moses. One of the laws of Moses commands respect, obedience, and support of your parents, yet you say—and encourage—those you teach to dedicate to God what would have been given to their father and mother, mocking God's law by preferring human invention to His commands. That's only an example of your transgressions, but a true one."

He turned away from them and faced the crowd gathered about him. He didn't notice the angry looks on the faces of the religious leaders and scribes as they walked away, arguing with each other.

Before entering the house he'd been headed for with his disciples, he said to the crowd, "Listen to me closely. What your body takes in through your mouth and how it's prepared isn't what is corrupt. Corruption comes from within, from the heart. Think on this."

After Jesus and his companions entered the house, Peter turned to him and said, "Lord what did you mean? The Pharisees and scribes were angry at your words."

"You mean you don't understand this either, after being with me all this time, Peter?" Resigned, he continued. "Don't you see that food only goes to the stomach and is eliminated by your bowels? But what comes out of your heart—how you speak and—

think—affects how you are and shows your true self to others. You see, inside a man's heart are the makings of corruption: evil thoughts, adultery and fornication, murder, thievery, greed, wanton desires, deception, blasphemy, pride, foolish thoughts. They are what must be avoided, not unwashed hands or utensils."

Humming to herself, Mary moved about getting ready to see Joshua. Daphne had been gone for nearly a month and Mary was sure she was making progress with him. Tonight would be the night that she'd make her proposition. She was going to win him; she was sure of it. As she was finishing her preparations, a knock on her door interrupted her. Sighing impatiently, she opened it. A young boy stood before her.

"Are you Mary from Magdala?" he asked. She'd told Joshua to say that if he ever needed to get in touch with her.

"Yes, I am. What do you want?"

Her heart sank as the boy took a flat rock with an X painted on it from his tunic and handed it to her, saying, "A man gave me this for you. Said it was important you get it before you left for Jerusalem today."

Mary looked down at the rock and saw the mark they had agreed upon. When she raised her eyes again the boy was gone; so was her heart. Daphne had returned.

Leaving Capernaum, Jesus and his disciples traveled over to the coasts of the ten cities and the sea of Galilee. Climbing a mountain, he sat down to teach the multitudes that had followed him. For three days they were in the mountainous desert area, and Jesus had taught all this time. Four thousand men, plus at least as many woman, and about ten thousand children were gathered to hear him, and he realized that they'd stayed so long that their food supply was gone. He called his disciples to him.

"It's been three days, and I'm concerned that any who leave now may pass out before they reach their homes. How much food is there?"

"Seven loaves and a few fish," John said after they inquired around in the crowd as they had before.

"Bring it to me," Jesus said. When they brought it, he blessed and broke it. Giving it to his disciples, he told them to distribute it to the people and gather the remainder of the fragments after everyone had eaten their fill. They filled seven hampers full when everyone was satisfied.

After they'd gathered the scraps, they climbed into a boat on the Sea of Galilee and began to cross. Jesus said to them, "Be careful of the leaven of the religious leaders."

Andrew turned to Peter and whispered, "Peter, we didn't bring food. We've only one loaf of bread between us."

Peter nodded. "The Master must be angry with us."

Jesus, who was across the boat, looked straight at Peter and Andrew. He knew what they were thinking. They'd missed his point because they did not see the teachings of the Jewish leaders as being poisonous to the spirit of the people. "Why are you concerned about bread? Are you so hardened that you also don't realize what I'm saying? Think about what happened with the five thousand men and the four thousand. How many baskets were left over with the five thousand?"

Peter said "Twelve."

"And with the four thousand, how many hampers?"

Peter bowed his head in shame as he answered again, "Seven."

"Knowing that, how can you not understand what I'm saying?"

Andrew placed a hand on his brother's arm. "Peter, he's talking about the doctrines and teachings of the Pharisees and Sadducees, not food at all."

Nodding his head, Peter said, "You're right. I see that now."


Joshua mumbled and rolled over. Someone was hammering loudly nearby. He drew a cloak over his head to muffle the sound, but it only became louder and faster. His eyes flew open as he realized that it wasn't hammering. Someone was pounding on the door.

"Daphne, answer that," he growled, but Daphne didn't answer. He looked about; he was alone. The pounding grew more insistent. Grumbling, he got up and swung open the door.

"What is it?" he bellowed before he realized that a woman had fallen into his arms. "Mary, what are you doing here? I sent you word that Daphne's back. If she finds us together—"

"She's gone to Bethany. I heard her tell someone she was headed there to visit some friends and check on your business. Oh please, Joshua, let me come in. I must speak with you." She looked up at him with pleading eyes.

He sighed and drew her into the house as he closed the door, "What is it you want?"

"Just your love," she said as she reached to caress him and lifted her face to be kissed. Joshua had no thought of resisting.


The disciples, traveling north of Galilee along the Jordan, eventually reached Caesarea Philippi, which had been renamed after Tiberius Caesar by Herod Philip in an attempt to gain Caesar's approval. Being built near the eastern source of the Jordan River, the land surrounding it was full of a great variety of vines, flowers, and trees. There Jesus chose to rest and pray. Martha, Caleb, and Lazarus, as well as many of his other disciples, were there as well as the twelve.

After praying apart from the others, Jesus turned and came over to a group seated near the river. "Who do the people say that I am?"

Caleb and Lazarus looked at each other and, shrugging, looked back to Jesus. "Some say Elijah," Lazarus said. Without a word, Jesus nodded and walked on to another group and repeated the question. "Some say Jeremiah," was the answer there. He proceeded to a third group, which answered, "One of the prophets."

He turned and faced them all, looking intently over their faces. Then he asked,

"Who do *you* say I am?" At first they were all silent, looking at each other and then back to him as he waited patiently for their answer.

Finally Peter spoke up. "You're the Messiah, the one, we've waited for, the Son of God."

Jesus approached Peter and placed a hand on his shoulder. "Only God could have shown you this, Peter, son of John. I called you Peter, which means a small stone, but upon this rock," pointing to himself, "I'll build my church and none shall prevail against it."

They all sat silently, not understanding that he was telling them that his ministry would continue through them all. Jesus knew they expected him to be with them for a long time, much longer than he would be. He sighed and sat down on one of the rocks near the shore of the river, beckoning the eighty-plus people who faithfully followed him.

"The time is coming when the elders, priests, and scribes will succeed in arresting me. I'll be betrayed, beaten, and whipped. Then they'll hang me until I'm dead, but I'll rise again three days later."

The disciples murmured among themselves. Then Peter spoke up, voicing all their thoughts, "Lord, this cannot be. They would never do such a thing to you."

Jesus looked sharply at Peter. "I rebuke your words, Satan." Peter blinked as Jesus continued and explained his words. "You see and hear things as a man sees and hears, not as God does. These things must and will happen, but I tell you now to look to yourselves. Do you value and cling to your physical lives and possessions more than you do the spiritual? If you cling to your life here, you'll lose all, but if you cling to that which is spiritual and let go of your life here, you'll gain eternity. There are those sitting among you who won't experience death until after they've witnessed the coming of God's kingdom."


About a week later, Jesus went up the mountain to pray, taking Peter, James, and John with him. John was enthralled. Usually the Lord went alone, so this was a great privilege. When they reached their destination, Jesus instantly went into praise and deep prayer. The others joined him at first, but soon tired. John's head nodded until Peter poked him in the ribs.

"John, James, look."

The brothers looked to where Peter pointed. There was Jesus, glowing brighter than the sun, his clothes radiant. Before him were two men John had heard and read of all his life: Elijah and Moses. They were talking with Jesus about something.

John began to listen more closely. They were discussing Jesus' death. It was to be in Jerusalem, and he'd be scourged and beaten and nailed to a tree. John shook his head. He had to be dreaming; he couldn't be hearing what he thought he was. They wouldn't kill Jesus; they had no reason to do so. While trying to grasp that this was truly happening, John heard Peter speak as if in a daze.

"Lord, should we build shelters for you, Elijah, and Moses?"

As Peter spoke, a cloud surrounded them, and John fell to the ground along with Peter and James. A voice spoke to them from the cloud. "This is My beloved Son. I am well pleased with Him. Listen to and obey Him."

John lay trembling until he felt a touch on his shoulder. He looked up to see Jesus alone and standing before them. "Come," he said. "We must return." He turned and began the descent down the mountain.

John, James, and Peter ran to catch up. When they did, Jesus said, "You must tell no one what you've seen and heard here until I've risen."

The three looked at each other and determined to try to make sense of what they'd witnessed among themselves. They didn't dare ask Jesus what he meant, but John decided to ask about Elijah.

"Master."

"Yes, John."

"The priests and scribes all teach that Elijah is to come."

"That's true. And he has come, but they didn't recognize him. Instead they killed him. I'll suffer in a similar way."

"Was he John the Baptist?" John asked after a few moments of of contemplation.

Jesus nodded. He paused and indicated the crowd ahead of them at the foot of the mountain. The disciples were gesturing and talking to some scribes and a man. A half-grown boy seemed to be in the middle of it. When they saw Jesus, they ran to him.

"Lord," the man said, "I brought my son to you, but you weren't here. Your disciples couldn't help me."

"What's the problem?" Jesus looked with compassion on the man and his son.

"He has a demon, and many times he falls into the water or fire. I fear for his life."

Jesus addressed his disciples with exasperation. "How long do I have to be with you before you'll learn? All you need do is believe, having faith as small as the smallest seed, and you can do anything." He raised his hand to the boy and said, "Come out of him, deaf and dumb spirit."

The boy's eyes rolled back, and he fell to the ground, flopping around like a fish out of water as the demon in him screamed. Suddenly, his body stilled as if there were no life in him at all, and someone murmured, "He's dead."

Jesus, however, reached down and grasped the boy's hand, pulling him up. The boy stood, wiping his eyes as his father embraced him joyfully.

When Jesus was again alone with his disciples, Philip asked him, "Lord, why did we fail?"

"That kind of demon can only be removed after fasting and much prayer," Jesus said.

# Chapter Eighteen

## The Adulteress

Joshua shook Mary's shoulder. "Mary, get up. Daphne's returning; you must leave."

Mary turned over. "Oh, surely she's not."

"Joshua looked down at her lying on his mat, her beautiful hair tumbling about her. His lips tightened. "She is. The boy I paid to watch the street has seen her."

"But we still have–"

"No." He pushed her away. "Do you want to be stoned? That's what will happen if she finds us."

Mary's eyes widened. "She'd have her own husband stoned?"

Joshua rolled his eyes. "No, she'll have you stoned. Daphne would find a way to do it without harming me."

"She couldn't. The law says both the man and woman—"

"She could and she would. Don't underestimate her, Mary. You must leave now."

Sighing, she got up and dressed, then pressed her lips to his chin. "Good-bye, my love," she whispered.

Joshua leaned an arm against the door frame and said nothing as he watched her leave. They were playing with fire and he knew it. Daphne would have her revenge if they were caught. Mary would be stoned and he shuddered to think what his wife would do to him.

After spending time in Caesarea Philippi, Jesus began to travel south again toward Jerusalem. As they neared a town in Samaria, he sent two of his disciples ahead to secure lodgings as there were more than eighty of them, but the men returned with the news that the Samaritans refused them because of where he was headed. They wanted nothing to do with him if be was going to the Jews to preach.

James and John were angry when they heard this. "Lord," James said, "should we call down lightning on them as Elijah did for their heathen ways?"

"No," Jesus said. "My mission isn't to destroy lives, but to save them. Many citizens shall suffer more than Sodom for their rejection of me and my ministry."

He called all of his disciples to him and sent them forth by twos to the cities, towns, and villages ahead to prepare the way for him to come and teach.

Caleb and Lazarus were among those sent, but Martha was to remain behind to cook for Jesus and the twelve, who also stayed until the seventy who had been sent out returned. She listened to the instructions Jesus gave.

"Take nothing with you and don't waste time visiting, but stay in only one place. Bless it when you enter. If those living there are worthy of that blessing, it will stay with them, otherwise it will come back to you. If a place rejects you, reject them also. Heal everyone in need of it wherever you are received and wherever you go tell them all that the Kingdom of God is at hand."

As they waited for the seventy disciples to return, Martha served the men who'd stayed behind and listened as Jesus taught them things he reserved for only them. At one point, he said to them, "Blessed are your eyes and ears for they have seen and heard what many prophets and kings yearned to see and hear but did not."

Later while Jesus was sitting apart from the others, Martha went over to Him. He looked up and, smiling, motioned for her to sit. "What is it, Martha?"

"Lord, we approach Jerusalem." She hesitated.

"Yes."

"Where do you plan to stay?"

"I haven't considered it yet, but don't you and Lazarus have a home near there?" Although his face was solemn, his eyes were amused because he knew what she wanted.

"Yes, Lord, we do." She paused and then blurted out, "We'd be so honored to have you there."

Jesus laughed and patted her shoulder. "It's I who will be honored, Martha. Of course I'll stay in your home."


Daphne turned the corner and stood waiting for the boy to appear. He came running out to the main street from the same one she'd just come down. He stopped and looked around as if searching for something, then his eyes lit upon her. She motioned him to come, and he turned and ran in her direction.

She bent down and, putting an arm over his shoulder, held a coin in front of him. "You have a message from my husband."

He looked at her, and his face went expressionless.

"Don't deny it. I know you do. I want you to deliver my husband's message, then come back to me. We must wait together until the woman you take the message to comes."

The boy looked startled. "How did you know?"

She smiled. "I know my husband."

"I must go, or he won't pay me."

"But I have something for you to do for me also."

"What?"

"I want you to go to the house of Uzziah, the elder. Do you know where it is?"

"Yes." The boy's eyes looked greedily at the coin, and he held his hand up for it, but Daphne pulled it out of his reach.

"No. You'll get it when I see that you've done what I ask, all that I ask, and not before."

"I'm to go to Uzziah's," the boy said impatiently. "What's so hard about that?"

"Nothing, but I want to make sure it's done. When you get there, you're to tell him

Daphne has sent you and all is ready for him to come. He'll follow you here, then you may have this." She looked at the coin and then to him. He started to run off, but she grabbed his arm to stop him. "Remember to come back here before going to Uzziah's." He nodded, and she smiled as she watched him run off.

Daphne stood waiting for the boy to return. She congratulated herself. Mary was about to get what she deserved. No one stole what was hers, and Joshua belonged to her. Mary would die by stoning as Jewish law dictated, but Joshua would live. Uzziah would see to that.

How convenient that one of the Jewish elders had an insatiable hunger for a woman's flesh. He'd been at Joshua's brothel the day she'd gone there to find men to help her. She'd nearly missed him—he'd been upstairs—but he came down just as she'd been about to leave, and she knew when she saw and recognized him that her plan would succeed. Mary would be stoned, but Joshua would not. Uzziah could see to that , and he would or he'd receive the same fate—Daphne would see to that.

"No, please." Mary wept and pleaded as they dragged her through the streets. "Oh, God, have mercy on me."

"Mercy? She wants mercy." A woman laughed a hideous, accusing laugh and cried out mockingly as a man spit in Mary's face. "There's all the mercy you'll get, you whore."

Fear permeated Mary's being as the crowd pulled her toward the temple. What were they doing? She knew stoning was the penalty for adultery, for both the man and woman, but the men who'd grabbed Joshua had disappeared with him. Now they were taking her, alone, to be tried by the ruling elders of the temple, and then she'd be stoned.

Into the Court of the Gentiles and up the steps to the treasury they dragged her. With every step, her insides seemed to get tighter and tighter as if twisting like a coil. Suddenly the crowd stopped, and some men came out of the treasury. The people surrounding her parted, forming a path through which they could approach her. Mary recognized many of them, having seen them in the temple during her younger years when she'd attended regularly. They were the elders, the scribes and Pharisees who taught the laws and led all the religious ceremonies.

They asked, "Are you guilty?" Mary mumbled an answer. One of the men slapped her across her face.

"Answer plainly," he screamed.

Sobbing, she raised her voice. "Yes, I'm guilty." She couldn't deny it. The men who took her from Joshua's house had seen her lying naked with him before they threw her clothes at her.

The crowd went wild and began to drag her away again. One of the men who had come from the temple raised his hand and called out "Wait." He approached the others, and they talked excitedly in low tones.

Mary watched them in wonder. What were they talking about? Were they going to release her? The man who had stopped them from taking her came over to her.

"I'll take her," he said. When those holding her began to object, he flashed his eyes at them. Silently, they let go of her, and he took her arm in a firm grip. "Come with us," he said.

She found herself surrounded again, this time by the elders. Their treatment of her was no different from those who'd previously had hold of her. They dragged her into the treasury and across the floor on which many people sat listening to a man at the far end of the room. They stopped in front of him, and Mary felt the eyes of every person on her.

She lowered her head in shame as she realized this was the man she'd encountered in Nain a year ago. She'd washed his feet and vowed to God she wouldn't continue living as she had been. But she hadn't kept her vow, and she knew God knew that. She sensed this man knew everything about her. She couldn't look into his kind, gentle eyes. She couldn't look at him at all.

A Pharisee told Jesus what she'd done and asked him what he thought they should do. Jesus bent down on his haunches and began writing in the dust on the floor. Mary closed her eyes and grasped her hands tightly in front of her, waiting for the answer she knew would surely come, but there was silence. Finally he stood and answered, then, without looking at her even once, he went back to what he'd been writing on the floor.

She sensed movement behind her and closed her eyes again, expecting unfriendly hands to grab her again, but no hand touched her. She opened her eyes and looked around in amazement. There was no one there. The only ones who remained besides herself and the teacher were the people he'd been teaching when the elders had brought her in. Again he defended her. Dazed, she turned back to look at him in wonder.


Jesus went up into the temple. He passed through the outer court and entered the treasury. There he sat down and began to teach the people who'd followed him in along with his disciples.

As he taught, a commotion stirred outside. Several Jewish leaders who were also present left and returned dragging a young woman with them. Jesus recognized her as the woman who'd washed his feet in Nain nearly a year earlier. Sadly he watched as they pushed her in front of him. The crowd he'd been speaking to looked on expectantly. No one said a word. Everyone wanted to be able to hear what was said between Jesus and the elders who had brought in the woman.

Jesus waited, but he didn't need to wait long. The religious people were always ready and anxious to judge and accuse others.

"Teacher," one Pharisee said, "this woman was caught in the act of adultery. Our laws state that she should be stoned to death. This is what Moses says; what do you say should be done?"

They had him. Jesus couldn't possibly argue with Moses. The leaders had trouble hiding their smug looks.

Jesus looked compassionately at the woman. She held her head down as if to hide in her disgrace. Her hands were clasped so firmly together in front of her that the knuckles had turned white. Jesus could see she was trembling and every few minutes a sob escaped her. He looked at the unfriendly faces of the religious leaders and realized that she wasn't the only one on trial by these men. His heart was grieved by their lack of understanding, and he couldn't bear to look at them any longer. He stooped down and began to write the laws of Moses in the dirt at his feet. But the insistent questions of the Pharisees forced him to rise once more and answer them.

"Yes, kill her if you like, but let the one among you who has never sinned be the one to cast the first stone."

Again he stooped and resumed writing, paying no attention as, one by one, the scribes, priests, and Pharisees disappeared. When they were gone, he looked up, straightened himself and addressed the young woman.

"Where are those who have judged you? Has none seen himself fit to cast the first stone? Does no one condemn you?"

"No, my Lord," the woman said, her voice trembling.

Then Jesus looked at her, love and peace radiating from him as he said gently, "Then I will not condemn you either. Go in peace and leave your sin behind you." The woman left, rejoicing as she went that God had given her back her life.

# Chapter Nineteen

## The Reconciliation

When she reached Bethany, Mary passed the well where the women congregated to gossip as they filled their jugs. A woman turned slightly, and Mary quickly turned her head. It was Martha. That meant Lazarus was also back, and Mary groaned as she realized it also meant she had nowhere to go. She turned down the first street she came to and kept going. It would've been nice to rest and think over the miracle that she'd just experienced, but that was not to be. There would be time when she reached Magdala. The cottage in Magdala would be the place to ponder this man, Jesus, and what he'd done for her. She'd go to her cottage.

Caleb turned toward his companion as they laughed while discussing an old woman they'd healed. The woman's foot had been bad, and she couldn't stand, let alone walk. When she realized the foot was healed, she'd not only stood up, but had immediately started dancing in the street as she praised God. Every once in a while she'd purposely come down on the newly healed leg doubly hard on the last syllable as she shouted `hallelujah.' But Caleb's laugh stopped and he stared at the well they were passing as they traveled through Magdala. Mary was there.

David looked at his friend. "Caleb, what's the matter? Is something wrong?"

Caleb shook his head as if to clear it, then looked at David. "I'm sorry, David. There's a woman here I knew long ago and lost track of."

"Here? Are you sure?"

"Yes. She just left the well. Come, we have to follow her. I must speak with her."

Mary caught herself humming as she did her daily chores. Her life with Marcus had mellowed her somewhat. She mused on it and smiled to herself. She hadn't realized how domestic she was becoming. Martha would be quite surprised. Mary had never willingly done any work that needed to be done. Living with Marcus and then becoming her own mistress had begun to give her pride in her own home. She jumped, startled by a knock on her door. It came again as she rose to answer it.

"Caleb!"

He smiled down at her. "Peace to you, Mary." He turned and spoke to someone behind him. "I won't be long, David. I want to speak with her privately."

Mary stepped aside as Caleb entered without waiting for her to invite him. She stared up at him. "Who's out there?"

"A friend. We've been traveling together."

"Traveling? Where?"

"To the towns the Master will be visiting."

"The Master?"

"Yes, You remember my telling you of the man in the temple at Passover? I found him. He's the Master. David is one of his disciples, as am I, Lazarus, and Martha."

He looked at her closely to see what her reaction to his words would be. He hoped they'd help him to speak with her on the matter for which he'd come. Mary had been more than just a harlot for Caleb. He hadn't realized until he'd seen her at the well how much he cared for her. Under other circumstances, it would have been more acceptable and proper to approach Lazarus with what he desired. However, Mary's estrangement with her brother and sister had left him at a loss on how to proceed, and he had decided to speak with Mary first before he sought Lazarus.

Mary's eyes widened. "Lazarus? Martha? You know them?"

"Yes, Mary. I know them. We've become good friends."

"Friends? But Lazarus—"

"Lazarus is changed, as I am."

Mary frowned. "Caleb, I don't understand. How has Lazarus changed? How have you changed?"

"The Master and his teaching has changed us," He took her hands. "Oh, Mary, come with me and hear him. Come with us and be a part of it. Lazarus will accept you back. He's forgiven you. I know he has. And I..."he reached out a hand to touch her face gently as he held her two small hands in his other one, "I want you for my wife, Mary. I want to ask Lazarus for you."

"Caleb." She gasped and felt color coming to her cheeks. Marcus had wanted her to marry him and she'd cared for him because he was kind to her and loved her, but no man had ever wanted to approach her brother and make her his betrothed. Caleb wanted that. He was young and handsome and she knew he'd cared for her before. Now he was telling her that he cared more than she'd ever dreamed. "You really want me?" she whispered incredulously.

He smiled. "Does that surprise you so much?"

Remembering how thoughtful and gentle he'd been with her at Joshua's, Mary smiled back. "No, Caleb, it doesn't surprise me that much."


Lazarus looked up from his work as Caleb entered the room. He smiled and nodded, "Good day, Caleb."

"Good day, Lazarus. Peace be with you." Caleb sat on a stool near Lazarus and watched him form clay into a pot. Lazarus broke the silence.

"David has told me you met a young woman in Magdala. He had the impression you know her from your past."

Lazarus stopped working and looked into Caleb's eyes. "Is it Mary?"

"Yes, it's Mary." Caleb became uncomfortable at Lazarus's gaze. "She lives in Magdala now. She seems different. I've asked her to come with us to hear Jesus."

"And?"

"She didn't say she would." Lazarus nodded and resumed his work."She didn't say no either," Caleb quickly added.

"If she didn't say she would, then she won't. Mary's like that. A refusal to commit herself one way is a commitment in the other direction. You only knew but one side of Mary in Bethany, so you wouldn't know that."

"I know her well enough, and I want to know her better."

Lazarus raised his eyebrows as he glanced over at him. "How so?"

Caleb cleared his throat. "I want her for my wife. I ask that you give her to me to wed."

Lazarus stopped working altogether and looked at his friend. "Are you sure? You know Mary's past. Did you know she's the woman who washed the Master's feet in Nain?"

Caleb stared at Lazarus and shook his head. "No," he spoke slowly. "I didn't know that."

Lazarus nodded. "Well, she is and you've heard what they said of her there. She hasn't changed, Caleb. Your feelings for her have made you blind to what she is."

"Are you saying you won't agree to our betrothal, Lazarus?"

"I'm saying, my friend, that Mary hasn't changed. How can you even consider her, knowing she may not remain faithful to you?"

"I love her, I've loved her from the very first."

Lazarus reached a hand out and placed it on his friend's arm. "Very well. If you love her enough to forgive her, and you realize that that part of her hasn't changed and won't unless she wills it, you have my blessing." Lazarus smiled.

They spent the rest of their visit discussing the betrothal agreement. Then Caleb left to tell Mary and to bring her back with him for her reunion with Lazarus and Martha.


Incredulous, Mary looked at Caleb. "You're sure? He really wants to see me?"

"He really wants to see you." He smiled, then took her in his arms and looked down at her lovely face. "By now, Martha is waiting for us also."

"Oh Caleb, I never dreamed Lazarus would want to see me again, let alone dower me."

"Well, he does and he has. We're to go now to their cottage to share in the evening meal."

She looked up at him apprehensively. "You're sure?"

He laughed. "Yes, I'm very sure."


Mary grasped Caleb's hand tightly. He looked at her and smiled reassuringly. "It's all right. Don't be nervous or frightened."

"He was so angry when I last saw him. I can't believe he's forgiven me. I know you say he has, but it's so difficult to forget his anger."

He stopped, took her other hand, and stood holding them both between his own as he gazed down at her. "Mary," he said, "Lazarus has been with the Master, who teaches forgiveness. He's no longer angry." He caressed her cheek and then took her hands in both of his again and put them to his lips. "You'll see."

Mary looked up into Caleb's eyes. He was the same and yet he was different, this man she'd once known intimately and to whom she was now betrothed. The kiss on her hands was the most intimate he'd been with her since he'd come to her cottage after seeing her at the well in Magdala. He was still kind and gentle, but in a different way, and his eyes were full of peace. His whole being was full of peace. She envied him.

"Caleb?"

"Yes, Mary?" Caleb looked down at her as they resumed walking. They were nearing Bethany and soon would be at their destination.

"Who is this Master you speak of?"

"He is Jesus of Nazareth."

"Jesus?" She stopped and stared at him.

"Yes. Didn't I tell you?"

"No. You never said his name before. You only called him the Master."

"Well, now I've said his name. Does it matter?"

"Yes, yes, it matters a great deal." She couldn't go on.

The Master was Jesus, the same Jesus whose feet she'd washed, the same Jesus who had saved her from being stoned, the same Jesus who raised widows sons and spoke wonderful words about God and His kingdom. Now she knew what was different about Caleb. He spent time with Jesus; he knew him well and intimately, and she was going to meet him. Caleb had told her she would, insisted that she must.

Mary wondered what Caleb would do if he knew of the two times she'd been before Jesus. The tear bottle wasn't a bad time, only sorrowful, but the incident in the temple—would Caleb forgive her for that? Her mind reeled at the idea of being near Jesus again.

Mary sat beside Caleb. They'd decided to take a brief rest before continuing their journey to Bethany. She cleared her throat.

"Caleb," she said.

"Yes." He turned to her and smiled, then noticed her troubled look, "What's wrong?"

"I've met Jesus."

Caleb remained silent, deciding not to tell her what Lazarus had told him. He wanted her to tell him her experiences herself. He reached over and took her hand as she continued.

"The first time was in Nain. I'd just lost someone, and I had heard him speak. I knew he had what I wanted, so I went to him and he forgave me." Caleb leaned closer as her voice grew softer. "Then, I..." She paused and raised apprehensive eyes to his.

"Go on," he, said and squeezed her hand in encouragement.

"I was with Joshua again." Her words came out in a rush. She knew that if she didn't get it out quickly she never would. "We were caught, and he was taken away. I don't know where. They were going to stone me, but on the way they took me to Jesus and he saved me. He forgave me again, but I'm afraid to see him now." She began to cry.

"Why?"

She shook her head. "I don't know. I want to see him, but I'm afraid."

Caleb took her face in his hands. "It'll be all right. Don't worry."

She gave him a tremulous smile. "Okay."


When they reached the cottage in Bethany, Mary placed her hand on Caleb's arm. "Caleb."

He turned and, seeing the fear in her eyes, took her into his arms. "It's all right, Mary. Lazarus wants to see you. Don't you believe me?"

"I do. It's just—"

"It's just what?" He looked down into her face.

"I'm so afraid of seeing Lazarus again. And him."

"You mustn't be afraid. Lazarus loves you, and the Master would never criticize you." He spoke gently.

Caleb opened the door after a quick knock to let those inside know they were there. Putting his arm around Mary's waist, he drew her in with him. Her large eyes reflected her apprehension as she looked at her brother and sister for the first time in nearly two and a half years. Both Martha and Lazarus had stopped what they were doing, and Caleb could see their eyes drinking in the sight of Mary. Their love could be seen on their faces.

Martha was the first to move, and her first step seemed to release a flood. All at once Mary was in her arms, and they were both weeping. Caleb turned his eyes toward Lazarus as he too approached the women. As he placed a hand on Martha's shoulder, she looked up at him and then both women were embraced in their brother's arms as Caleb silently moved away a few paces to let them have their reunion. None of them seemed able to utter any words other than their names. After nearly ten minutes, Caleb coughed to remind them of his presence.

Lazarus looked over at Caleb with a joyous smile. "My friend, come. Join us. We must celebrate this reunion. Jesus will be joining us soon for our evening meal. The twelve will be with him."

A grin spread over Caleb's face, and he again drew Mary next to him, his arm firmly about her waist, his other arm extending around Lazarus. These friends he'd grown to love were reunited, and he was a part of it.

# *Chapter Twenty*

## The Portion

Mary balked when she heard the men's voices. Now that the time had come and Jesus was there, she was afraid. It was nearly overpowering. It was strange, she thought. Never had she been so aware of this fear within her, but she knew it had always been there. It was what had kept her from pursuing Jesus before this. She had an overwhelming urge to run, but where? And why? He was only a man, after all. He wouldn't harm her. The only times she'd ever encountered him before, he'd defended her, yet she feared him.

Martha came over to her with a face glowing with joy and pride. "Come, Mary, meet the Master. I've told him about you, and he wants to talk with you." Taking Mary's hand, she drew her into the house from the garden.

"Master, this is Mary, our sister."

Lazarus and Caleb watched as Mary was presented to Jesus. Surprise overcame them as they watched her face contort in fear as she shrank away from Jesus and cried out, "Get away from me! Don't touch, me!"

Mary pushed Martha aside. Martha looked in stunned silence from Mary to Jesus. "But Mary," she said, "Jesus won't hurt you. He–"

Jesus held out an arm to stop everyone in the room from approaching. Calmly he looked at Mary. He sensed seven spirits within her. Fear, lust, and deception were the main ones, with four lesser spirits helping to control her. "Come out of her," he sternly commanded.

"We don't want to." The voice didn't sound like Mary's voice to the three in the room who knew it.

"But you must. She doesn't want you there any longer. She's proven it by her own actions and by agreeing to meet me. Now come out. "

Mary writhed and, crying out, fell to the floor. She lay like a rag doll as Caleb rushed to her and Lazarus spoke, "Master?"

Jesus turned to the brother and sister as Caleb picked up Mary and laid her on a mat near the wall. "She's all right now. There were seven demons controlling her. I know you suspected something like that. She'll be all right now." He went over to the mat where Mary was just awakening.

Mary opened her eyes. "Caleb?" she said weakly in her normal voice. "What happened?"

Caleb smiled and smoothed her forehead as he answered, "The Master has set you free, Mary. You're no longer in bondage to what was driving you to live as you did."

He turned as Jesus came up beside him and smiled down at Mary. She smiled back and held out her hand to the Master.

Mary sat on the floor beside Jesus. Like a sponge, she drank in every word he spoke. She couldn't get enough. As she'd suspected in Nain, Jesus had what she'd desired and searched for all her life. Every word he spoke, every idea he conveyed, was like a refreshing spring she never thought existed. To be accepted just the way she was, without criticism, without judgment, without being told she wasn't good enough. The love that emanated from Jesus was present all around him. It flowed out to Mary and enveloped her as she sat at his feet and hung on every word he said. She couldn't get enough. She'd never stop wanting more. She wanted to sing, to dance, to shout it out to everyone. She was free. She was loved.

As Martha worked on the evening meal, a resentment she had long ago thought was gone began again to plague her. More and more often she turned to look over at Mary, seated at Jesus' feet with the men while Martha made the evening meal for them all, alone, just like before Lazarus had thrown Mary out. Every time the nagging thoughts and memories would come, Martha pushed them back, but it was getting increasingly difficult to do so. Finally, when she could take it no more, she approached Jesus.

"Lord," Martha said.

Jesus looked up. "Yes, Martha?"

"There's a lot of preparation yet to be done for our evening meal. I could use some help. Don't you think Mary could be spared to give me a hand?"

Jesus looked at Martha, and she sensed he knew her thoughts. She loved Mary, but the past was difficult to forget. The demons that had bound Mary before were gone, but the memories of how she'd been while under their influence were there yet.

"Martha, it's good of you to make these preparations and they're important to an extent, but they aren't urgent. Only one thing is needful in this life. Mary has finally found this better portion, and I won't deny her of it in her hour of discovery," Jesus said.

Shame filled Martha as she looked at the glowing face of her sister and realized that Jesus was right. This was the reason she'd wanted to bring Jesus and Mary together and now that it was happening, she was asking Jesus to stop it. Suddenly love flowed in her heart for her sister and the resentment fled. She wouldn't resent or deny Mary her healing at Jesus' feet.

It was winter and Mary, along with Caleb and his other disciples, followed Jesus to Jerusalem and the temple. It had been two months since she'd met him. Although it still seemed unreal to her, she was slowly becoming accustomed to the life and love she'd found through being with Jesus and his disciples, including her own brother and sister. She thought back over the past two months, remembering his many miracles and words. One instance in particular stood out in her mind.

Jesus had just finished speaking in the temple—had, in fact, angered many of the elders to the point that they were ready to stone him—and was passing by one of the gates of the city where a man who had been blind since his birth sat daily to beg. The disciples asked the Lord whose sin had brought this on, and Jesus had replied that no one had brought it on by sin, but that this was an opportunity to show God's love and power and through this glorify Him. He said then that he was sent to do God's works. He had picked up some dirt and spit on it and rubbed the mud over the man's eyes. The man, of course, was dumbfounded and moved to wipe the mud away, but Jesus stopped him and told him to go to the swimming pool made centuries ago by King Hezekiah and wash it off there. It was appropriate, Mary reflected, since the name of the pool was Siloam, which meant the one who has been sent.

The healing had caused a great commotion among the Pharisees. They didn't believe the man had really been blind at all until they talked to his parents who confirmed it, but wouldn't say how he'd been healed for fear of being excommunicated. The man, however, had had no such fear and told the Pharisees plainly how he'd been healed. They were indignant. These healings were all too frequent. They desperately wanted to catch Jesus in any way they could. They tried to get the man to help them, but when the Pharisees had said Jesus was a sinner and God wouldn't listen to a sinner, the man had come back with the answer that no one had ever before healed someone blind from birth and that only God could have given Jesus the power to do so. The Pharisees, in anger, threw him out of the temple.

When Jesus had heard of it, he, went to the man and asked him if he believed in the Son of God. The man had asked who he was so that he could, and Jesus had said that it was Jesus himself. It was the first time Mary had heard him openly declare that he was God's Son. He usually called himself the son of man.

The man had worshipped Jesus on hearing who he was, and then Jesus made a strange statement. He said that he came into the world so that the blind could see and those who saw would be blind. There had been some Pharisees near Jesus when he said that, and they asked him if they were blind. His reply was that if they'd been blind, they'd be innocent of sin, but because they claimed to see, they were guilty.

Mary had pondered that for a while before she realized Jesus had been talking about spiritual blindness. Now she looked on the Pharisees in a new light. They claimed to know so much, but in reality they knew nothing because they put their trust in the things they saw rather than what they didn't see. It made her look at Jesus in a different way again. He knew the laws, but he cared about the people more than rules, and if there was a choice between them, the people always won. Everything he did was people-centered, love-centered. She'd never met anyone more gentle and kind, but he was a lion when it came to the Father he spoke of so often and His people.

Mary felt humbled and honored that he considered her one of them. She squeezed Caleb's hand as they separated and Mary went with Martha to the Court of Women where they'd listen to the men—especially Jesus.

Since nearly everyone there had come to hear Jesus, it wasn't long before he stood and began to teach. He likened himself to a shepherd and the people to sheep and said those who heard and believed in him and what he taught were his, given to him by his Father, He said he'd come to give them life in abundance. He was the door to eternal life, and he'd lay his life down for them because they were his and God had sent him to do this.

The Pharisees were outraged and again went after him, but Jesus evaded them. It seemed the Father didn't want him to lay his life down just yet.

# Part Four

## The Last Months

## The Opposition Increased

*Behold, I lay in Zion for a foundation a stone...*
Isaiah 28:16.

*The stone which the builders refused is become the
head stone of the corner*
Psalms 118:22.

# Chapter Twenty-one

## The Restoration

After leaving the temple, Jesus and his disciples again went back to Bethany where it was decided that they should leave the area. Although Jesus himself was unafraid of the recent threats to his life, the disciples were able to persuade him that the tempers of the Jewish leaders would cool more readily if he weren't around to inflame them.

Shrugging, Jesus agreed to leave, stating that he needed to visit the towns and villages the seventy had visited in preparation for his own arrival. "We'll travel to Bethabara," he said.

Lazarus, his sisters, and Caleb decided to remain in Bethany. Mary and Martha wanted to begin preparations for Caleb and Mary's wedding, and the men were going to begin building their house. Also they wanted some time together to renew and strengthen their ties again, including Caleb into their family circle.

About a month after Jesus left, Caleb and Mary were sitting out in the garden together. They were silent, both content just to be together. Reaching out, Mary touched Caleb's arm. He turned and smiled at her, his brows raised in question.

"I've never thanked you, Caleb." Mary spoke hesitantly.

"Thanked me? For what?"

"Insisting I meet Jesus. You know how drastically it has changed my life."

"Mary, it's all right. I know how you feel about it and about him. I feel it, too. He did the same for me."

"He did?"

"Well, I had no demons to be cast out, but he's changed my life and changed me. I could never be the same man you knew so long ago, just as you aren't the same woman. Jesus does that to people, just his presence will do it."

"Yes, that's true, but Caleb." She paused again.

"Yes, Mary?"

"Why do the elders hate him?"

"They're jealous of his miracles and that they can't form him into their own mold. They try to trick him into saying or doing something they can come after him for. So far the worst they have is that he cares about the people so much that he performs miracles even on the Sabbath—like with the blind man."

Mary nodded. "But can't they see how good he is? How loving, kind, gentle, and forgiving?"

"No, their jealousy makes them blind. They think they need no forgiveness because they don't think they do any wrong."

"Well, I'm glad I know him and know I need what he has."

"So am I." He took her in his arms and placed a kiss on her forehead.

Caleb opened the door to the house Lazarus was helping him build. It was nearly finished, and Caleb wanted to show it to David, who'd been his partner when Jesus sent them out by twos. As they entered, he stopped and gasped. There on the floor lay Lazarus. Caleb ran to him and, rolling him onto his back, took Lazarus's head in his arms. He was unconscious, and his body was on fire with fever.

Caleb looked over at David, who was crouched on the other side of Lazarus. "We must get him back to his house. He needs to have this fever brought down."

David nodded, and together they carried Lazarus back to the house he lived in with his sisters. The women took turns bathing him with cool water, but it didn't help, and the physician they sent for could do nothing.

They all felt helpless as they sat at the table. The men had done all they could as well, but their faith, or lack of it, couldn't bring about a healing for their friend.

"If only Jesus were here," Martha said.

Mary nodded. "Yes, he'd help Lazarus."

"I could get him for you." David began to rise as he spoke. "I'm sure I could find him. He can't be far from where he was when I left him two days ago."

"Oh, David." Martha clapped her hands together. "Yes, find and tell him Lazarus is sick. He'll come. He'll save Lazarus."

David crossed the Jordan and arrived in Bethabara around noon. It wasn't hard to find Jesus at the side of the river. As usual a crowd of thousands had gathered. What was hard was getting through the throng and finding one of the disciples. It was nearly impossible to get close to Jesus himself, but David knew that if he got to one of the twelve, his news of Lazarus would reach Jesus.

Sure enough, he spotted Judas near a palm tree beside the water. It was at the front and to the side of the crowd, making it easy for David to approach him. Judas would have little trouble getting word to Jesus.

"David," Judas said. "How's everyone in Bethany?"

"That's why I'm back so soon. Lazarus is ill. He may even be dying or dead as we speak. The Master must come at once."

Judas, reaching out, took David's arms and gave them a squeeze. Nodding, he went over to Andrew who was listening intently to Jesus. They spoke, then Andrew glanced at David and nodded as he headed toward Jesus. Soon, several of the disciples were surrounding David, asking questions.

John came over to join them. "Peter's going to tell the Master," he said and stood listening as David answered the other men's questions.

Later, after Jesus had dismissed the crowd, he also questioned David. Then he said, "Lazarus has gone to rest."

The disciples were overjoyed at this announcement, thinking Jesus meant he was better and was sleeping. Jesus realizing they'd misunderstood him, clarified. "He's dead. It's good I wasn't there for your sakes." At the shocked silence of the disciples; he softened his tone and continued. "This illness won't be to the death, but it's so the Father and Son may be glorified."

Two days passed, and Jesus went on teaching and healing. On the evening of the second day he told them, "We'll go now to Bethany and I'll awaken Lazarus."

Puzzled, but not daring to ask Jesus to explain what he'd said, the disciples followed him as he left Bethabara and crossed the Jordan. The next day as they neared Bethany, David was sent ahead. Finding the sisters, he told them Jesus was near. Martha went out to meet him, leaving Mary at their house with the professional mourners and people who'd come to console them. She met him on the road a mile or so east of Bethany,

"Martha." Jesus held out his hands to her.

"Master," Martha said. "If you'd been here, he wouldn't have died. Even now you'd be granted what you will."

"Have faith, Martha. He'll rise again."

"Yes, Lord, I know he'll be resurrected at the final judgment."

"Martha, I am the resurrection. I give life. Anyone believing in me lives on, even when he dies. Do you believe that this is so?"

"Yes, Lord. I know you're the Messiah, the one we've waited for."

"This is good. I wish to see Mary. Where is she?"

"She's still in Bethany. I'll get her for you." Martha left him waiting on the road.


Mary and Caleb sat side by side. She sighed and he squeezed her hand. They both looked up as Martha entered.

"Mary," Martha seemed breathless, as if she'd run a great distance. "The Master asks for you. He's on the road just outside of Bethany,"

Immediately, Mary rose and left, running ahead of Martha and Caleb. They followed at a slower pace because Martha could run no more, having already come the distance from Jesus to their home.

Upon reaching Jesus, Mary repeated nearly word for word what Martha had said about Lazarus living if Jesus had been there. Neither woman had said it accusingly or with rancor, but the hurt on their faces and in their manner moved Jesus and he raged inside at Satan who had stolen their brother and his friend.

"Where have you buried him?" he asked as Martha and Caleb caught up with Mary and the group Jesus was with.

"Come, Lord, and we'll show you." Mary took his hand as she brought him to the rock they'd hollowed out for Lazarus's tomb. The professional mourners and the Jews who had come from Jerusalem to mourn Lazarus had caught up by this time also. A large following was gathered outside the tomb. Jesus wept for the senselessness of it, and rage again filled him toward the thief who stalked even his closest friends.

"Roll away the stone," he said, and some of the disciples began pushing on the stone.

"But Lord," Martha said, "he's been there for four days now. With the heat, he's surely begun to rot and smell."

"Martha, didn't I say he'd rise again?" Turning away from her and the crowd, Jesus faced the stone. Looking up, he said, "Father, for the benefit of these who are with me, I thank you now for hearing me. You always hear me, but I say it here that they might believe." Then he looked at the tomb and said loudly, "Lazarus, come out."

A gasp ran through the crowd as a body wrapped in swathing emerged from the hole the rock had covered.

"Free him," Jesus said, and the disciples quickly began to unwrap the clothes from Lazarus's body. Many of the people there became disciples of Jesus that day, but others, sent as spies, returned to the Jewish elders to report what they'd seen.


"What are we to do?" a Pharisee cried out. "He draws all the people and causes commotions wherever he goes and now this; raising a man from the dead."

"Surely Rome will send more soldiers and we'll lose not only our temple, but also our nation," another elder said.

"Quiet," Caiaphas commanded. "You know nothing. Don't you realize that one can be sacrificed for the many? If we find fault with this Jesus and have him arrested, the crowds will stop after he's dead." He paused and spoke as if to himself. "We just have to find a way to have him arrested."


After restoring Lazarus to his sisters, Jesus journeyed to Ephraim, about twenty miles north of Jerusalem. He began visiting the places where the seventy were sent. He healed all who came to him for healing and turned no one away, not even on the Sabbath. This frustrated and angered the Jewish leaders all the more, but there was nothing they could do against him. To arrest him for such a reason would accomplish nothing. The crowds would be angered, and the Romans didn't care what days Jesus worked. They needed witnesses to testify against him.


Judas sat listening to the conversation of the others. Jesus had gone off alone to pray, and the twelve were discussing a topic they dared not bring up when he was around: when he'd make his move to come into power. They were of two minds. Some thought he was just biding his time and would eventually take up arms to free Israel from the Romans. Others thought Jesus had a different plan in mind and didn't intend to use force. All agreed on one thing. Jesus was the Messiah and was there to free the Israelites from the bondage they were under.

Judas leaned toward the use of force, but at times he wondered. Jesus had never committed a violent act that Judas knew of other than throwing the money-changers from the temple. The only other incidents of violence he'd been involved in were directed *at* him, not by him. Jesus always managed to disappear at those times. Whenever authorities came to cool down the riot that had begun, Jesus was never there.

Judas was becoming frustrated and impatient. The Romans had no right to be in their country, but neither had the Assyrians or Persians or any other conqueror who'd overthrown the Jewish people. It was tiresome waiting for God to fulfill the promises He'd made. Now Jesus was finally here. Why didn't he do something? Why didn't he free the country of the Romans and then go back to his preaching, teaching, and healing?

Maybe he needed a push, some persuasion to get him to accomplish it more quickly than he was presently going about it. Yes, that was it, but what and how to get the ball rolling more quickly? Judas bit his lip. He'd have to think about it some more. Maybe there was a way. He just needed to find it.

# *Chapter Twenty-two*

## The Explanation

Nicodemus cringed at the knock. His mind was troubled, and he didn't feel like entertaining. It would be too difficult to concentrate. However, when Rachel, his daughter, brought in the visitor, he felt a lifting in his heart. It was Joseph of Arimathaea, an old friend and one of the few Pharisees he knew who felt as he did about the young carpenter that many of the common people called the Messiah.

"Joseph."

"Greetings, Nicodemus. How goes it with you?"

"All is well, And you?"

"I'm also well, physically, but my mind is troubled."

Nicodemus sighed. "You also sense it."

"Sense what?" Joseph looked intently at his friend.

"There's something that grabs me," Nicodemus pounded his heart with his palm, "here. I can't rest easily, and my mind ponders what to do."

"About what?"

"Jesus."

"Ah." Joseph closed his eyes. "The scriptures say the Messiah will be ridiculed and scourged. We can do nothing to stop it when it comes. If his ministry is truly of God, it will come."

"I know, but Caiaphas is being eaten alive with jealously. I fear for him also."

"They're all jealous, and now this with Lazarus of Bethany."

"You've heard of that?"

"Yes. It's one of the reasons I'm here, to see if it's true."

"It's true."

"So I found before I came to visit you."

"They want to kill him now, too."

"What? Why?"

"Because of what he represents. The people revere him because he was dead four days, yet now he lives. The council is jealous of this reverence."

Joseph sat silently pondering this. "It's gone far. How blind they are. This man, this Jesus, has already fulfilled many of the prophecies. Why can't they see he's the one?"

"As you say, they're blind. I've even heard Jesus himself tell them that."

"He did? I would have liked to have been there. I imagine they were angry."

"Livid."

"But it didn't help him any?"

"No, it just made it worse. He seems not to care."

"Well, my friend, all we can do is pray that we'll know what to do when the time comes, as it surely will."

Nicodemus nodded sadly.

Mary stood near a boulder silently gazing at Jesus kneeling a few yards away. His face glowed with an intensity she'd noticed quite often when she'd heard him speak of heaven and his Father. He turned and showed no surprise that she was there.

"Mary." He smiled and stood, holding his hand out to her.

"Lord," she hesitated, "I'm sorry if I've disturbed you. I didn't mean to." She bit her lip.

"You want to talk to me," he said. "There are questions you've long wanted to ask me." He led her to some rocks nearby that formed a natural perch for them to sit on.

Mary wasn't surprised that he knew. Jesus seemed to know a lot of things without anyone telling him. She looked down at her hands in her lap.

"What is it, Mary? You *can* talk to me, you know. You can ask me anything. I won't turn away from you."

"I wanted to ask you about what happened to me when you cast the demons out of me."

His kind eyes seemed to caress her as he smiled and answered. "You accepted who you know I am." Her puzzled expression prompted him to explain further. "You sensed in your heart what you didn't yet grasp in your mind. When your mind accepted what your heart was saying, you finally found what you sought."

"Oh." She looked thoughtful a moment, then asked, "But what happened?"

"You became born again."

"Born again?"

"Your spirit took on life. It's what you've been seeking, but you were seeking it in the wrong places. You sensed there was something missing, something more to life than what you had, but you didn't know what it was, where to find it, or how to find it."

She gave a short laugh. "I still don't."

He smiled. "But you do. You found it that day in Bethany."

"But I'd met you before that." She stopped. Neither of them had ever mentioned their first two encounters. Mary was unsure if he remembered them.

"Yes," he said solemnly, "We'd met before. Both times you sensed that what you sought was before you." He looked at her closely. "Didn't you?"

"Yes, Lord, but how?" she paused. "You knew. Both times you knew."

"Yes, Mary, but you had to know also. I couldn't tell you. Your heart had to reach your mind."

"I don't understand."

"Your heart is your spirit. It's eternal and continues when your body dies. Your mind, where your feelings and emotions are, is the soul that belongs to your spirit. They live in your body. Your spirit was yearning to become alive, and it was trying to get your mind to cooperate. When your mind finally did, you were born again because you accepted what your spirit was trying to tell your mind."

"But what was my spirit telling my mind?"

"Who I am. Do you know who I am, Mary?"

"Yes, Lord. You're the one we were promised long ago by God. You're the Messiah."

Jesus nodded. "Because you believe and accept this, you're born again. The Father's love has been accepted into your heart. Now it's up to you to give that love out to others. Accept others as He's accepted you. You're valuable and precious to Him, Mary. You're His child and He loves you. He wants you to have an abundant life, and He'll give it to you, but you must let Him do it. You began to let him when you accepted who I am."

Mary's eyes sparkled. "Lord, I've been so happy since that day. The emptiness is gone. My heart overflows with joy, and I see everything as if it were new. Is that the way it's supposed to be? Will it always be this way?"

"That's how the Father wants it for you, for everyone. Someday it will be, but there's more, and soon you'll experience that also."

"What, Lord? What will we experience that's more than this?"

Jesus shook his head and stood, "It isn't time for you to know that yet, Mary. We must return to the others. Time is short, and there's still much work to be done."

Mary sat on the grass listening closely to what Jesus was teaching. Caleb, Lazarus, and Martha were with her, and a few of the other disciples were nearby. He was finishing up his answer to a Pharisee who'd been trying to find some fault in his teachings. As usual all the attempts were fruitless. Several Jewish leaders were present, and their frustrations were clearly seen on their faces, but Jesus gave them no heed as he noticed some of the twelve turning mothers with small children away. Displeasure was present in his voice and on his face as he stopped them.

"Don't turn them away." Mary heard Jesus rebuking Peter, "Never turn away or disregard little children. Always welcome and bless them, for they're as all should be. For unless your heart and faith are as a little child's, you'll never enter the kingdom of heaven."

They all exchanged glances. Mary had heard Jesus say similar things before, but had never realized until now what he meant. Her talk with Jesus helped her to understand more clearly that she needed to trust as well as believe in God, and who was more trusting than a child?

Her attention was drawn back to Jesus when she heard a man speak she'd never heard before. He was dressed in rich clothing and he asked what he needed to do to get to heaven.

"Obey the commandments," Jesus said. "Don't lie, kill, steal, or commit adultery, and honor your parents."

"I've always obeyed these," the young man said. "Is there anything else?"

"Yes. Sell what you own, and give what you get for it to those less fortunate than you. Then come and follow me and be my disciple."

Dismay filled the young man, and he turned away. He couldn't put others before himself. He valued luxury and things too highly.

As Jesus watched him walk away, he shook his head. "It's hard for the rich to enter heaven." Looks of astonishment on the disciples' faces prompted him to continue. "It's easier for a loaded camel to enter the eye of the needle than for someone who's rich to enter God's kingdom."

The disciples pondered this. The eye of the needle was a small door in the gates of Jerusalem through which an unloaded camel could crawl.

"But then who can be saved?" Judas asked incredulously.

"For man to do so on his own it's impossible, but for God, all things are possible. He alone can bring it about."

"We've left all we had to follow you, Lord," Peter said.

"Yes" Jesus said to his unspoken question. "All who leave family, friends, and possessions behind to follow me will receive them back again–along with persecutions–but they'll also receive eternal life. You twelve were chosen to sit on thrones and judge the twelve tribes when I'm glorified and sitting on my throne in my kingdom." He rose to leave, and the others prepared to follow him.


They were heading toward Jerusalem. Jesus and the twelve were a little ahead of the rest of the group. All the disciples were filled with apprehension because the Pharisees and Sadducees in Jerusalem had threatened Jesus when he'd last been there, yet Jesus had insisted on going back. None of them were too happy about it, but Jesus was their leader and they wanted to be close to him in case something should happen.

They walked in silence for a while, the twelve grouped around their Master.

"We're going to the lion's den," Jesus said, his voice low so only the twelve heard. "We go to Jerusalem. I'll be turned over to the chief priests and scribes and be condemned to death. They'll deliver me to the Gentiles who will mock, scourge, and spit upon me. Then they'll kill me, but after three days, I shall rise up again from the dead."

The twelve looked at each other. What Jesus was saying was incomprehensible to them. He was their savior. He'd defeat the Romans, not be killed by them. No one could harm Jesus. Forgetting the prophesies of Isaiah and others, they couldn't believe that Jesus would really suffer as he said he would

# Part Five

## Passion Week

## The Last Seven Days

*...and he was numbered with the transgressors; and he bare*
*the sin of many, and made intercession for the transgressors*
Isaiah 53:12.

# Chapter Twenty-three

## Thursday

Caleb held Mary's hand tightly so they couldn't be separated by the crowd. They were about to pass through Jericho, and many people from the ancient city had come out to hear Jesus and follow him after he was finished. Caleb looked over to the side where he thought he'd glimpsed a bright head bobbing up and down as though someone was hopping along the outskirts of the crowd. He couldn't be sure of what he saw because of the press of the crowd.

"What's wrong, Caleb?" Mary had noticed him looking more and more frequently to the side.

"I could swear I saw a head bobbing over there," Caleb said.

Mary, being much shorter, could see nothing. Caleb stood more than a head taller than her and was able to see over the crowds. Suddenly Caleb stopped and pointed.

"There," he said. "That's the person whose head I saw." He pointed to a sycamore ahead of them. A smallish man in bright blue and brown clothing was perched on one of the branches.

Jesus wasn't too far ahead of them, but he didn't seem to notice the tree or the man who now sat among its branches. He was deep in conversation with a Pharisee who was questioning Jesus' views on various topics, trying to trap him as usual. Unexpectedly the Master stopped as he came directly beneath the tree. He turned and looked up.

"Zacheaus," he said, "come down. I have need of rest and will be staying with you in your home this day."

The man's face beamed as he descended from the tree. "Lord," he said, "I'd be honored to have you." The little man puffed out his chest as he strutted beside Peter. He barely reached the disciple's armpits in height, and Caleb realized this was the reason for the bobbing head and resultant climb. The man was uncommonly short and had wanted to get a better view of Jesus.

"Caleb, do you hear the comments?" Mary said.

"No, I've been paying more attention to our new host."

"It's about him they speak."

"Oh?" Caleb perked his ears. It seemed they were to be guests of the head tax collector, a rich man who made his living taking money from his own people for the Romans. The usual comments about Jesus associating with sinners were being bandied around, and Caleb sighed and shook his head as he looked at Mary. Both were familiar with the crowd's reactions to Jesus.

Suddenly Caleb grinned and, pulling her along, began to move ahead and get closer to Jesus. "Come on," he said. "I'd like to see what happens to the sinner now."

Mary laughed and followed Caleb as quickly as she could. It was always intriguing to see the reactions of those the Master encountered, especially the ones he singled out as he had this tax collector just now. When they reached Peter, he motioned to them, and they found themselves included with those invited into the house. It was large and spacious, reminding Mary of the house Marcus had left her. She'd sold it and given the money to Jesus to do with as he deemed fit. He, in turn, had used little of it for himself, giving it instead to those who had more need.

As they settled themselves among the luxuriant pillows and couches around the room, Mary turned her attention to what Zacheaus was telling Jesus.

"Lord," he said, "I'm giving half of all I own to the poor, and if I've cheated anyone, I'll pay them back four times what I took."

Mary and Caleb looked at each other and Caleb whispered, "A far cry from the young ruler who thought he was so good." Mary just nodded. The point Jesus had tried to make that day about the rich having a difficult time getting to heaven finally hit home. Zachaeus, though considered a sinner by many, had a heart God was pleased with because he loved others as he loved himself. The young ruler saw only his own wants met. She looked to Jesus to hear his reply to Zacheaus.

"Salvation has entered this house with the faith of Abraham. For I come to seek out and save those sons who were lost. I've found one here this day."

## Friday

Jesus spent that night at Zacheaus's house, but Mary and Caleb went on to Bethany to prepare for the next day when the disciples would come with Jesus. They were to stay at Lazarus's home during the weekly Sabbath. In the morning, Jesus beckoned Andrew and Judas Iscariot to him.

"Go into the village yonder." He pointed to the area he spoke of. "You'll find a donkey and her foal tied up. Bring them to me. If anyone questions you, just tell them I have need of the animals and they'll be satisfied and let you take them."

As they approached the village, Judas said, "Do you think the Master will declare himself, Andrew?"

"Declare himself?"

"Yes, declare himself, let the Romans know he's our rightful king."

"Judas, the Lord has never given any indication he intends to do that."

"But all the scriptures tell of the Messiah overthrowing our oppressors." Judas was becoming exasperated with Andrew.

"Not all, Judas," Andrew said as they found and began to untie the animals Jesus had said they'd find.

A man came out of the house near where the animals were tied. "Hey, you there, what do you think you're doing?"

Andrew smiled and said, "Peace, brother. They'll be returned to you. The Master has need of them for now."

"The Master?"

"Yes, Jesus of Nazareth. He's going into Jerusalem this day.

"He's here?"

Judas didn't have the patience Andrew had, being already resentful of being sent out on what he considered a lowly task. The frustrations he felt because of the conversation he and Andrew had just been having made him even less tolerant. "You heard him," he snapped as he grabbed the rope which was tied to the foal as Andrew led its mother along.

"You'll see him if you go to the temple." Andrew nodded and smiled apologetically at the man as they turned to go. Then he gave Judas a stern look and when they'd gone out of hearing distance, said, "What ails you, Judas? The man didn't deserve that."

"Nothing," Judas said.

"Nothing? I wouldn't call an attitude like yours nothing." Andrew shook his head.

"It's been three years. I'm tired of waiting."

"Waiting for what?"

"Waiting for Jesus to finally make his move."

"Did you ever consider that Jesus might not do that?"

"What do you mean? He's the Messiah. How else can he deliver us except through power?"

"Maybe he knows another way."

Judas snorted. "What other way could there be? You've seen what he can do. If he has the power to raise the dead, he can do anything. He's invincible. Nothing can harm him. Nobody can go against Jesus and win."

Judas was getting more excited the longer he talked, and his eyes glared with a fanatical light Andrew wasn't pleased to see. He pondered whether he should tell Jesus of this, but decided against it. Jesus knew. Andrew was sure he did.


As they journeyed toward Jerusalem, the crowds grew. When they reached the Mount of Olives, the disciples placed several layers of clothing over the back of the donkey and threw down cloaks and tree branches in front of the animal as it, with its foal following, carried Jesus the rest of the way to the city. They shouted out Hosannas and gave him the welcome usually reserved for royalty. The air vibrated with exclamations of praise to God and declarations that their salvation had arrived. Judas wasn't alone in believing Jesus would deliver them.

When they reached the temple, Jesus dismounted and proceeded to clear the courts of the merchants and money-changers who were there. It had become a relatively common occurrence for him to do this because he couldn't tolerate their thievery. They took advantage of those who needed their services by giving back less than what was due when they made their transactions. He then proceeded into the inner portion of the temple and healed everyone who came to him. The priests and scribes could barely hide their jealousy when they saw the miracles and heard the praises of the small children. They wanted to be the ones being praised, but they couldn't do what Jesus did.

"Don't you hear them?" they complained to Jesus. "They're worshipping you."

"Aren't you aware that it's written that out of the mouths of babes come perfect praise?" Jesus said.

Ignoring their enraged looks, he left the temple and went, along with his disciples, to Bethany to stay with Lazarus, Martha, and Mary.

# Chapter Twenty-four

## Saturday

As she lifted the water jar to her shoulder, Mary turned and saw a large crowd approaching. They were shouting, and many were looking toward the center of the group. Her eyes widened and she smiled. Swiftly she made her way back to the house.

"Martha, they've come. Quickly, we must lay out the mats."

The women pulled out the extra mats for their guests and saw to as many last minute preparations as they could while Lazarus and Caleb went out to meet Jesus and the disciples who were to be joining them for the Sabbath. Soon the voices of the crowd reached their door, and then Jesus was standing just inside the threshold. He entered the room, followed by their brother, as Caleb and the twelve turned the people away, telling them Jesus needed to rest and they'd see him again in the temple after the Sabbath was over.

Lazarus looked out the door, shook his head, and turned toward Jesus, who was gazing outside. Then their eyes met, and Jesus smiled. "They're like lost sheep in need of a shepherd, Lazarus. They seek guidance, but don't understand what they want or why."

Lazarus nodded without speaking for a moment. Then he turned and indicated the mats the women had laid out. "Lord, come and sit. I'll bring water so you can wash from your journey."

The chief priests and elders were perplexed. This man, Jesus, was drawing too many people away from them. Now there was another problem: what to do about Lazarus. The people being drawn from them to Jesus had increased ever since Lazarus was risen from the grave.

"We need to be rid of him also," one priest said.

"But how?" another asked. "He's evidence of a great miracle that can have no explanation other than God's hand."

He received many scornful looks and a rebuke from Caiaphas. "He's the spawn of Satan, just as Jesus is." Others murmured both for and against this statement.

"No matter what power raised him up," Annas said, "we can't have him around. Too many are believing this Jesus is the Messiah because of him."

Again there were murmurs, this time only from those who had hardened their hearts to the teachings of Jesus. Others sat silently, vowing to themselves to no longer trust in or meet with Caiaphas. They couldn't condone killing innocent men.

Martha and Mary were finishing their preparations for the Sabbath meal. Jesus had stayed with them and their brother in their home during the day, taking his rest and teaching them and the other disciples who were with him. Several times he made statements which none of them understood, referring to a time when he'd be gone from them. None of them wanted to believe there would ever come such a time. They didn't want to understand his statements.

The men gathered on the mats that were laid out as Martha began serving them. When she saw Jesus lie down on the mat next to her brother and reach for some bread, Mary left the room and returned carrying a box. A few days before, while in Jerusalem, she'd purchased two boxes of a costly perfumed oil. She'd had no specific reason to buy them at the time, but now she knew what the purpose of at least one of the boxes was.

Approaching Jesus, Mary broke the seal on the box and, removing her veil, knelt at his feet. Lifting the lid, she began to pour the liquid on his feet and to wipe it off with her hair.

As Jesus calmly accepted her ministrations, Judas said, "Lord, what a waste. That perfume could have been sold and the money used to feed many of the poor who are in need."

Jesus, knowing Judas's heart didn't match his words, looked over at him. "Judas, you'll always have the poor to care for, but I won't always be here. Let her be."

At this rebuke, Judas remained silent as he greedily watched the expensive ointment being lavished upon Jesus' feet. Although he respected Jesus, he couldn't help thinking that what Mary did was a waste. He held the purse for their funds and, no matter what amount they had, felt there was never enough. Because of the waste he witnessed both now and at other times, he felt justified when he delved into it, never suspecting that Jesus knew of that flaw in him.

## Sunday

The next day, Jesus again sent Andrew and Judas out, saying, "Go over into the village. There you'll find a colt. Bring it to me. If you're stopped, just say I have need of it, and they'll allow you to continue."

Again Andrew and Judas found the colt as Jesus said they would and were stopped by its owner. When they told him what Jesus had said to say, he not only allowed them to take it, but also accompanied them and joined the throng which was gathering. When they reached Jesus, the disciples placed cloaks upon the animal and lifted Jesus upon it as people gathered palm branches from nearby trees and lay them on the road leading to Jerusalem along with their cloaks and other articles of clothing. Slowly the donkey bearing Jesus picked its way over the strewn branches and clothes as the people cried out praises declaring Jesus their king and welcoming in his reign and kingdom. The disciples surrounded Jesus and the animal to keep them from being trampled as more people joined the throng.

Some Pharisees who had become his followers were dismayed at what they were hearing and said to Jesus, "Tell them to stop. You're not a king."

But Jesus only shook his head and said, "If they should be silenced, the stones would cry out."

At this the Pharisees held their peace. What more could they say? They knew what Jesus' enemies would think and how they'd react when they heard the crowd, but they could do nothing to stop it.

When the procession reached the Mount of Olives, Jesus stopped the colt and gazed upon the city in all its beauty, the temple rising up in the foreground and Herod's palace behind it higher up. He wept. The sounds of his loud cries were drowned by the praises around him, but his disciples heard him say, "If only you had recognized this time, but you did not. Because you didn't, the day will come not long from now when not a stone will be left and all within your walls will perish."

After saying this, he continued on, descending to the city. Stopping at the temple entrance, he thanked the donkey's owner before entering the temple. The merchants and money-changers, having heard Jesus was on his way, were careful not to overcharge anyone or be dishonest in their dealings while he was present, so Jesus stood a while watching, then left to return to Bethany. He wouldn't spend a night in Jerusalem before his death.

# Chapter Twenty-five

## Monday

The following morning, as the disciples accompanied Jesus back to Jerusalem, they passed a fig tree. Jesus desired some of the fruit, but as they got close to it, he saw there was none, only leaves. He cursed the tree, saying it would never again bear fruit and continued on toward the city. When they reached the temple, the merchants scrambled frantically about as Jesus again overturned tables and scattered animals upon discovering they'd resumed their dishonesty.

As Caleb and the other disciples followed Jesus in, the cries of both humans and animals rang in his ears. He took his place between Lazarus and Andrew when Jesus calmly began teaching on the love of the Father and forgiveness. After the teaching many people approached him for healing for themselves or someone they'd brought. Jesus healed them all, then took his leave and headed back toward Bethany.


The scribes, Sadducees, and Pharisees murmured angrily among themselves as they watched Jesus scattering the merchants and money-changers. Jesus had to go; it was the one thing they could agree upon. Too many of their own followers were being drawn to him. Following him into the temple, they speculated on how it might be accomplished.

Joseph, raising his brows, turned toward Nicodemus, who shrugged and sadly shook his head. They were afraid to say anything in the Master's defense for fear of turning the whole Sanhedrin against them as well. They both knew only too well that soon they'd have to openly take a stand, but until then they hoped they might dissuade the violence the rest of the Jewish rulers were planning.

The group retired to a private area where they could speak freely without any of the common people or the disciples being witness to them.

"We must be rid of him," one of the scribes declared as soon as the door was shut.

"Well, it can't be during the Passover Sabbath. That would surely cause us more problems than we want," another said.

"But how? The people revere him as a prophet, and many believe him to be the Messiah," a Pharisee said.

"Yes, and there's also Lazarus," the first man said.

All murmured in agreement. Too many were believing in Jesus because of Lazarus.

"Maybe if this Jesus is killed, his followers will disburse and there will be no need to do anything about Lazarus." This came from a Sadducee.

They continued on for some time, suggesting and discarding ideas until Joseph and Nicodemus departed, both sick of the evil which had overtaken these men. They walked to the home of Nicodemus and, when they were inside, sat silently together. They said nothing to each other, but raised their voices in prayer to God for guidance. Only He could help them know what to do for Jesus.

# Tuesday

When Jesus entered Bethany after leaving Jerusalem, he went with Lazarus to his house, intending to spend the evening there. As they approached it, Martha and Mary appeared at the doorway.

"Greetings, Master," Martha said when she saw them. "We were just going out to find you. Simon the leper sends greetings and requests that you and your closest companions join him for the evening meal."

Jesus nodded and turned to Judas who was beside him. "Go tell Simon we accept his invitation and shall be there shortly, Judas."

"Yes, Master." As Judas turned to do Jesus' bidding, he felt a surge of resentment again at being made a messenger boy. He didn't deserve to be treated that way; he held the purse. He struggled inwardly as he made his way through the village to Simon's house. Jesus was wasting his time; didn't he see that the time was ripe to overthrow the Romans? Clearly Jesus needed some prodding.

The men lying on the couches were just finishing their meal. Simon made sure Jesus had all he desired. He looked up and saw Mary carrying an alabaster box and coming toward him and Jesus. He opened his mouth to speak, but closed it again as she broke the seal to the box. When she reached Jesus, she knelt at his head and bowed low saying, "My Lord," so softly only Jesus heard her. Then she stood and, opening the box, poured the contents slowly onto his head. Immediately, the fragrance of perfume filled the room as Mary continued to anoint Jesus' head until the box was emptied. When she was done, she looked into his eyes and felt warmth and love radiate from him. A small smile touched her lips, and she sensed a oneness with him until an unexplained sorrow overwhelmed her.

"Lord," Judas said, "what a waste. The poor should have profited from the money that was spent on the contents of that box."

Jesus looked over at Judas and knew his heart. Again Judas's concern wasn't really for the poor. "Don't berate her for this," he said. "She's preparing me for what will shortly take place. You'll have the poor with you always, but I won't be here much longer. This woman will be remembered throughout the ages for what she's done for me this day." He returned the look of gratitude she gave him before she left his side and the room.

After Mary left Simon's, Judas found a way to slip out. He walked around Bethany for some time thinking, and finally he came to a decision: He'd go to the Jewish rulers and offer to turn Jesus over to them.

Upon deciding this, he turned toward Jerusalem. Now all he had to do was to find an elder who'd listen to him and believe he was serious. He went to the temple and watched as members of the Sanhedrin entered the building. He stood near the doorway and followed some of them in. The door to the room they entered was shut before they realized he'd joined them and had heard part of their plotting.

Several of the elders' faces darkened in their anger and suspicion of being spied upon. They recognized Judas as being one of Jesus' closest disciples, but Judas put up a hand to stop them from saying or doing anything against him before he'd had a chance to tell them why he'd joined them.

"Peace to you," he said. He knew he had to persuade them that they were in no danger of being exposed and of his sincerity in helping them. "I'm right, am I not, in believing you wish to lay hold of Jesus and arrest him?" Not waiting for a reply, he continued. "I may be able to help you in this. I know all of his plans and habits. I could lead you to him during a time when he'll be alone and you'll be less likely to encounter opposition."

"You would do this? How do we know you aren't planning to trap us with this offer? You're one of his closest disciples." The voice of the priest who spoke up was joined with those of many others.

"I'll do it—for a price," Judas said. It would be easy money, he figured. Many times Jesus had slipped away when there was an attempt to take him. Judas knew no reason why this time would be any different, and he himself intended to get some profit from it besides the overthrow of the Roman rule in Judea. He was sure this would force Jesus to declare himself. He spoke confidently, believing the only loser would be Rome.

"What price do you ask?"

"I'd say thirty pieces of silver would be acceptable," Judas said.

The next morning, as they left Bethany to return to Jerusalem, the disciples noticed the fig tree Jesus had cursed the day before. It was dead.

Peter exclaimed, "Lord, look. The tree you cursed is withered up."

Jesus said, "My words weren't lightly spoken, Peter. I knew it would die. Faith does that. With even the smallest amount of faith, you can move mountains. All you need do is believe what you say and it's yours. But before you do, you must examine your heart because if you're carrying a grudge and have unforgiveness in your heart, your Father in heaven will likewise not forgive you."

The disciples were silent as they pondered this. Jesus always stressed forgiveness, and they had thought it was for the other person's sake. But the statement he'd just made put a different light on it. The forgiveness was for them, not the other person. It was for their benefit. Several now began to understand why Jesus insisted that the amount of times they forgave should be limitless. If they held a trespass done against them, God would likewise hold his own trespasses against them also. Considering what Jesus had said, they knew they didn't want that. They wanted God's forgiveness.

Before Jesus could begin teaching, the chief priests and elders approached him, determined to trap him in his own words.

"By whose authority do you say the things you say?" they asked.

Caleb, who was nearby, came and stood next to Jesus as if to ward off an attack, but Jesus calmly raised a hand to stop him. "I will ask you a question also," Jesus said. "If you can answer it, I'll tell you your answer. John came and many heard him preach and were baptized by him. Who do you say his authority came from, heaven or man?"

Moving to a corner, the elders consulted together where Jesus couldn't hear.

"What do we say?" one said. "If we say heaven, he'll want to know why we didn't follow John. If we say man, we'll be mobbed by those who believe John was a prophet."

The others murmured their agreement, discussing and discarding possibilities, but coming up with no satisfying answer. Finally, being at a stalemate, they returned to Jesus.

"We do not know," their spokesman said.

"Then I won't answer your question either," Jesus said, knowing they lied to him. Their acceptance of John would mean they would have to accept him also, and the Jewish rulers as a whole wouldn't do that.


Lazarus and Caleb sat listening to Jesus throughout the rest of the afternoon. Several times men came, sent by one or another of Jesus' enemies. They asked questions about the Jewish laws and the resurrection. When they couldn't trip him up with that, another group presented themselves and tried to corner Jesus with a politically explosive question about whether the Jewish people were obligated to pay Roman taxes. But Jesus, with the wisdom of God, turned that question around, stating what belonged to Caesar was Caesar's and what belonged to God was God's.

Then, in one last effort, they pressed him again.

"Master," one of the priests addressed him, although all there knew he didn't really respect Jesus as the title implied. "What's the greatest commandment?"

Lazarus and Caleb looked at each other in astonishment. There were, according to the scribes, over six hundred commandments. How could Jesus possibly answer this with so many to choose from? But they turned as he began to speak.

"There are many commands, but all of them are summed up into only two. The first and greatest is to love the Lord your God with all your heart, mind, and being. The second is to love your neighbor. If you do these two, all other commandments will be kept as well."

After these men were thwarted in their attempts to trip him up, a murmur of approval went up from the crowd that had gathered and Jesus was approached by another. This was a scribe who, up until then, had remained silently listening.

"Lord," the scribe said, "you speak well. For nothing is more important than loving and serving God and loving our fellow man."

Jesus gazed warmly at the scribe and saw that his heart was good and accepting toward God. "You aren't far from the kingdom of God," he said.

The scribe blinked at this. It wasn't the response he'd expected, but it pleased him nonetheless that this man whom he secretly revered approved of him.

As Jesus continued to teach the people, he warned them about the teachings of the rulers, pointing out their hypocrisy. This angered many of the scribes and priests who were present, and they left. The offer of help they'd received from Judas was very welcome.

Around three in the afternoon, Jesus turned to Peter and John. "It's time to prepare for the Passover," he said.

This surprised the two men because it was a day early, but they made no comment, instead asking, "Where would you like for us to make the preparations, Lord?"

Jesus said, "Go into the city and you'll see a man carrying a water jar. Follow him into the house he enters. There, ask the owner to show you the room in which I and my disciples may partake of the Passover meal. He'll show you. We'll join you there when it's ready."

Peter and John did as Jesus said. After finding the house with the upper room all furnished and ready for them, they returned to the temple where they purchased a lamb and had it sacrificed. In the meantime, Jesus continued to teach and heal all those who came to him.

When he rose to leave, Caleb and Lazarus met Martha and Mary outside the Court of Women. Immediately, both women recognized the look of concern on the men's faces. Mary took Caleb's hand.

Martha looked to Lazarus and said, "What's wrong?"

Lazarus shook his head as Caleb said, "The Lord is—"

"Caleb!" Mary grabbed his arm with her other hand. "What's wrong?"

"We fear for Jesus." Lazarus took Martha's arm and directed her from the temple courts as Caleb and Mary followed.

"Why?" Mary looked up into Caleb's face.

"Today, Joseph and Nicodemus both told me things that hinted that the elders are more serious than we thought with their plotting." Caleb's lips were tight as he continued. "Now they're including Lazarus in their plans."

The women gasped at this, and Martha stopped, turning a frightened face toward her brother. "Lazarus."

"It's all right," he said. "I'll be all right, it's Jesus we're most concerned for."

# Chapter Twenty-six

## Wednesday–The Arrest

Like most of the houses in Jerusalem, the room Peter and John were in was on a flat roof with an outside entrance and stairs leading up to it. Because the temple was in this city, many of these roofs were reserved by their owners for travelers during the Passover season.

After the lamb was sacrificed and roasted, the two men prepared the sauce, herbs, and other foods normally served at the Passover meal. They were just finishing these preparations when the door opened and Jesus, accompanied by James, entered.

The other disciples stayed outside to turn away the crowd while Jesus' eyes gazed over the room with approval. He nodded and smiled as he approached the table and lay on one of the couches at the head. When the disciples had all arrived and filled the couches, a discussion about who among them was the greatest resumed. They'd apparently been arguing about it before entering the room.

Hearing this, Jesus arose and, removing his outer robe, took a towel and basin of water and placed the basin at the foot of Judas's couch. Stunned, the men watched in silence as he washed first Judas then John. When he reached Peter, they found their voices and began to murmur. Peter pulled back his feet.

"Lord, what are you doing? That's the job of a slave," Peter said indignantly.

"I do what I came to do, Peter. I'll explain my reasons to you shortly."

"No, Lord, you shall not wash my feet," Peter said.

Exasperated, Jesus looked up at him and said, "If I don't do this, you shall have no part of me."

At once Peter was contrite, realizing that Jesus was again trying to teach him something, so he held out his hands and exclaimed, "Then, Lord, wash my hands and head also."

With a slight smile, Jesus shook his head and said, "No, Peter. You're already clean, but not all of you. It's only your feet which need the dust removed." He continued on around the table until all of the twelve had been washed. Then he placed the basin and towel aside and, putting his robe back on, resumed his place between John and Judas.

He began explaining his actions to them. "You call me Lord and Master, and you're correct in this, for I'm both. But unlike those who are lords and masters of the world, I'm not here to be served, but to serve. That's why I washed your feet. And if I'm here to serve, so must you be. A servant is never more than their master nor a pupil more than their teacher. I've taught you this before, but you didn't learn it well. Do as I've said: Humble yourselves and do what you can for one another. Don't seek to exalt yourselves, but to serve wherever you're needed."

Then the wine was poured and drunk after a blessing and the food was brought out. A second serving of wine was poured, and the story of how God saved the Israelites on the first Passover was retold. The second serving of wine was drunk, psalms were sung, and they began to eat.

As they began their meal, Jesus said, almost offhandedly, "One of you who now shares this meal with me will betray me."

For a second there was a shocked silence, then they all began to question him as to who would do this. Even Judas asked, and, when he did, Jesus looked him straight in the eye.

"This is so," he said and resumed his meal.

Troubled, Judas continued to eat as he pondered the Lord's words. What he planned wasn't a betrayal. No one could harm Jesus; he had the power to stop even the strongest foe. Many times before he'd seen Jesus walk away when the crowds were ready to destroy him for some anger he'd caused them. God had a firm hand on Jesus; He'd never allow him to be harmed. The way Judas saw it, he was helping God to bring in His kingdom a little sooner.

Mary and Caleb sat on the bench behind the house. It was twilight and the sky was clear.

"What do you think will happen, Caleb?"

"About what?"

"Jesus and Lazarus. Will they really kill them? Or at least try to?"

Caleb sighed. "They're jealous enough to try."

"But Jesus has never done anything but good."

"I know." He was silent a moment. "It's a fact that our people have destroyed everyone God has sent us, Mary. I fear this will happen again."

"But his power. He can raise the dead. He can—"

Caleb's hand silenced her. "I remember quite clearly now Jesus saying as recently as yesterday that he wouldn't be with us much longer," he whispered. "I think he'll die, and I think he knows this."

"Oh, Caleb, I hope you're wrong." She grabbed his hand with both of hers and held it tightly.

"So do I, Mary." He placed his free hand over hers and looked up at the stars that had begun to appear. "So do I."

John felt a tap on his shoulder, and when he leaned back, Peter whispered, "Ask who it is that will do this."

John looked over at Jesus and back again to Peter, who nodded his encouragement. "You're closer to him. Go on, ask." The double meaning wasn't lost on John, who was aware that Jesus favored him over the others; he always had, from the time they were growing up together. He leaned away from Peter toward Jesus.

"Lord, who is it who would do this?" he whispered.

Jesus answered quietly, "The one I'll share bread with." Then, reaching over, he handed some bread dipped in sauce to Judas.

Because they were all sharing the meal, none of them understood that the Master was directly referring to Judas. The shock of the disclosure, the knowledge of his power, and the firm belief in his invincibility were too strong. They couldn't believe anyone or anything would be able to harm him.

As if through a fog, they heard Jesus tell Judas to go and do what needed to be done. Because of Judas's position as their treasurer, they thought nothing of it when he rose and left the room. All thought he'd been commanded to do something concerning their funds.

Jesus then raised some bread toward heaven and, blessing it, said, "This bread represents my body, which will be broken for you. Remember me when you eat of it." He broke the bread and passed it around to each of them. Then he reached over and picked up the fourth cup, which was sitting upside down and was traditionally reserved for the Messiah. He filled and raised it, saying, "Likewise, this represents my blood—my life which will be shed for you." He drained the cup. Do this to remember me also. This is a new covenant I give to you. Soon I'll go where you can't follow. The world will rejoice, but it will be to your sorrow. Yet your sorrow will turn to joy, for after I'm gone you'll receive a new Comforter, and he'll never leave you, but will continue on where I left off. You'll learn much from him for he'll lead you into all truth. Where I go you won't be able to follow, but you'll be able to have me with you if you follow the commandment which I give you now: love one another. For if you love one another, I'll be with you and we'll be one, even as I'm one with my Father. This is how they'll know you are my disciples, if you show love one to another.

"Until now, you were servants and pupils. Now I call you friends and tell you all I can. My love for you is great. I lay down my life for you. No greater love can a man give than that he lay down his life for his friends. I lay down my life, and I will pick it up again. But when I lay it down, you cannot follow."

"Lord," Peter said, "where are you going, and why can't I follow? I would give my life for you."

The others all murmured similar thoughts, but Jesus just shook his head. "Peter," he said, "you'll deny me, but don't let that overwhelm you. I've prayed for you that Satan won't be able to deceive you with guilt. I tell you truly, before the cock crows twice tomorrow, you'll deny me three times."

"Never. I will never forsake you." Peter was adamant, and the others took up his cry.

"We'll never leave you, Lord," they all exclaimed.

Deciding not to dwell on what he knew would happen, Jesus tried to comfort them and went on to tell them what he needed to be sure they knew. "Don't despair. My Father has many mansions, and I go to prepare a place among them for each of you. Rejoice, for if I didn't go, the Comforter wouldn't come. Believe in me and my words. My words are truth. I am the way, the truth, and the life. No one can come to the Father and eternal life except by me. He must believe that I am and that I come from the Father and am one with Him. This you must believe to be one with me. Love each other as I've loved you. Live as I've lived among you. You've asked for nothing because I've been here with you. When I'm gone, you'll do greater works than I've done if you ask in my name. For whatsoever you ask in my name, I will give you."

"Don't allow my words to disturb you. I'll give you peace in your hearts, not peace as the world gives. They don't understand the peace I'll give to you. It's an inner joy which will bring you a calmness even in the midst of the worst turmoil you can imagine, but the time has come for my departure." He stood to leave.

As they walked toward the garden near the Mount of Olives, Jesus continued to exhort them to love one another and to treat each other as he'd taught them. He'd stressed that and forgiveness during the whole time they'd known him. Again he stressed that love was the most important factor. "Keep this commandment that I give you: Love each other."


As they walked along, Jesus again reassured them and told them that if they prayed using his name in faith they'd receive whatever they prayed for. He told them more of the Comforter he'd promised them and that they should rejoice that he was going to the Father. Then he said, "You will scatter and I will be alone, but only physically, for my Father will be with me."

Upon reaching Gethsemane, which was a garden owned by Nicodemus, he left them, taking only Peter, James, and John with him into the garden.

"Stay here and pray," he said when they entered. "I will go yonder. I need to be alone." The three men sat as Jesus went farther into the garden and knelt beside a large boulder. As they waited, their heads began to nod, and their eyes grew heavy.

"Can't you stay awake even an hour and give me your support in prayer?"

Peter woke instantly at the words and saw Jesus standing before him. He nudged James and John, who rubbed their eyes and looked shamefacedly at Jesus who shrugged and went back to the boulder. Again they fought to stay awake, and again Jesus came and woke them, then returned to the boulder. After more prayer Jesus returned a third time.

"Can't you even pray with me in my last hour? It doesn't matter. Go ahead and sleep. No, I see the time is here." He pointed toward the garden entrance where they saw Judas leading a band of six hundred soldiers toward them.


Caleb and Mary held hands in the moonlight until Lazarus appeared at the doorway. "I'm going to Gethsemane. I'm worried about Jesus. I believe he'll be spending the night there, and I want to warn him about what we heard in the temple today, Caleb. Watch over Mary and Martha for me while I'm gone."

He left before Caleb could answer.

Lazarus walked through the garden to see if Jesus and the twelve were there. He turned and was walking back through it toward the city when he spotted Jesus kneeling beside a large boulder. Just as he was about to make his presence known, a light fell upon Jesus and a being appeared upon the rock. Lazarus drew back and watched as the being bent over in a gesture of comfort to Jesus.

Awed, Lazarus realized this had to be an angel ministering to his Lord. There was no other explanation, for his size was nearly twice that of a normal man. Lazarus drew a step closer and realized that the expression on Jesus' face was pure agony. He appeared to be going through a struggle so intense that the sweat on his face and body seemed to be mingled with blood. Lazarus fell to his knees and, covering his face, cried out to God in anguish.

Upon hearing voices, he raised his head. A crowd was approaching, and Jesus was no longer kneeling at the boulder, but was standing at the garden entrance. Lazarus rose and moved closer to hear and see better what was taking place. There were soldiers, and Judas was leading them. He hid himself behind a tree to listen and watch as Judas approached Jesus.

"Master." Judas reached out and kissed Jesus on his cheek then stepped back. Lazarus saw that not only were there soldiers with him, but the officers of the chief priests also.

"Judas, so you betray me with a kiss?" Jesus' voice was low as he asked this, then he spoke out to the others. "Why are you here?"

"We seek Jesus of Nazareth," one of the men said.

"I am he," Jesus said.

Lazarus was close enough to feel power emanate from him. It was so strong that many of the men standing nearer to Jesus fell down, including Judas.

Again Jesus said, "Who do you seek?"

One of the soldiers rose to his feet as he replied, "Jesus of Nazareth."

"I told you, I am he." Jesus turned. Recognizing some of the chief priests' officers, he continued, "Daily I spoke in the temple, and you never took me. Am I so much of a threat now that you come for me with clubs and swords?"

One of these men moved toward Jesus, and Lazarus noticed Peter for the first time as he raised a sword and cut off the man's right ear. Lazarus had seen the man before. He was a servant of Caiaphas named Malchus.

Jesus turned and rebuked Peter saying, "Put up your sword, Peter. Those who live by the sword shall die by it. Don't you realize that I could call down legions of angels if I wanted to? But if I did that, my purpose for being here would be defeated. I must do the will of my Father." He picked up the severed ear and turned back to Malchus. Placing the ear back on the servant's head, he healed the man before them all.

Lazarus gasped. One of the soldiers heard him and grabbed at him, but he turned and ran back toward Bethany, leaving behind only his cloak in the soldier's hand.

# *Chapter Twenty-seven*

## Wednesday—The Trial

James went to see if he could find the others who'd run off. Meanwhile, Peter and John followed the band of men who'd bound Jesus' hands before shoving him ahead of them toward Jerusalem.

"John, this can't be happening." Peter felt as though he were walking in a dream.

"It's happening, just as Jesus said it would." John kept his eyes ahead to see where they were taking Jesus.

"But why? Why now? They've let him alone until now."

"They finally found a way to get him. Judas betrayed him, or weren't you watching?" Distraught, John turned and looked at Peter, whose face looked dazed. Again he looked ahead. "They're taking him to the palace of the high priest. I know him; they'll let me in. Come on." He pulled on Peter's arm and began to run.

When Peter just plodded slowly along as if in a dream, John waved a hand as if to dismiss him and ran ahead.

Upon entering the palace, John turned and, seeing Peter not far behind, spoke to the maid who kept the door. She opened it for Peter as he approached.

"Aren't you with Jesus of Nazareth?" she said.

Peter shook his head. "I don't know the man." A cock crowed in the distance, but it didn't register with him as he went over and stood in front of the fire in the hall. He noticed John standing over to the side, and they nodded to each other. Then Peter held out his hands to the flame.

Another maid came and stood beside him to warm herself before she resumed her duties. She looked at him inquiringly and then asked, "Aren't you one of the Galileans who were with Jesus of Nazareth?"

Peter shook his head vehemently. "I've never heard of him." He drew away to a corner.

After a time, one of the men came up to him saying, "You were there in the garden with him. I saw you, and your accent tells me you're from Galilee."

Peter began to swear as he denied ever even laying eyes on Jesus. Then his head snapped up as a cock crowed a second time. He looked over to where they were interrogating Jesus just as the Master turned and looked at him. Covering his face, Peter ran from the building, weeping with shame at what he'd done.

The soldiers and officers of the priests brought Jesus before Annas, who sent them with him to his son-in-law, Caiaphas, the high priest. Many of the men were brought forth to bear witness against him, but none of them could be found to tell the same tale. Caiaphas, in frustration, demanded that Jesus answer the charges, but Jesus stood silent.

John stood along the sides, watching and listening helplessly as they badgered Jesus, trying to find a reason to bring him before Pilate. When the cock crowed a second time, John saw Jesus turn and look behind him. Following Jesus' stare, he saw Peter cover his horror-stricken face with his hands and run from the palace.

The questioning became more intense. Caiaphas, at a loss for anything else, said, "Are you the Christ, the Son of God?"

Jesus said, "You have said rightly, and the time will come when you will see the son of man coming at the right hand of the Father."

Caiaphas tore at his clothes and said, "We need no more witnesses. He's blasphemed. You've heard it yourselves from his own lips."

They blindfolded Jesus, slapping and spitting on him, demanding, "Who hit you? Tell us!" and "Prophesy to us!" But Jesus remained silent.


Lazarus ran as he'd never run before, back to Bethany. Only when he reached the door of his own home did he stop. He grabbed his side where a cramp had begun and sought to catch his breath before he entered the house. Jesus had been arrested. It couldn't be, and yet he'd seen it with his own eyes. Tears blurred his vision, and he bent over as much with sorrow as pain. The Master had been taken, betrayed by one of the twelve. It was inconceivable, yet it had happened. He reached for the door and opened it.

Three faces turned toward him as he stood at the threshold. He didn't have to say anything. They knew by the look on his face.


After giving the prearranged sign of a kiss, Judas had stepped off to the side. He watched in amazement as Jesus was taken off. It wasn't supposed to be this way. Never before had anyone succeeded in taking Jesus, but they had. He fell to his knees, shaking his head in disbelief. Jesus was the Messiah. He was to overthrow the Romans not be captured by them. Judas covered his face and wept.


The priests' officers replaced the bounds they'd removed while they mocked Jesus and pushed him out before them. Many of the council members followed closely as they made their way to the Praetorium where Pilate would hear their accusations. It was nearly midnight and Jewish law forbade any legal actions being done at night, but what did that matter? Other laws had also been broken because of this Jesus. All they cared about was that they finally had him. They'd see to it Pilate did what they wanted. They were sure they could persuade the crowds to demand it.

When they reached the porch of the Praetorium, they shouted out for Pilate, who'd just retired with his wife, Claudia, to their bed chambers. Telling her to go to bed without him, he left the room and strode out to the porch where they awaited him.

"What is it you want?" he said. "It's nearly midnight."

The chief priests and other Jewish rulers present shouted out accusations as the band of soldiers with them pushed Jesus forward and dragged him up the steps to stand before Pilate, who had seated himself. He motioned to his servants to bring more torches so that he could better see the man before him and strained to hear the accusations. It seemed to him to be some religious controversy.

He shrugged and said in a low tone, "I see nothing to charge him with." He turned to Jesus. "What do you say? What of these charges they're accusing you of?"

Jesus remained silent, watching Pilate, appearing calm even though his hands were bound and the crowd seemed wild. More people had joined the throng, and it seemed like they'd become rowdy. Pilate questioned Jesus some more, and upon receiving only silence for his answers he turned to the crowd. Their religious laws were their concern, not his, he told them.

"Well, kill him. We cannot," the Jewish rulers said.

"This man is innocent of anything that would concern me," he said, knowing they lied. They were accusing him of blasphemy. Jews stoned blasphemers.

At this statement, a priest cried out, "He says he's a king and travels all over Galilee declaring it." The man looked smugly at Pilate. The Romans crucified traitors, and the priest had just accused Jesus of that.

Upon learning Jesus was from Galilee, Pilate turned to him and said, "So, you're a Galilean? Herod is here for the Jewish feast. Maybe we should send you to him." He turned to the soldier standing behind Jesus. "Take him to Herod and we'll see what he says about this man." Dismissing Jesus from his mind, he returned to his bed chamber and his wife.


"My Lord."

"Yes, what is it?" Herod turned impatiently to the servant bowing before him.

"There's a mob outside, my lord. They bring a prisoner sent by Pilate because he's a Galilean, Jesus of Nazareth."

"Jesus? Here?" A pleased look crossed Herod's face. "Have them bring him in. I'll be there shortly."

"Yes, my lord." The servant bowed and left.

"What do you intend to do?" Herodius had remained silent until they were alone.

"I have long desired to see this man. They say he does miracles. I want to see one." He grabbed his outer robe and pulled it on as he spoke.

Herod entered the chamber where they held Jesus and seated himself. Placing his chin in his hand, he took time to look over the man before him. So this was the supposed Messiah of whom John had spoken. He didn't look at all like John, although Herod had heard from somewhere that they were cousins. But then that could have been only rumor. There were many flying around about this man. Herod was curious to find out if any of them were true.

"I've heard you perform miracles. Is that true?" He continued to look at Jesus, who remained silent. When he didn't get an answer, he said, "Well, what's your crime?" Again there was no response. "What is his crime?"

Immediately he got a barrage of answers from the Jews who had come with the soldiers escorting Jesus, but all he could glean from them was that Jesus claimed to be king of the Jews. He laughed at that and questioned Jesus more, but the prisoner never said a word. Out of anger and frustration, Herod had a white robe brought out. Usually given to candidates for office in Rome, the Galilean governor thought it a great joke and mocked Jesus by having it placed on him.

Suddenly impatient with the entire situation, Herod said, "I find nothing against this man. Take him back to Pilate."

The Jews cried out to stop him as he turned to go, but Herod narrowed his eyes and snapped, "I said he's innocent. He doesn't deserve death. Good night." He left abruptly.

Pilate turned over at the pounding. "What is it?" he said. The door to the bed chambers opened and a servant entered.

"My lord, they've returned."

Pilate didn't need to be told who; he already knew. That Jewish rabble was intent on keeping him up all night. "I'll be there momentarily," he said. "Go back to sleep, Claudia. I have business to attend to." He caressed her shoulder, got up out of bed, and began to dress.

Coming out to the porch, he knew without being told what conclusion Herod had come to. One look at Jesus clothed in the white robe told him. Although Herod had intended it as an insult, it also spoke of his decision to declare Jesus innocent. Pilate sighed. Would this night ever end? He'd begun to think not. The crowd was screaming for blood so he raised a hand for silence.

"I've told you I find no fault with this man, and Herod has concurred. Each year at this time I release a prisoner to you. Would you like me to give you Jesus, your king?"

"No."

As the crowd yelled and became rowdier, a small scroll was handed to Pilate. Claudia had been troubled in a dream about the man before him. So much so that she'd felt it necessary to warn him. She wasn't the only one troubled. This Jesus was clearly innocent and was only before him because of the jealousy of the Jewish leaders; of that he was certain.

"Why?" he said. "I'll release him to you."

"No," the crowd repeated, spurred on by the priests, elders, and experts of the Jewish laws. "We want Barabbas. Release Barabbas to us."

Pilate rubbed the bridge of his nose and thought. Barabbas was a robber and murderer, the leader of an insurrection. And they wanted him instead of this man who, from all Pilate could tell, was guilty of only doing good. He sighed and shook his head. Maybe they'd be satisfied with a scourging, but first he made one last try. "What then do you want done with this Jesus, who is your king?"

"Crucify him."

"Why? What has he done?"

The people were worked into a frenzy by this time and would only yell louder for blood. Disgusted, Pilate turned Jesus over to the soldiers to be scourged.


After they took Jesus to Pilate, John left the city and went directly to Bethany. His aunt, Jesus' mother, needed to be told–she was staying with friends–also Lazarus. John didn't know Lazarus had been in the garden and knew some of what was taking place, so he headed for his house first. He didn't want to be alone when he told his aunt what was happening in Jerusalem.

The door opened almost instantly at John's knock. Without a word, Lazarus grabbed his arm and drew him in. There sat his aunt with his own mother on one side and Mary on the other. Martha and another aunt sat near her. John went to Jesus' mother as she held out her arms to him and they wept together.

"I'm sorry, Aunt. There was nothing we could do," John said.

"I know." The Lord's mother's soothing voice comforted him. "Lazarus told me how it was."

Caleb came over to John and placed a comforting hand on his shoulder. "Lazarus was there in the garden. They tried to take him, too, but he ran. All they managed to get was his cloak. We went and got your mother and aunts as soon as he told us what had happened."

"I was looking for Jesus to warn him. Joseph and Nicodemus had told me what was being planned," Lazarus said when John turned questioning eyes toward him.

John nodded and turned back to his aunt. "We must go to him. They've taken him before Pilate. They're trying to get him crucified."


At Pilate's bidding, Jesus was led inside the Praetorium and his clothes were removed. When he was completely naked, one of the soldiers raised a whip with a dozen leather thongs. Each thong had a long metal spike at the end. The soldiers drew a flask of wine and passed it around as the one chosen to do the scourging tossed the whip in the air to loosen his arm muscles. In the meantime, Jesus' hands were tied to a post. All the while they ridiculed Jesus by bowing, spitting on and laughing at him, calling him Lord and Master in mocking tones.

Finally the soldier wielding the whip was ready. The rest stood back to watch. By Roman law, forty stripes could be given, but many died or at least fainted before that amount was reached. At about the tenth stroke, the soldiers grew quiet; not a sound had come from Jesus' lips. At the end of forty, he was not only still alive, but fully awake as well.

The men stood around him. His body was a bloody pulp. Each stroke had gouged away more of his flesh and even had wrapped around and gouged the front. The spell was broken when one man, drunker than the rest, got up and drew a purple robe around Jesus after releasing his arms from the post. The others suddenly came to life also and wove a crown from a thornbush which grew in the courtyard. Someone produced a reed and placed it in Jesus' hand as others crowned his head, sinking the thorns deep into his scalp.

They bowed and mocked him some more, crying, "Hail, king of the Jews," as they hit and spit upon him repeatedly. Then, laughing, they took him back out to Pilate, who turned him so he faced his accusers.

"Behold, the man," Pilate said. "Now shall I release him to you?"

"No," the crowd said. "Crucify him!"

"You take him and crucify him," Pilate said.

To which they said, "Our laws say he should die because he made himself to be the Son of God."

This frightened Pilate, and he took Jesus back into the Praetorium to question him.

"Where do you come from?" he asked in desperation. When Jesus didn't answer, he said, "I have the power to kill you or free you."

Jesus looked into his eyes as he replied. "You'd have no power over me at all if my Father didn't give it to you. Therefore they have the greater sin."

Pilate tightened his lips and pushed Jesus ahead of him, back out onto the porch. He presented him to them, saying, "Behold, your king."

The throng shouted, "Crucify him!"

Seating himself, Pilate reached out to a basin of water and dipped his hands in. "I wash my hands of this innocent man's blood," he said. "Do with him what you will."

The mob shouted, "His blood be upon us and our children."

The soldiers took the purple robe off Jesus and replaced it with his own robe. Then they gave him a large wooden cross and led him out of the city to be crucified.

Judas stepped up to the palace door which was opened by a young maiden at his knock. "Yes?" she said.

"I must see Caiaphas," Judas said.

"Who are you? It's late and he's gone to bed. Come back at daybreak. He'll be up then." She moved to close the door.

"No, wait, I must see him. Tell him Judas Iscariot is here. I must speak with him. It's urgent."

She looked him up and down. Then, opening the door, she let him into the hall. "Wait here. I'll see if he's still awake and will see you."

Judas fingered the moneybag in his hands. They had to take it back. Jesus was innocent.

At the sound of soft footsteps, he turned to see the maid returning. "Come," she said. "He'll see you." Turning, she led him to an inner chamber where several men were gathered. She left him standing there before them as he licked his lips while trying to decide what to say and how to say it.

"Yes, Judas," Caiaphas said.

"You hold an innocent man," Judas said. "I should never have agreed to help you."

"What do we care? It's already done. He stands before Pilate as we speak." Caiaphas slid into a chair next to Annas.

"But he shouldn't be. He—" Suddenly Judas knew all the begging and pleading he'd planned wouldn't work. They'd never let Jesus go. They'd wanted him too badly.

He threw the bag down at their feet and ran from the room.

Caiaphas bent over and, picking up the bag of silver, said, "What do you suppose we should do with this? We can't put it back into the treasury. It's blood money."

Annas thought a moment. "Why not purchase a burial place for strangers?" Taking the bag from Caiaphas, he tossed it up and down as the other council members present agreed that he had a splendid idea.


After a short distance, the centurion in charge of the four guards around Jesus realized the scourging had weakened their prisoner too much. He needed help carrying the cross that they'd use to crucify him on. That didn't surprise him. Seldom had he witnessed anyone being able to take the beatings Jesus had without breaking down. Looking around, he spotted a strong-looking man who hadn't been among those calling for Jesus' blood and approached him. "You," he said. "What's your name and where are you from?"

"I'm Simon. I come from Cyrene," the man said.

"Help him." The centurion indicated Jesus. "He's too weak to carry it. We'll be all day if he's left to do it alone."

So Simon was pressed into service to carry the cross on which the Messiah would spend his last hours.


Judas left the palace and wandered around the city. He could hear the crowd hollering in the Praetorium courtyard and new guilt washed over him. He had to get away where he wouldn't be reminded of his sin. Heading west, he found himself on the outskirts of Gethsemane. Entering the garden, he fell to his knees and buried his face in his hands.

He stayed in that position for a long time. Then thoughts—condemning thoughts—began to run through his mind, tormenting him until he could no longer stand the overwhelming guilt. Desperate, he looked around him. He got up and went over to a large rock with a tree next to it. The tree had a branch that could be reached if he stood on the rock. Removing his belt, he made a loop in it and climbed up on top of the rock. Attaching the other end of the belt to the tree, he put his head inside the loop and jumped from the rock. His legs kicked a few times as he fought for air to fill his lungs, but then his neck snapped and consciousness fled. Satan had won a small victory at least: Judas had believed the lies in his mind and didn't realize he could have been forgiven.

# Chapter Twenty-eight

## Wednesday–The Crucifixion

Only when they reached the place of the skull, called Calvary, did the centurion allow Simon to let the cross down from his shoulder. Two thieves who also were to be crucified lay down their crosses as well. The centurion sighed. It was to be a full day. Two criminals were scheduled to come later. He eyed the area. There was room for five crosses. Wanting to have these three up before the others arrived, he ordered each man down onto his cross. While two of his men dug the holes, the other two nailed those to be executed onto their crosses. The thieves were first, both crying out in agony as the wood was dropped into the holes.

The centurion removed his helmet and wiped his forehead. Looking at Jesus, he shook his head. The man was nearly unrecognizable. His face was so bruised and swollen that he doubted Jesus could see. It was nearly all one large purple mass. His clothing was covered with spittle, and beneath it, the soldier knew, the body was raw with not only welts, but also deep gouges that would have festered with infections had he been allowed to live longer. Many of them were inches deep. He ordered all his clothes, including his loincloth, removed. When they were, Jesus was shoved forward toward the cross awaiting him and told to lie down upon it.

Jesus moved forward and lay down on the cross as he'd been ordered to do. Two soldiers came up and took hold of his arms, stretching them as far as they could. Then another came and hammered a spike into each hand. When they finished with his arms, they left his sides and went toward his feet. His face was too swollen to see clearly, but he felt them bend his knees slightly so that they could place his feet one on top of the other. He felt hands holding them together, and then a spike was driven into his feet just at the ankle of each foot. He heard a noise above his head. Something was being nailed above it.

A sponge was put to his lips, but he turned his head away, knowing it was drugged wine. He wanted to remain alert until he couldn't bear it any longer. He felt himself being lifted and, as the cross came upright, his body pulled forward. With the thud of the wood landing in the bottom of the hole, his arms were jerked from their sockets. As the soldiers refilled what was left in the opening around the cross, Jesus struggled to catch his breath. Every muscle in his body cried out in agony as his lungs struggled to work.

Although he couldn't open them far, Jesus raised his eyes to heaven. "Father," each word causing pain in his chest and throat, "forgive them. They don't know what they're doing." His head fell to one side and rested on an upstretched arm as he closed his eyes.

It was mid-morning, about nine, and the soldiers knew it would be a long day. They were ordered to remain until the prisoners were dead so no one could free them. The time was dragging, so they got out some dice and began to gamble for whatever belongings were left by those being executed.

While this was taking place, many of the Jews came to gloat at Jesus' feet and revile him, but several of them left in anger when they saw what had been nailed at his head. They went directly to Pilate and demanded an audience.

When Pilate came out to them, they said, "You must change the inscription."

"Why? What's wrong with it?" Pilate was losing all patience with these men.

"You have it saying `Jesus of Nazareth, King of the Jews.' It should say, `He said he is the King of the Jews.'"

Pilate shook his head. "What I have written, I have written. It stays the way it is." He dismissed them and went inside, leaving them to stew in their frustration.


In the meantime, two more criminals were brought and hung even closer to Jesus than the thieves who were already hanging.

The Jews came and stood at the foot of Jesus' cross to mock him. "Save yourself, if you are of God," they said. "He said he would destroy the Temple and rebuild it in three days. If you are so mighty, come down from the cross!" These and other comments rose up to him and even the thieves had ridiculed him, daring him to save them all.

When the two criminals were placed beside Jesus and one began to take up the theme, mocking him, the other said, "Have you no conscience at all? We deserve to be here, but I've heard of this man. He's done nothing but good and is innocent. He doesn't deserve to be here with us." Looking at Jesus, he said to him, "My Lord, remember me when you're with God."

Jesus struggled to reply, "I'll remember. This day you will be with me in paradise."

To which the man said, gratefully, "Thank you, Lord."


John placed an arm around his aunt as they approached the cross where Jesus hung. Tears streamed down his face as he looked up at his cousin. He felt as if he were walking in a dream. This man he'd lived with nearly constantly for three years was dying, and there was nothing he could do, nothing any of them could do. Jesus had never done a single thing to harm anyone. All John had ever known him to do was good, even when they were boys growing up. Unbidden, memories came to mind, and John remembered times of laughter as well as the miracles and intense teaching of the these last three years.

Even before his ministry began, Jesus had lived his life to the fullest and had brought joy to all who knew him. John remembered how, a short time before he'd begun his ministry, Jesus had brought John's mother, Salome, a cabinet he'd made for her for no other reason than to give her a present. John knew Jesus had worked many hours on that gift. He'd done it only because he loved her, and it wasn't the first or last time John had seen him do that kind of thing.

His mother was with him now, as was his uncle Cleophas's wife, Maria, who was his mother's and Aunt Mary's other sister. Lazarus's sister Mary had insisted on coming also. They hadn't been able to talk her out of it.

John tightened his arm around his Aunt Mary's shoulder as she looked up and gasped with shock upon seeing Jesus. She covered her mouth to muffle her cries, and he cradled her head upon his shoulder as he looked up through blurred eyes at the man he'd come to know and love as his Master.

As she looked upon her son, Jesus' mother thought of the night the angel had come to her to announce that she'd been chosen by God. All during Jesus' life, she'd known this day would come, but the knowing hadn't made this moment any easier. She forced herself to gaze up at him, remembering what he'd looked like less than twelve hours earlier. Her son.

She closed her eyes as she remembered his body as it had been all his adult life: sleek and muscular, not an ounce of fat, shoulders wide and biceps bulging, as only a carpenter's would. Jesus had worked all his life lifting, cutting, and shaping wood, as Joseph, her husband, had taught him. Always he'd been strong, but they'd heard he'd been beaten so badly that he couldn't lift the cross he now hung upon. Simon from Cyrene had carried it for him. She must remember to thank him if she ever met him, thank him for helping her son, who'd done nothing but help others all of his life.

"Aunt Mary," John said, "he sees us."

She looked up at Jesus.

Jesus saw her look up at him and wanted her to know he was concerned for her. John, he knew, would care for her, if he asked. The pressure on his chest from hanging forward was excruciating. It was hard enough to breathe, let alone speak, but he knew he must.

"Woman," he said, forcing the words, "behold your son." He looked at John and knew he'd understand. "Behold, your mother."

The words weren't loud, but John heard and nodded. Jesus closed his eyes and again leaned his head on one arm to rest it as much as he could. The blood from the thorns had dried, but every once in a while one would stab into him and a trickle would fall down his forehead to his eyes, making it even more difficult to see. It had been several hours. The end was near.

The Jewish rulers clamored into the courtyard demanding an audience with Pilate. After several minutes, the governor came out onto the porch.

"What is it you want now?" Pilate didn't even try to hide his irritation. Because of these men, he'd not only had the worst night of his life, but had been forced to compromise himself.

One of the Jews stepped forward. "We have a request, sire," he said. "Well, two, actually."

Pilate stared down, waiting for him to continue. When he didn't, he said impatiently, "Well?"

The man cleared his throat. "In less than three hours, our high Sabbath begins for the Passover. We request that the legs of those crucified be broken to speed their deaths. We can't have them hanging during the Sabbath. It's against our laws."

Pilate nodded. "It will be done. What's your second request?"

"That man, Jesus, said he'd come alive again in three days. We know that's impossible, but we ask that a guard be placed around him for three days so that his disciples cannot come, steal his body and then claim he's risen as he said he would."

With a gesture of impatience, Pilate said, "You have guards of your own. Have them do it."

The Jews, afraid to anger Pilate more than he already was, agreed to do this and left as quickly as they could. They'd set their guards, all right. They'd prove this Jesus wasn't the Christ. They'd keep the prophecy about his rising up in three days from happening. They'd make sure no one else believed him to be the Messiah.


Mary looked up at Jesus. Her eyes were swollen from crying. She loved him with her whole being. Oh, she was in love with Caleb, but her love for Jesus was different than that. It was special. She'd searched all her life for what he'd given her. It tore her apart inside to see him like this. They'd not spared him at all. Every part of his body had been torn from the whip and its metal spikes. He'd lost all control of his bowels and bladder. Their contents covered his legs, mixing with the blood from the wounds the metal spikes had caused. She longed to do something for him, but all she could do was cry and hold John's mother. She wished this were a dream. She would rather have a thousand nightmares than to be living through this now. She didn't think she could ever have joy again.


The hours dragged by. Finally, as it neared three in the afternoon, the time when the Passover lambs were traditionally sacrificed, Jesus cried out in a loud voice, "My God, my God! Why have you forsaken me?"

The people around John and the women began speculating about what they'd heard him say. None seemed to be able to understand him, yet he'd spoken clearly. John heard and understood. Jesus, who'd always been in contact with God, was experiencing separation from Him for the first time in his life. John knew it without knowing how he knew.

Then the voice grew quiet and the effort it took to speak was evident. "I thirst." Someone passed John and raised up a sponge again to Jesus' mouth. This time it wasn't refused. Jesus' tongue came out and licked his parched lips.

"It's finished." John could barely hear him. But then, louder so all could hear, Jesus cried out, "Father, into Your hands I commit my spirit!"

John saw his cousin's body relax and knew Jesus was dead.

The centurion stood near the foot of Jesus' cross as his men threw their dice and murmured in low tones. Since noon the sky had been as dark as if it were midnight, and all of them had become increasingly nervous because of it. He looked over the area. Several men were seated on the ground not far away, all of them weeping. The women near the cross and the man with them were weeping. The centurion felt like weeping himself. It had been a long, hard day for him. He'd done his duty as a Roman soldier, but he hadn't felt right about it. This man was innocent. He knew it as surely as Pilate had. He shook his head in amazement at what jealousy could do. How people would commit the most insane acts because of it.

He heard the man hanging above him speak. The centurion turned and ordered one of his men to bring the drugged wine, then watched as Jesus was presented the soaked sponge. Then he heard him cry out and saw his body relax in death. He was awed. In all his experience, the centurion had never witnessed anyone willfully giving over to death as this man just had.

Immediately, the skies seemed to whirl and lightning began to streak across the sky. The ominous darkness that had surrounded them for three hours seemed even more threatening as thunder blasted the air and the very earth seemed to vibrate with the force of it. The air that had been almost unnaturally calm during the previous three hours of darkness suddenly came alive, and its force was staggering. He had to grab at the cross he stood beside to remain erect, The earth rumbled and quaked, breaking apart in places. His eyes raised to the body hanging above him, and fear gripped his heart.

"Truly," he said, "this man *was* the Son of God. Beyond a doubt, he was a righteous man." He clung to the cross at Jesus' feet as the world crashed and flared about him.

John drew the women over to the rest of the disciples as the storm raged. As they reached them, the other men gathered them into their midst so that their bodies could offer the women some protection. James had found them all except Peter huddled in the upper room where they'd eaten the Passover meal with Jesus. Lazarus, Martha, and Caleb were also there, having come with John and the other women.

As they huddled together, John reviewed in his mind all that had taken place, all Jesus had told them would take place and all the scriptures he remembered concerning the Messiah. How blind they'd been. So many prophesies had been fulfilled on this day alone that it was nearly staggering. He could barely comprehend it all. Jesus had predicted other things would happen as well.

"We need to go," he said to James and indicated their Aunt Mary. "She's exhausted, and the other women need to rest as well. We all do."

James nodded. Together, the brothers led the group back to the upper room.

Peter watched from a distance, tears blurring his vision. Jesus had been right. He'd denied him. If only he could live it over, undo it in some way, but he could not. He hid himself behind a rock and watched John comfort his aunt as they watched her son die.

*I will never deny him again,* he vowed. *Never.* If only he could be sure that he would not. But it really didn't matter. Jesus wouldn't be there to see it anymore. Peter knew he couldn't undo that no matter how badly he wished he could. The man they all thought would save them was on a cross dying, himself a prisoner of their conquerors.

Peter looked over to the group of men gathered nearby. James had found and brought them. Jesus had been right about them too. All of them had scattered; only John hadn't. Steadfast John. One of the youngest of the disciples, the one Jesus always favored because John was his beloved cousin. He was the only one who wouldn't have to repent of leaving Jesus. Peter envied him because of that.

He watched as Nicodemus and Joseph approached John, then followed behind when they headed back to the city. He couldn't bear to be alone any longer with his guilt.

Joseph and Nicodemus stood a little apart from the disciples and watched as they huddled together and then began to lead the women away.

"I believe," Joseph said to his friend, "it's time we come out of hiding, Nicodemus.

"We should have long ago."

"Yes, we should have."

"So what do you intend to do?"

Joseph nodded toward Jesus, still hanging before them. "He's dead now. I'll offer my tomb until we can prepare one that's more fitting for him." As he said this, he moved to intercept the group that was now heading back into the city, and Nicodemus accompanied him. The closest disciple was Andrew, who was trailing the others, his head hanging and the tears flowing freely down his cheeks. Joseph touched his shoulder.

Startled, Andrew jumped and turned quickly. "What is it you want?" Andrew didn't bother with titles to show his respect. He no longer respected the Sanhedrin who had killed his Lord.

Joseph and Nicodemus exchanged looks, and Nicodemus nodded for his friend to speak. Joseph took a deep breath.

"You are his disciples." He indicated the group walking before them.

"Yes, Andrew answered shortly and with suspicion.

"We did not approve of this." Joseph waved his hand toward Jesus. When Andrew only glared at him, he continued.

"We believe he was the Messiah. I am Joseph of Arimathaea, and this," he nodded toward his companion, "is Nicodemus."

Andrew gave a curt nod and Joseph saw it as a good sign, so he went on. "We want to help. I have a tomb we can put the body in temporarily until we can prepare one more fitting for him."

Andrew looked at the two men. They seemed sincere. He raised a hand to show he didn't want them to follow him and said, "Wait here." He went up ahead to James and John. The whole group stopped, and the two men stood silently waiting as the larger group spoke among themselves.

"I wouldn't blame them if they turned us down, Joseph," Nicodemus sighed. "We should have declared our convictions long before this."

"I know, but we wouldn't have been able to prevent what happened either way, my friend. What happened this day was prophesied long ago."

Nicodemus didn't answer, but turned and faced the group of disciples. The one who had stood at the cross with the women came over to them.

"I am John," he said. "Jesus was my cousin as well as my Lord and Master. Andrew tells us you offer a temporary grave for his body. We accept your offer. We don't want him buried with the criminals."


Pilate looked up as a servant entered. "Yes?"

"My lord, one of the Sanhedrin is here."

Letting out a sigh of exasperation, Pilate spoke to himself. "Will they never leave me alone?" Resigned, he said in a louder voice, "Tell him I'll come to him." He prepared himself for another confrontation.

Before Pilate could move, however, Joseph, led by the servant, allowed himself to be brought before Pilate inside the Praetorium halls. Pilate was surprised at this. He knew it meant the man wouldn't be able to partake of the feast they were presently celebrating. He wondered why one of the Sanhedrin would allow that until Joseph spoke.

"Lord, governor, I am Joseph of Arimathaea, a disciple of Jesus who was crucified this day."

The mystery was solved. This man wouldn't be of the Sanhedrin much longer, if he still was at all.

"Why are you here?" Pilate said.

"I wish to make a request."

"And what is this request?"

"That you allow me to have the body of my Lord."

Pilate pursed his lips. The request was simple enough. He nodded. "When he's dead, you may have it."

"Sire, he's dead now."

Pilate's eyebrows raised. "Already? Are you sure?"

"I watched him die."

"Well, Joseph, forgive me if I seem to not believe your word. It's unusual for one crucified to die in so short a time."

"Nevertheless it's true, but ask the centurion in charge if you don't believe me."

Pilate sent the servant for the centurion and waited with Joseph in silence. When the soldier entered, Pilate asked, "Is this true? Is the Galilean really dead?"

"It's true, sire," the centurion said. "I was standing at his feet when he died. I've ordered that the others have their legs broken."

Surprise etched Pilate's face. Turning to Joseph, he said, "Well, it seems your king has left you." He paused. "Yes, you may have the body." He turned to the centurion. "See to it."

The soldier bowed, "Yes, sire," he said, following Joseph out.

The soldiers went from cross to cross breaking the leg bones of the criminals to hasten their deaths. When they reached Jesus, one observed, "This man is already dead. We don't need to do anything."

Another replied, "Well, we'll just be sure."

Raising the spear in his hand, he pushed it into Jesus' body, which was still warm. Blood mixed with water gushed out and mingled with the blood, spittle, and excrement already on his body. Quickly the soldier drew the spear back out. The still form above him with the lifeless eyes caused chills to go through him. He shook himself and walked away, not realizing he'd just fulfilled more prophesy concerning the Jewish Messiah.

The centurion led Joseph and Nicodemus out to where Jesus still hung. The soldiers had just finished breaking the legs of the criminals and were in the process of taking down Jesus' body. The centurion took the body and looked at the man he held. Not understanding why, grief filled him as he gently handed him over to Joseph. Their eyes met and Joseph understood that, even in death, Jesus had touched a life.

"May God truly bless you," he said to the stunned soldier. "May you find the peace only He can give." Turning, he took Jesus to his sepulchre with Nicodemus following.

Joseph had told the disciples where Jesus would be lying, and many of them waited there for him and Nicodemus. Several of the women had come with them to help clean the body and prepare it for burial.

When the two men arrived, some of them went inside the tomb with them while others remained outside. Joseph had purchased fine linen, and Nicodemus carried seventy-five pounds of myrrh and aloes which would be placed within the folds of the linen as it was wrapped around Jesus' body, but before they could do that, it needed to be cleaned. Not an area of his body had been untouched by the beatings or the scourging, and what skin wasn't broken was purple from the broken vessels within. He was unrecognizable.

They worked over his body gently, even though he couldn't feel their ministrations. Then they carefully wrapped the linens, liberally placing the spices into the folds. Although it was only temporary, until the day after the weekly Sabbath in three days, they worked as carefully and thoroughly as they could. It was their last chance to do something for him. It was the least they could do.

# Part Six

## The Risen Savior

*For thou wilt not leave my soul in hell; neither wilt Thou suffer thine Holy One to see corruption*
Psalm 16:10

# Chapter Twenty-nine

## Sunday

The earth trembled and the women drew closer together as they approached the tomb where the body was laid. Four full nights and three full days had passed since Jesus had been crucified, but because Thursday had been the Passover Sabbath and Saturday the weekly Sabbath, they had had to wait until Sunday morning to finish embalming Jesus' body with the spices which had been bought and prepared on Friday.

"How will we move the stone?" one of the women asked as they entered the garden.

"We won't have to. Look." Mary pointed toward Joseph's tomb, and the others followed her gaze. The huge boulder that had been placed in front of the tomb was no longer blocking the entrance. It had been rolled over to the side, and lying nearby were several men. On top of the large stone sat what they knew could only be an angel. He was larger than any human man and glowed with a light that was overpowering. When he spoke, his voice was deep and pleasant.

"Don't be afraid. Jesus, whom you seek, is no longer here. He has risen. He'll meet his disciples in Galilee as he said he would. Wait for him there. I was sent to tell you this."

When he'd finished speaking, the women turned and fled, leaving the spices on the ground where they'd dropped them. When they reached the building with the upper room, all but Mary passed it by. She stopped. The eleven remaining disciples, Jesus' mother, and a few others were gathered up there. Should she tell them what they'd seen?

Slowly she climbed the stairs as she tried to form the words in her mind. Would they believe what she'd tell them? She didn't know. She herself couldn't believe it.

She knocked before entering. All eyes were turned in her direction, and she realized there was no easy way to tell them what she and the other women had just witnessed. The body was gone. The angel had said Jesus was alive, but that couldn't be true. She'd seen him laid in the tomb. Someone had taken him.

"They've taken his body. We don't know where," she said and proceeded to relate what they'd seen and what the angel had said.

Peter rose. "I must see this."

John got up also. "I'll go with you," he said.

They left the room and ran down the stairwell and out onto the street before Mary could stir herself to follow them. Slowly she turned and left the room. Tears streamed from her eyes and coursed down her cheeks. It seemed she hadn't stopped weeping since Wednesday when this nightmare they were living had begun.

Peter and John raced to the garden which contained Joseph's tomb. When they reached it, John passed Peter, but stopped next to the boulder which had covered the entrance. It had been moved, as Mary said, but no angel sat upon it and no men were lying on the ground. Standing between the stone and entrance, he turned as Peter came up beside him.

Silently Peter looked over at him as he passed on into the tomb. He stopped just inside the entrance, awestruck. John came up behind him and looked over his shoulder. There in front of them were the linen clothes and the napkin for the head in which they'd wrapped Jesus, laying where the body had been, but the body itself was gone.

Without a word, Peter turned and left the tomb, slowly walking toward Jerusalem. John took a last look at the linen clothes and then followed Peter back to the upper room.

Mary reached the garden. She watched as first Peter, then John silently walked past as if they couldn't see her. She went up to the tomb entrance and leaned in. Two angels sat, one at the head and one at the foot of the linens, and they glowed with an unearthly light. Their size and brilliance stunned her.

One asked her, "Why are you weeping?"

She looked at them through blurred eyes. "Because they've taken my Lord and I don't know where they've put him." She turned away and saw a man standing behind her.

"Woman, why do you weep? Who are you seeking?"

"Sir," she said, thinking he was the caretaker of the garden, "if you know where they've taken him, tell me and I'll take him away."

"Mary." The word was said with such love and compassion that she instantly knew who it was before her.

"Master," she cried, and her tears of sorrow turned into tears of joy as she reached for him.

He held out his hand to stay her. "Don't detain me. I must go present myself to my Father and your Father, my God and your God. Go and tell my disciples and especially Peter that I'll meet them in Galilee, but I must do this first."

"Oh, yes, Master," she exclaimed and ran, weeping for joy, to tell the disciples that Jesus was alive.

On her way back to Jerusalem, Mary encountered the other women. They'd been looking for her, having been told by the disciples that she'd gone back to the tomb.

"Mary," Salome said, "we've been looking for you. John says—"

"He's alive, Salome. I've seen him!" Mary could barely contain herself, for the joy she felt inside.

"What? Are you sure?"

"I'm sure. I saw him, and he spoke to me."

All the women spoke at once as they followed Mary back to the garden where the sepulchre was. As they reached the tomb and looked around, the expectancy on their faces vanished. No one was there, not even the angel they'd seen earlier. They turned to go and, as they did, a man appeared on the road before them. He stood watching them as they approached.

"Greetings," he said.

Salome stopped and gazed at him intently for a moment.

"Jesus," she exclaimed. "It *is* you."

Immediately all the women gathered around him, crying and praising God as they knelt at his feet and worshipped him. After a few moments, he told them to return to Jerusalem.

"Tell my brothers to go on to Galilee where I'll meet with them," he said. Then he disappeared, and the women went on to the city to tell the disciples that what Mary had told them was true. The Master lived.


The guard stopped a moment to rest. He shook his head as if to clear it, but it didn't really need clearing. He was fully awake and aware of what had taken place. It was just that it was too hard to believe, even though he'd seen it with his own eyes; angels—he'd seen angels-and the power, that overwhelming power.

It had forced him and the other guards to fall prostrate and lay as if dead while the stone was rolled away and one entered the tomb while the other sat upon the large rock that had covered the entrance.

What happened then was hazy in his mind. He thought he remembered voices, but he hadn't been able to open his eyes, and his hearing had been impaired as well. And yet he'd been fully awake; but he couldn't move, hear, or see.

When he reached the home of Caiaphas and was shown in, he saw the other guards cowering in front of Caiaphas as he glowered at them.

"Gone?" the high priest said. "Gone where?"

"We don't know, sire," one man said. "We were struck down and couldn't see or hear, yet we were awake. The angels—"

"Angels?" Caiaphas interrupted. "How do you know these were angels?" he roared at them. He was afraid of what he'd done and of its consequences. If there had really been angels, then Jesus was the Messiah and he'd executed him, but the Messiah wouldn't have allowed himself to be crucified.

"They were large, my lord," one guard said.

"And bright," another said.

"Yes, very bright," a third added.

"And strong. It took only one to move the stone," the first man said.

Caiaphas looked over the guards and then motioned to the elders who were there with him. They gathered together, and he said, "I'm open to comments in this matter."

"We must silence these men. If word of this reaches the common people...."

The elder let his sentence drift.

"You speak the truth," another said. "Only how do we silence them?"

"A bribe." Caiaphas bit his lip. "It's the only way. We must pay them all to be silent, or we'll be the ones to pay for this."

The others nodded in agreement as they turned toward the guards. Caiaphas sent for the treasurer.

"We want you to tell anyone who asks you about this that the disciples of this Galilean came in the night and took his body while you slept. If Pilate should hear of this, we'll handle the matter and cover for you."

The guards, seeing the large amount of money Caiaphas was handing out to each of them, agreed. The story was spread around that the body of Jesus was stolen, and many people believed them.

# Chapter Thirty

## Forty Days

After the women had come to the upper room with the tale that Jesus still lived, the disciples there decided they'd gather together all of his other followers to attempt to find the body. None of them believed the women, thinking they'd imagined what they said they saw. Caleb agreed to go with Cleopas, who was married to Jesus' Aunt Maria, to Emmanus which was eight miles southwest of Jerusalem. There were several disciples living in that area who'd either not come to the city for the Passover or had left right after Jesus was crucified. While they traveled, they discussed what had happened three days before, trying to come to grips with the tragedy.

Caleb shook his head as they discussed Jesus and what Mary and the other women had told them that morning. "He could never have survived what he went through, Cleopas. And angels? I fear Mary's having a hard time accepting what has really happened. I don't know if I can accept it myself."

Cleopas placed a reassuring hand on Caleb's arm and then became aware of someone walking just behind them. He turned. "Greetings, friend. Peace be to you."

The other traveler nodded. "Peace be to you also. I couldn't help overhearing. What is it you were discussing that's so hard to accept?"

"Don't you know? You're traveling on a road that leads directly from Jerusalem. Have you heard nothing of what has transpired there these past few days?" Cleopas was incredulous.

"No. Tell me."

They told the man of the crucifixion and ended by saying, "We thought he'd free us from the Roman rule, but they crucified him instead. Now our women are insisting that he lives and that they've seen not only him, but angels as well."

"Are you blind?" the man said. "The scriptures tell of these very events. Moses wrote that God said Satan shall be crushed under the heel of the woman's seed, and the sufferings of the Messiah were foretold as well by Isaiah, Daniel, and Zechariah. The lamb of the Passover represents the ultimate sacrifice of the Messiah as well. These happenings were necessary in order for man to become eternally acceptable to God once again."

Caleb and Cleopas walked silently into the village with the stranger beside them as they pondered what he'd said. When they stopped in front of the inn, the man continued on.

"Wait," Caleb said. "We'd like to hear more of this from you. Join us."

The man stopped, seeming to consider the invitation, then smiling, he nodded and entered the building with them. As they ate their meal, the two men felt an overwhelming peace as they listened to their companion. When the meal was nearly finished, he picked up a small loaf of bread and, breaking it, handed a piece to each of them.

Suddenly it was as if blinders had fallen from their eyes: The man was Jesus. Immediately upon their recognizing him, the Master disappeared. They stared at each other in wonder. The women had been right; Jesus was alive.


Peter sat alone in the garden because he felt unworthy to be with the others in the upper room. They may have scattered, but they'd not denied they'd ever known Jesus. He buried his face in his hands and wept again.

"Peter." The voice was gentle.

Startled, he looked up. He didn't recognize the man before him. The sun was right behind the man's head, and it's brilliant rays were blinding. He moved slightly and saw a hand reaching out to him. He put his own hand out and drew it back again before they touched each other. There was something familiar about the voice, the carriage of the man before him. He looked down. The man's feet were bare, and they were scarred. Peter looked up at the face. It was bruised, and he couldn't see the features clearly.

"Peter," the man before him repeated.

"Master." All at once Peter knew who stood before him and he began to weep as he grabbed at the hand before him and held it to his face.

Jesus laid his other hand on Peter's head. "Don't berate yourself, Peter."

"Lord, you were right. I did deny you. Forgive me. Please, forgive me. I denied you."

"It's all right, Peter. You're forgiven. I love you. I'll always love you." Jesus' voice was gentle, and Peter felt an overwhelming sense of peace flood his body, mind, and spirit.

Suddenly he was alone again, but he was forgiven. Jesus still loved him. He bolted upright. Jesus was alive as the women had said. He had to tell the others.


Peter pounded on the door. When no one came, he shouted. Finally Andrew opened it and pulled him in.

"Peter, what has gotten into you? Do you want us to be arrested?" Andrew said, a little angry.

"It's true, Andrew." Peter grabbed his brother's shoulders and shook him for joy.

"What are you saying? What's true?"

"Jesus is alive. I've seen him. The women were right. Jesus is alive."


Cleopas and Caleb ran up the steps to the roof where the upper room was. Caleb tried the door, found it locked, and pounded with his fist as he yelled. "Open up."

Immediately the door was flung wide and the two men ran in, but before they could tell their story, the others in the room were telling them that Jesus lived. He'd appeared to Peter. After they heard what had been happening to the others, the two men related their story. Just as they were finishing, Mary looked up and turned pale. Caleb and several of the others turned to where she was staring and saw a figure standing in the shadows. Several of them cried out in fear.

"Peace. Do not fear. It is I." Jesus stepped forward into the light cast by the lamps.

Although the fear vanished from their faces, many of them were still wary. Jesus held out his hands as he tried to persuade them to see he was real. "Here are my hands. Touch them. See the wounds? Look at the holes in my feet. It is I. Ghosts don't have flesh and bones." Finally, seeing they still doubted, he said, "Do you have anything here to eat?"

They handed him a piece of fish, which he ate. "There," he said. "Ghosts don't eat. I'm real."

Suddenly there was a flood of questions. He held up his hands to silence them and then began to repeat what he'd told Caleb and Cleopas about the scriptures. As he did, their minds finally grasped the meaning of the words and the scriptures became clear.

When he'd finished revealing the scriptures to them, Jesus said, "This is what was written about me, and I was also to suffer as I did and rise up again on the third day, as it is also written. Repentance and forgiveness of sins shall be preached in my name, beginning here in Jerusalem and reaching out throughout the whole earth, and you were chosen to be witnesses of these things."

After saying this, he vanished from their midst.

When Jesus had appeared to the disciples, Thomas had been coming back from Bethany. When he arrived and heard that Jesus had come and gone, he scoffed at what they said.

"I'll not believe," he said, "unless I can touch the holes in his hands and feet and place my hand in the wound at his side." Nothing they said could persuade him to believe.

Eight days later all of them, including Thomas, were again in the upper room when Jesus again appeared out of nowhere. Mary sat quietly next to Caleb and watched Thomas's face with interest. It went through a series of changes as he beheld the Master.

Jesus silently held out his hands. "Here Thomas. Touch me. I'm real."

As Thomas took the wounded hands in his own, his voice quavered as he knelt before Jesus and said, "My Lord and my God."

"Do you believe now, Thomas?"

Thomas nodded his head.

"Because you see, you now believe, but I tell you, many will not see. Yet they'll believe and will be blessed because of it."

Thomas bowed his head at the rebuke, yet he knew he was forgiven and loved. An unexplainable peace had filled his heart.

Several days later, the disciples traveled back to Galilee where Jesus had told them he'd join them. They were sitting near their boats mending nets when Peter jumped up. He'd been restless ever since leaving Jerusalem, and he could stand waiting no longer.

"I'm going fishing," he said, and the other six men who were with him said they'd go along.

"Nothing else to do here. The nets are finished," John said as he got up to follow Peter into the boats.

All night long they cast out their nets, but caught nothing. They began hauling in the nets for the last time when John looked up and saw a man standing on the shore. Without saying a word, he nudged Peter, who also looked up. One by one the others turned to stare at the man standing on the shoreline.

The man called to them. "Have you caught anything?"

"No."

Then he said to them, "Cast your net to the right of the boat."

They did, and the net became so full that the men couldn't haul it into the boat. John exclaimed, "It's the Lord."

Peter drew his tunic back over his head. They always worked in their loincloths because of the heat and exertion. He jumped into the water and swam ashore as the others rowed behind him.

As they landed, they saw a fire with fish and bread cooking over it. Jesus told them to bring the fish they'd caught. When they brought the net up and counted the fish, there was an unusually high amount—one hundred and fifty-three—yet the net was still whole. It overwhelmed them all and made them even more sure this was Jesus, even though he didn't look the same.

After counting the fish, they sat and ate. Jesus turned to Peter. "Peter, do you love me above all others?"

"Yes, Lord, I love you," Peter said.

Jesus said, "Feed my lambs." Then he repeated the question, "Do you love me, Peter?"

"Lord, you know I love you," Peter said.

"Feed my sheep."

Jesus looked Peter straight in the eye and asked again a third time, "Do you love me, Peter?"

Peter, not knowing what Jesus was driving at, felt hurt as he answered, "Lord, you know everything. You know I love you."

Satisfied now that Peter had declared his love three times and had admitted Jesus knew everything, Jesus repeated, "Feed my sheep." Then he continued. "When you were young, you went wherever you wanted to go, but when you are old, you'll put forth your hands and another will carry you where you don't want to go."

Then Jesus rose. "Follow me," he said.

As Peter got up to follow Jesus, he looked over at John and asked, "What of him, Lord?"

"Don't be concerned with him. Even if he were to live until I come again, that's not your affair. You follow me."

James laid down his tools and went over to the water jar for a drink. It had been four weeks since Jesus had been murdered. That was how he thought of it. Anger rose in him at the thought of the Romans crucifying his brother. Yet his mother kept insisting he wasn't dead; she'd seen him alive. James found that hard to believe.

He took another drink and threw the rest in the cup over his head and shoulders to cool off. He shook his head and wiped his eyes with the back of his hand. When he opened them again, a man was there in front of him.

His features were marred, and he had wounds on his hands and feet. James didn't recognize him.

"Who are you?" he said.

"You don't know me, James?" came the answer in a familiar voice.

James stared. It couldn't be. That voice was unmistakably the voice of Jesus, but that was impossible. Jesus was dead; he died four weeks ago.

"James?" That voice again, that beloved voice.

"Jesus?" A slight glimmer of hope wove through James's own voice.

"Yes, James. It is I. Do not doubt it." Jesus reached out toward him, and James found himself hugging his brother fiercely.

"James, you must believe. I am here; I am real. I'll be here only a short time longer. It was meant to be. You must forgive, James."

"But how?"

"You, who know the scriptures so well, need to ask that?" Jesus shook his head. "James."

"Then you are the Messiah as so many believe."

"Yes, James. I am."

James knelt at Jesus' feet. "My Lord and my God," he exclaimed as he looked into his brother's eyes, eyes so like his own and yet not. Pools of life, compassionate, warm, forgiving pools of pure love. His brother. His Messiah.


Mary opened the door. There stood Peter and John. James, Andrew, and the others were approaching the house. She smiled.

"The peace of God be with you, Peter. John. Come in. We've been expecting you. The Lord showed himself to Caleb and Lazarus and said you would be coming." She moved aside to let them enter.

The other apostles had reached the house and followed them in as well, greeting those already there. Several of the women and the Lord's mother and brothers had arrived earlier. Word had spread that Jesus wanted them to come to Jerusalem. It had been forty days since his crucifixion, and he'd appeared several times, once to as many as five hundred of his disciples at one time. There was a feeling of expectation in the air.

Then he was among them. It happened that way, always. First they were without him, then he'd appear. He didn't enter with a knock or warning of any kind. He just was there, but he was real. He'd proven it time and again. He lived, and yet no door kept him out. He needed no door to admit him.

"Peace be to you," he said.

They turned to listen. During the last six weeks he'd talked of many things, the necessity of his crucifixion and resurrection in fulfillment of the prophets' predictions, the spreading of his words and teachings and many other things. Now they sensed he had something more to say.

"I leave you now." He raised a hand at their exclamations and dismay. "If I do not, I can't send you the Comforter that's been promised, the Holy Spirit. You must go out and preach and teach what I've taught you. Those who believe and are baptized will be saved. Those who don't believe will be lost forever. And these signs shall follow not only you, but also all who believe. In my name, they'll cast out demons. They'll speak in languages they don't know, handle deadly serpents, and if they should drink any poison, it won't harm them. Any who are sick and come to them shall be healed by the laying on of hands. Teach them all I've commanded of you, and I'll always be with you. Teach them to love one another, but you must stay in Jerusalem until the Holy Spirit comes to you. He'll give you the power to do the things I've just told you of, and all others who believe what you tell them will have these powers also. Come." He rose to leave, and the disciples followed him out to the Mount of Olives.

"Lord," Peter said, "will you now restore the kingdom of Israel?" The disciples had discussed this at great length during the last few weeks.

"Peter, it's not for you or any other man to know the Father's plans for the future," Jesus said. "But as I told you, you'll receive power when the Spirit is sent to you, and you shall be witnesses of me in not only Jerusalem, Judea, and Samaria, but also throughout the whole earth."

Then he began to rise up into the sky. Caleb grabbed Mary's hand as they watched Jesus disappear into the clouds. Then two angels in glowing white robes appeared from nowhere into their midst.

"Why are you staring into the clouds?" they said, "This Jesus who you've seen taken into heaven will come again to this very spot in the same way as you've seen him go into heaven." Saying this, they disappeared.

The disciples stood worshipping and praising God for the privilege of knowing Jesus Christ.

# Epilogue

*For John truly baptized with water; but ye shall be baptized with the Holy Ghost not many days hence*

Acts 1:5.

## Pentecost

Ten days after Jesus ascended into the skies, the apostles and several other disciples were praying and worshipping in the temple. They'd selected by lot a replacement for Judas so they again numbered twelve. Matthias had been chosen.

With the twelve were 108 others, including Jesus' mother and four brothers. Caleb, Mary, Lazarus, and Martha were also present. A loud clap of thunder burst overhead, and forks of fire streamed down, touching each person present who believed Jesus to be the Christ of God.

From all over the city, Jews of many nations were present for the feast of Pentecost. They'd seen the fire come down upon the building and could hear voices, loud and strong, coming from it as well. Awed, they stopped inside, too stunned to move further as they heard their native languages being spoken in praises to God by these unlearned men and women, most of whom were from Galilee and had never before spoken any but their own dialect. Much speculation was made concerning how this could be, and many concluded that those they heard could only be drunk.

But Peter, boldly speaking by the power of the Spirit which God had just poured down upon them, denied this and quoted the scriptures which foretold the experience that they were witnessing. He reminded them of David's prediction of the Messiah and told them that the man they'd crucified fifty days earlier was the very Messiah for whom they had been waiting.

Strongly convicted of the wrong of which he accused them, they asked what they could do now that it was in the past. Peter boldly taught them the words of Jesus, concluding, "Repent and believe on the name of the Lord Jesus Christ. Through him alone you can be saved." Then he told of the many works and miracles of Jesus until three thousand people accepted Jesus and many more went out to spread the good news that God had sent His Son as the Messiah–Jesus the Christ.

Two thousand years later that good news is still being told. Jesus Christ was a real man with feelings and desires the same as ours, yet He was God as well. He came as a man to show us that it's possible to live the way He did. There was nothing supernatural in His own personal walk with God. He had to develop a relationship in the same way you and I do.

If you've never given your heart to Jesus and made Him your personal savior, I urge you to do it now. What He did for Mary and Caleb and the others, who represent us all, he can–and will–do for you as well. I guarantee, you'll never regret it.

Each detail of a prophecy doubles the chances of the prediction not coming to pass.

## Law of Compound Probability Chart*

| Number of details in a prophecy | Fulfillment--one chance in number stated: |
|---|---|
| 1 | 2 |
| 2 | 4 |
| 3 | 8 |
| 4 | 16 |
| 5 | 32 |
| 6 | 64 |
| 7 | 128 |
| 8 | 256 |
| 9 | 512 |
| 10 | 1,024 |
| 11 | 2,048 |
| 12 | 4,096 |
| 13 | 8,192 |
| 14 | 16,384 |
| 15 | 32,768 |
| 16 | 65,536 |
| 17 | 131,072 |
| 18 | 262,144 |
| 19 | 524,288 |
| 20 | 1,048,576 |
| 21 | 2,097,152 |
| 22 | 4,194,304 |
| 23 | 8,388,608 |
| 24 | 16,777,216 |
| 25 | 33,554,432 |
| 26 | 67,108,864 |
| 27 | 134,217,728 |
| 28 | 268,435,456 |
| 29 | 536,870,912 |
| 30 | 1,073,741,824 |
| 31 | 2,147,483,648 |
| 32 | 4,294,967,296 |
| 33 | 8,589,934,592 |
| 34 | 17,179,869,184 |
| 35 | 34,359,738,368 |
| 36 | 68,719,476,736 |
| 37 | 137,438,953,472 |
| 38 | 274,877,906,944 |
| 39 | 549,755,813,888 |
| 40 | 1,099,511,627,776 |

*Taken from *Dake's Annotated Bible*

## Prophecies Concerning Jesus Christ*

**OT Prophecy**                                    **NT Fulfillment**

Gen 3:15 ............................Seed of Woman ......................Matt 1:20
Is 7:14 .....................................Virgin Born .........................Matt 1:18
Gen 49:10 ........................Tribe of Judah ......................Luke 3:23,33
Micah 5:2 ........................Born at Bethlehem ..................Matt 2:1
Psalm 72:10 .....................Presented with Gifts .................Matt 2:1, 11
Jer 31:15 ..........................Herod Kills Children.................Matt 2:16
Is 7:14 ..............................Shall Be Immanuel ...................Matt 1:23
Is 40:3 .........................Preceded by a Messenger ..............Matt 3:1-2
Is 35:5-6 .......................Ministry of Miracles .................Matt 9:35
Zech 9:9 ...................Enter Jerusalem on a Donkey ...........Luke 19:35-37
Psalm 16:10 ..........................Resurrection .........................Acts 2:31
Psalm 68:18 ..............................Ascension .........................Acts 1:9
Psalm 41:9 .....................Betrayal by a Friend .................John 13:21
Zech 11:12 ...............Sold for Thirty Pieces of Silver ..........Matt 26:15
Zech 11:13 ........ Money Thrown Down in God's House.... Matt 27:5
Zech 13:7 ....................Forsaken by His Disciples..............Matt 26:56
Psalm 35:11 ..................Accused by False Witness ..............Matt 26:59-60
Is 53:7 ...........................Dumb before Accusers.................Matt 27:12
Is 53:5 ...........................Wounded and Bruised ................Matt 27:26
Is 50:6 ...........................Smitten and Spit Upon .................Matt 27:30
Psalm 22:7-8 ...........................Mocked .........................Matt 27:31
Psalm 22:16 ...................Hands and Feet Pierced ...............John 20:25
Is 53:12 .........................Crucified with Thieves .................Matt 27:38
Psalm 22:18 ............. Garments Parted and Lots Cast ......... John 19:23-24
Psalm 22:1 .......................His Forsaken Cry .....................Matt 27:46
Num 9:12 ........................Bones not Broken....................John 19:33-36
Zech 12:10 .............................Side Pierced .......................John 19:34
Amos 8:9 .....................Darkness over the Land ..............Matt 27:45
Is 53:9 .........................Buried in Rich Man's Tomb ............Matt 27:57-60

*The source of this chart is unknown

# Author's Note

Although I used several other books for my research, I'd like to give a special recognition to two especially helpful volumes: Thompson's Chain Reference Bible and Dake's Annotated Reference Bible. All quotations at the beginning of each section are taken from the King James Version.

This book may seem to many to center on Mary and her sin; however, it is really about God's love for us and the expression of that love through Jesus who said that when we see him we see God. Many of the scenes in this book can be found in the Bible, and it is my hope that they will instill a desire in my readers to look them up and read them. I have included a notes section for those who wish to do this. There may be some readers who are confused concerning the days of Passion Week. The days are named according to how we know them; however, Jewish reckoning for a day is from sunset in the evening of one day to sunset in the evening of the next. Therefore, the events happening in the evening of one day are included as being a part of the next day.

An example of this is the Lord's last supper and the events leading up to His arrest. These took place on our Tuesday evening, and His trial began after midnight on our Wednesday, but all are figured as part of Wednesday according to the Jewish reckoning. This is why it was important to the Jewish leaders that Jesus and the others crucified with Him be removed from their crosses before sundown on Wednesday. Thursday was the actual Passover or Holy Sabbath, and they could not perform any labor after sunset. Even carrying a needle was considered labor.

Although the leaders didn't realize their demands would accomplish this, to fulfill prophesy, Jesus had to be in the tomb by that time and be buried for three full days and three full nights. In other words, He could not rise again until after sunset on our Saturday.

With the feeding of the four thousand and five thousand, the numbers may seem unrealistic to some readers. This is because I have estimated women and children as well as men. In Bible times, men were the only people who were counted because they were the fighting force, but in both of these cases it is clearly stated, "Plus women and children." My estimates are large because children were considered to be the life-line of the parents, and so families tended to be large. Jesus' own family consisted of at least eight children. There was no welfare or social security, and the parents were cared for by their children in their old age.

Contrary to what many may think, my character is not Mary of Magdala, even though that Mary is one of five women I combined to make her a more rounded character, but rather Mary, the sister of Lazarus and Martha. There is no evidence that Mary of Magdala was a prostitute, and my reason for making my character involved in sexual sin has more to do with the adulteress. This and melding the gospels together were done so the reader could get a better idea of how things may have been and see Jesus and my other characters as real people. I apologize to any Bible scholars who may object to the liberties

I've taken and can only say that I attempted to stay as close as I could to the events as they happened, according to the gospels.

# Notes

Portions of the following chapters were based on the scriptures indicated.

Chapter One
>According to Matthew 13:55-56 and Mark 6:3, Jesus had four brothers and at least three sisters (Matthew 13:56 would have said "both" instead of "all" if there had been only two sisters).
>Matthew 3:1-12; Mark 1:8, Luke 3:2-18; John 1:19-28

Chapter Two
>Matthew 3:13-17; Mark 1:9-11; Luke 3:21-22

Chapter Three
>John 1:29-34
>John 1:35-40

The following scriptures are the basis I used for making James and John Jesus' cousins. In these three scriptures, the same woman is referred to in three different ways.

>Matthew 27:56–Mother of Zebedee's children
>Mark 15-40–Salome; James and John's mother is named Salome
>John 19:25–Jesus' mother's sister

Chapter Four
>John 1:41

Chapter Five
>John 1:42
>Matthew 4:1-11; Mark 1:12-13; Luke 4:1-13

Chapter Six
>Matthew 4:18-22; Mark 1:16-20
>John 2:1-11

Chapter Seven
>John 2:13-17

Chapter Eight
>John 3:1-21

Chapter Nine
>Luke 5:1-11
>Matthew 8:5-13; Luke 7:1-10

Chapter Eleven
>Luke 7:11-16
>Luke 7:19-29
>Luke 7:36-50

Chapter Twelve
>Luke 11:33-54

Chapter Thirteen
>Matthew 8:23-27; Mark 4:35-41; Luke 8:22-25
>Matthew 8:28; Mark 5:1-20; Luke 8:26-39
>Matthew 9:10-13; Mark 2:15-17; Luke 5:27-32
>Matthew 18:21-35

Chapter Fourteen
>Matthew 14:3-12; Mark 6:17-28

Chapter Fifteen
>Matthew 14:3-12; Mark 6:17-28
>Matthew 14:15-21; Mark 6:35-44; Luke 9:12-17; John 6:5-14

Chapter Sixteen
>Matthew 14:22-33; Mark 6:45-52; John 6:16-21
>Matthew 14:34-36; Mark 6:53-56
>John 6:25-71

Chapter Seventeen
>Matthew 15:1-9; Mark 7:1-13
>Matthew 15:32-38; Mark 8:1-9
>Matthew 16:13-28; Mark 8:27-9:1; Luke 9:18-27
>Matthew 17:1-21; Mark 9:2-29; Luke 9:28-42

Chapter Eighteen
>Luke 9:51-10:24
>John 8:1-11

Chapter Twenty
>   Luke 10:38-42
>   John 9 and 10

Chapter Twenty-one
>   John 11:1-46
>   John 11:47-52

Chapter Twenty-two
>   Matthew 19:13-30; Mark 10:13-31; Luke 18:15-30
>   Matthew 20:17-19; Mark 10:32-34; Luke 18:31-34

Chapter Twenty-three
>   Luke 19:1-10
>   Thursday sunset to Friday sunset is based on Matthew 21:1-17

Chapter Twenty-four
>   Friday sunset to Saturday sunset is based on Matthew 21:17; John 12:1-11
>   Saturday sunset to Sunday sunset is based on Mark 11:1-11; Luke 19:29-44;
>   John 12:12-19

Chapter Twenty-Five
>   Sunday sunset to Monday sunset is based on Matthew 21:18-22;
>   Mark 11:12-19; Luke 19:45-48; John 12:20-50
>   Monday sunset to Tuesday sunset is based on Matthew 21:23 to 26:13;
>   Mark 11:20 to 14:9; Luke 20:1 to 21:38

Chapters Twenty-six, Twenty-seven, and Twenty-eight
>   Tuesday sunset to Wednesday sunset is based on Matthew 26:14 to 27:66;
>   Mark 14:10 to 15:47; Luke 22:1 to 23:56: John 13:1 to 19:42

Chapter Twenty-nine and Thirty
>   Matthew 28:1-10; Mark 16:1-11; Luke 24:1-12; John 20:1-18

Epilogue
>   Acts 2:1-41